Eye of the Mountain God

ALSO BY PENNY RUDOLPH

Lifeblood

Thicker Than Blood

Listen to the Mockingbird

Eye of the

Mountain God

PENNY RUDOLPH

THOMAS DUNNE BOOKS

ST. MARTIN'S PRESS

NEW YORK

This is a work of fiction. All of the characters, organizations, and events portrayed in this novel are either products of the author's imagination or are used fictitiously.

THOMAS DUNNE BOOKS.
An imprint of St. Martin's Press.

EYE OF THE MOUNTAIN GOD. Copyright © 2010 by Penny Rudolph. All rights reserved. Printed in the United States of America. For information, address St. Martin's Press, 175 Fifth Avenue, New York, N.Y. 10010.

www.thomasdunnebooks.com

www.stmartins.com

Library of Congress Cataloging-in-Publication Data

Rudolph, Penny.
    Eye of the mountain god / Penny Rudolph.—1st ed.
        p. cm.
    ISBN 978-0-312-54546-8 (alk. paper)
    1. Women photographers—Fiction.   2. Pima Indians—Antiquities—Fiction.   3. Archaeologists—Fiction.   4. Kidnapping—Fiction.
5. New Mexico—Fiction.   I. Title.
    PS3618.U347E94 2010
    813'.6—dc22

                                                            2009041642

First Edition: April 2010

10   9   8   7   6   5   4   3   2   1

To Ralph, for Ralph knows what and Ralph knows why

Acknowledgments

I owe much appreciation for advice and assistance to the following people.

Warren Murphy, two-time Edgar-winning author and cocreator of The Destroyer series, who read this manuscript when it could barely be called a novel, and who has given me wonderful support and advice on all my books.

Jeff Corwin, an excellent photographer, who taught me, and therefore Megan, my protagonist, just about everything I know about the art and science of taking pictures.

My agent, **Sorche Fairbank**, the best coach an author could ask for.

My editor, **Toni Plummer**, whose insight and patience make her an author's dream to work with.

Evelyn Garcia, who helped me to understand the lives of New Mexico's Hispanics.

Michael Siverling, who as a supervising criminal investigator and an author in his own right had answered my questions about the world of law enforcement with the flourish of a writer.

Stan and Pat Gralski, who lived across the street when I wrote the first draft of this book, and their daughter, Allie, on whose sunny disposition I patterned my protagonist's daughter, Lizzie.

Rob Kresge, who organized the critique group where *Eye of the Mountain God* was first read. Also **Roz Russell** and **Penny Rogers**, whose comments at those meetings were so helpful.

Linda Warren, a wonderful designer, from whom I learned the importance of shape and color.

Goldialu Stone, whose sage advice has been valuable.

Marilyn and Pat Hutton, good friends and longtime New Mexico residents, who helped with aspects of this work.

Rudolfo Anaya, for his wonderful novel *Bless Me, Ultima*, and **John Nichols**, for writing *Milagro Beanfield War*. Both were inspirations for this book.

Lynne and Sid Gudes, northern New Mexicans and good friends, who fielded my questions, even the ridiculous ones.

Bernice Sena, for her help with Spanish slang.

Lois Mile, who made me very aware of teeth.

Eye of the Mountain God

Prologue

Ten minutes after John Runyon began his newspaper deliveries, he knew he was being followed.

And he knew why. Or thought he did.

He grabbed a rolled-up paper from the canvas bag slung across the handlebars of his bike and flung it across the still-brown Bermuda grass of the Portillo yard. On Saturdays, the paper was pretty light. It landed just short of the welcome mat. A hand at the window waved. Everyone knew John even if they didn't know his name. The Runyons were the only blacks in town.

The sharp dry air smelled of tumbleweeds and dust. The sun was unpinning the dark rim of the sky.

John patted the pocket of his jeans to be sure the packet was still there.

It was.

The pickup truck was still there, too, a block behind him, no lights. In the mirror clamped to his bike's scarred handlebars John could make out its dark hulk, hovering. Just some drunk in a beat-up truck trying to get home? Or should he ride up a driveway and hammer on someone's front door?

Stucco houses the color of old clay lined the next street. He chucked a paper dead center on a doorstep, then glanced at the mirror. The pickup hadn't followed. Yet.

John unrolled a newspaper, took something from his pocket, wadded it up, and placed it on a headline about forty-two Mexican men arrested crossing the border near El Paso, Texas.

Which of his customers did not get up early? His gaze skipped past a wind-blown geranium in a chipped planter. The woman there was fairly new in town. Once, when he went to collect, he'd noticed a few unopened papers in her living room. Maybe she didn't get around to reading every issue. Maybe he could make up some story, take her another paper and ask for this one back.

The paper hit the ground with a hollow sound a dozen feet short of the front steps. Bad throw, but he didn't want to call attention to it, so he pedaled on, slinging papers as the bike's canvas pouch grew lighter.

The sky brightened, the corners got easier to turn. The pickup was nowhere in sight. Maybe he was silly to get so spooked. He pedaled toward the last street of his route.

Turning the corner, he jammed on the brakes. Wheels skidding, he tried to turn the bike back, but it jackknifed.

The pickup was sideways across the empty road.

Two men uncoiled from the fender they had been leaning against and moved toward him.

Chapter One

Megan Montoya got out of her car and was halfway to the front door before she noticed the living room drapes were closed. She always left them open. Her daughter should be home from school by now, but why would Lizzie close the drapes?

She hated the idea of Lizzie coming home to an empty house. If the stoplight on Alameda hadn't stuck on red, backing up two lanes of horn-happy drivers as last year's tumbleweeds rocketed through the intersection, Megan would have been there sooner.

Hurrying up the steps, she shoved her key in the lock and opened the door. One foot was inside the house before her brain registered what she was seeing.

The head of one of Lizzie's dolls, ruthlessly decapitated, gaped up at her. Strewn across the aged carpet were lamps, books, and photographs. Spools of thread and a heap of buttons spilled from her overturned sewing basket. Scattered sheets of paper fluttered like surprised ghosts as a gusty breeze whipped past her.

"Lizzie!"

Her belongings lay like wreckage in debris that spread through both bedrooms and the spare room she used as an office. In the dining area, newspapers once neatly stacked now littered the table.

A stuffed rabbit, stabbed in the heart and oozing cotton, squeaked in protest when she stepped on it.

"Lizzie!" she screamed. "Where are you?"

"Mom?"

Megan whirled and ran back to the living room. At the door, eyes wide, mouth open, a mix of puzzlement and fear written on her face, her Lizzie gawked at her.

Megan's own freckles stood out on the little girl's whitened cheeks. At eight and a half, there wasn't a trace of baby fat. Lizzie was all angles, from the chin of her heart-shaped face to her elbows and knees.

"What happened, Mama?"

Megan hugged her so tightly the child yelped.

"You knocked my hearing aid loose." Lizzie straightened the wire and placed the little device back in her ear. "What happened?" she asked again.

"I don't know, sweetheart. I just got home." A gust of wind slammed the door shut, making both of them jump.

"Poor Eliot." The little girl scooped up the wounded toy rabbit, then glanced at her mother. "I passed the spelling test."

*   *   *

The shorter officer had a dark leathery face and the broad chest and mournful eyes of a basset hound. His name was Córdova, which he pronounced carefully, as if Megan were a foreigner, which, in a way, she was.

The younger deputy sheriff didn't bother giving his name. He was built like a stump. Bristling red hair topped a broad face above a short, thick neck. Pacing, wide black shoes squeaking, he shot questions at her, ending with, "Any idea who did it?"

"I told you, I'm new here." She ran fingers through hair she had cut herself to save money. "I hardly know anyone."

A few months ago she had packed Lizzie and everything they owned into an old blue Chevy Nova and headed out of Pennsylvania toward California, where she planned to take some classes and begin a career in photography.

But in New Mexico's Rio Grande Valley the Nova had succumbed to a worn piston ring, and Megan, bewitched by the brilliant colors and bold contrasts, had succumbed to the high desert that once was home to her grandparents. She wished she had paid more attention when they talked of their early lives there.

By the time the mechanic pronounced her car worth more dead than alive, she had found this house in Santa Ynez, far enough from Santa Fe to be affordable.

The officer with the doleful eyes was intoning more questions. While Lizzie clung to her mother's hand, Megan repeated everything for the third time: Someone broke the glass in her back door and ransacked her home. Nothing seemed to be missing. "Why would anyone do this and not take anything?"

The younger man, right foot bouncing incessantly, as if he were about to break into a run, scratched his Marine-style haircut. "You sure nothing's missing?"

Megan shook her head. "My cameras are here, computer, photo equipment. Nothing else is worth taking."

Deputy Córdova demonstrated how to secure the sliding windows with a dowel and recommended a new lock for the back door. The present one would be easy to manipulate with an ordinary credit card.

The younger deputy watched as if sizing her up. Eyes beneath blond eyebrows searched hers. "You get the paper delivered?"

"Yes." The frown that now seemed permanently etched on her face deepened. "Why?"

"You know the delivery boy?"

"Seems like a nice kid."

Córdova passed a look to his partner. The two moved toward the door.

"Excuse me?" Megan said. "What *about* the paper boy?"

Córdova turned back, eyebrows meeting in a peak. "We do not want to frighten you and the little girl." He glanced toward his partner, who had stopped at the door. "Four break-ins on this street. All today. All of them get the newspaper delivered. And the paper boy . . ."

"He's missing." The redhead finished the sentence for his partner, tossing the words over his shoulder like things he wanted to be rid of. "The kid's parents say he got up early Saturday to ride his paper route. He never came home."

Chapter Two

From her dining room window Megan could see the sky, swept by the wind, rinsed clean by a cloudburst, and now the color of polished sapphire. After days of cleanup, repair, and jumping at the slightest sound, she was ready for some open air.

With Lizzie off to school she headed for the desert tableland that locals called "the mesa."

Her neighbors had met in little outraged knots up and down the street, men ramming fists into palms and swearing to shoot to kill, women suggesting where to buy locks for the best price.

Mrs. Gonzalez, from across the street, insisted Lizzie must come to her house after school.

"Thanks," Megan said, "but I'm afraid I can't afford to pay much."

"You . . . no *español*?"

"No, sorry. I don't speak Spanish."

The woman mimed aiming a camera. "You do the camera. *¿Sí?*"

Megan nodded. "Yes."

"You *fotos mis nietas*? My gran'childs?" Mrs. Gonzalez frowned with effort, as though English words were stubborn and must be trained to come out right.

"Of course. I'd be happy to. Any time."

"*Sí.*" The woman's head bobbed happily. "I look over the *niña.*"

Now, lying prone amid the low brush, sun lighting her hair the color of freshly stained mahogany, Megan delighted to see the play of light and shadow across the mesa. A few months in New Mexico's sun had ripened the freckles that skipped across her cheeks. She actually felt safer than before the break-in. It was comforting to have such good neighbors.

A recent rain had sent a thin stream into the arroyo just below her. Puddles strewn across the hard clay flashed like newly shined silver. Misty haze hovered around some wizened junipers.

An adobe hut took shape in the camera's viewfinder; Megan could make out the pitted texture of the stucco. A large bird strode purposefully across the ground toward the little house, tail bobbing up, then down, every few steps. He stopped, head thrust forward, intent on the door of the hut. Megan pressed the camera's shutter button.

The door, sun-bleached almost white, swung open, and a woman in faded jeans emerged. A goat appeared from behind a tin-roofed shed as Megan shot again. The woman was tall, her posture as regal as any queen's. She carried a big straw hat. An old fifty? Young eighty? Undone, her braided hair, the color of pewter, might reach almost to the ground. Megan wished she had her 35 mm, or even her old large-format camera. The digital cam was good, but nothing matched the sheer art of old-fashioned black-and-white film.

Despite a niggling guilt about photographing an unsuspecting stranger, she went on snapping. The scene was just too good to pass up. If the results were really good, she could come back and ask the woman to sign a release.

Tall grass tickled Megan's nose, and a sneeze spoiled the next shot.

"Bless you."

The voice was male and quite close, but she could see no one. "Excuse me?"

A shapeless hat rose above the edge of the arroyo a few yards away.

Whatever color the hat might once have possessed was long gone. The face, now on a level with Megan's own, was very tan. Black-framed glasses covered his eyes with lenses as dark as twin eye patches. Irregular features made the face less than handsome, but a gentle mouth beneath a slightly oversize nose somehow made the overall effect appealing.

Slightly wary eyebrows rose above the sunglasses. "I'm just on my way over there." He gestured with his chin, then pulled his long frame over the rim of the gully. His suede jacket, worn shiny in places, looked about as old as its owner. Somewhere just the other side of forty. "What are you doing?"

Megan glanced back at the house where the woman was disappearing inside.

"Oh." After a beat, he smiled. Not a big smile, but it flashed unexpectedly bright in his tanned face. He was Anglo, tall, rangy but solid. Having apparently exhausted his store of small talk, he turned away.

"Hey . . . ," she called, running a hand through wind-tangled hair. "Megan Montoya."

"Pleased to meet you." With a perfunctory nod, he moved on.

"Hey," she called again. "You know anything about that house over there?"

He looked back, a black silhouette now, cut out by the sun. "Like what?"

"Like who lives there?"

"Alma Peters."

"Is she . . . Native American?"

"Alma? An Indian?" He grinned uncertainly, like someone not particularly comfortable around children who found himself in the company of one. "What gave you that idea?"

"She's beautiful. I've never seen a white woman who looked so . . . impressive, so in charge of herself and her corner of the world. You think she would sign a release? A photo release?"

"Don't see why not. Some folks think she's crazy, but she's not." He took a few steps closer, and Megan could see his face again. Gazing at the mountains as if they held the answer to some profound question, he said, "We get a lot of photographers around here. Don't know why."

Megan rose to her full five foot four and recited with the fervor of the newly converted: "The textures, the light, the contrasts, that's why. The color of the sky. The mountains. And especially, the shadows. They're better just after sunup, but I have a daughter. I can't get away that early."

"How long have you lived here?"

"How do you know I'm not from here?"

"In spite of your name?" Something seemed to twitch at the corner of his mouth before he nodded at her loafers. "You'll ruin those pretty quick. Not a lot of sidewalks out here. You need some nice boots. And some dark glasses; this sun could ruin your eyes. And a hat."

"Thanks." She was thinking he might have a face worth photographing—if she could get him to take off the sunglasses. "My grandparents grew up somewhere in this area. You like it here?"

"It's okay." He stared at his own scarred engineer's boots. "But it's a good long way from much of anywhere," he said, and ambled away in a loose-jointed gait.

Megan watched the shapeless, colorless hat disappear beyond a rise, then brushed herself off, made her way back to the car, and drove home.

The house was quiet and cool. Craving some hot tea, she put a cup of water into the microwave. The green frog on the cup seemed to grin at her as it spun on the turntable. Unexpected emotion prickled like acid rain behind her eyelids. Her mother gave her that cup when she was about Lizzie's age.

"Don't believe that stuff about the princess and the frog," Barbara Montoya had said. "A frog is a frog. They don't turn into princes, no matter how many times you kiss them."

Barbara was working in her father's bookstore in Pittsburgh when Ian O'Connor came to sign his latest novel. By the time she learned he was married, she was pregnant.

"A tale-spinner. The most charming tale-spinner of all time" was the only description Barbara ever gave of Megan's father.

"What does 'tale-spinner' mean?" the child Megan had asked.

"Liar." Barbara's lips always grew thin when she spoke of him. "It means liar."

The entire Montoya clan refused to comment further except to report, much after the fact, that he was among the passengers never found when a storm-pitched ferry went down in the Irish Sea.

Barbara never married, becoming instead an ardent feminist. She inherited the bookstore and managed to send her daughter to Penn State.

Megan sometimes wondered why her mother gave her an Irish first name if she didn't want to be reminded of the man who had fathered her. And why was her mother so flabbergasted when Megan, with no interest in marriage, deliberately conceived a child? Without, for that matter, any further interest in Lizzie's father?

"I'm only doing what you did, but without the pain," Megan explained.

Barbara eyed her daughter for long seconds. "Maybe. But without the joy, too."

When a drunk plowing through a stoplight on a rainy night killed Barbara, Megan was devastated. Eventually, grief gave way to a gnawing sense of disquiet about her own life. Her job as an accountant paid well but now seemed stifling, rigid, boring. She and Lizzie needed something more in their lives than numbers in neat columns. Aside from Lizzie there was only one thing she really loved: Photography. She had won awards in half a dozen amateur competitions, but there was so much she didn't know. By the time the bookstore sold, Megan knew what she wanted to do.

Most of the time she knew she had made the right decision.

The microwave's timer chimed. As she plunked a tea bag into the cup, her gaze wandered to the ever-present stack of newspapers in the corner of the alcove that served as a dining room. She was hopelessly behind on the news. She scanned the headlines of the topmost, tossed it aside, and pawed through the remaining papers. Where was Saturday's? If she couldn't read them on time, she preferred to at least read them in order.

Was it the Saturday paper she used to sweep away those cobwebs? Yes, there it was, still rolled up on top of the kitchen cabinet. She retrieved it and pulled it open.

Something clattered to the floor. She stared at what appeared to be a dirty, nicked plastic bag and picked it up. Inside were several jagged, dingy stones.

Chapter Three

Tea sloshed as Megan set down her cup. The stones looked like thin little pieces of coal.

She emptied the bag onto the table. There were five pieces in all. The edges were chipped. Tiny smooth places dotted the surface of each. She rubbed away some dust with her thumb and held one stone up to the light. A dim, dark green appeared in the cleaned spot.

Sipping the tea, she remembered the missing paperboy. Was he mixed up with thieves or smugglers? Was she being used as a front to hide some sort of loot? Should she call the cops? What would she say? "Excuse me, I found some stones in my newspaper"? Already she could see the younger deputy smirking.

She tossed the packet into a drawer next to the kitchen sink and took a bowl from a shelf. Lizzie would love an early supper of waffles.

The drop of water she flicked onto the waffle iron bounced twice, hissed, and evaporated just as she heard the front door open. "Want some waffles?" When there was no reply, she reminded herself to check the batteries in the child's hearing aid and called again.

Lizzie poked her head into the kitchen. "Waffles?"

Megan held out her arms. "Hugs."

The little girl bounded across the kitchen, almost knocking her mother over as she threw her arms around her. "What's that box in the living room?" Lizzie asked, eyeglasses slightly askew.

"Used books." Megan set two plates on the table. "How's the math coming?"

Lizzie dropped into a chair. "I can't do it, Mom. And Jimmy Ramirez says I'm stupid."

"What a rude thing to say. You're very bright. But you do have to work hard."

Lizzie doused her waffle with honey. "Harder than everybody else?"

"Maybe."

"That's no fair." Lizzie tilted her head, a long straight strand of ash-blond hair sticking to the honey on her lips. "I know, I know. Life isn't fair." She attacked her waffle again with relish. "It's going to snow tonight," she said, mopping up the honey.

Megan looked out the window at the cloudless sky. "This is Santa Ynez. In New Mexico. As in Southwest. As in dry. And it's April."

Lizzie shook her head vigorously. "I don't care, Mom. It's going to snow."

When they finished eating, Megan said, "I want to take your picture."

"Again?" Lizzie squirmed out of her chair and dashed for her room.

"Math," Megan called after her. "Then pictures."

When she posed her less than willing model on a step stool in front of the window, the sinking sun played across the child's upturned face. "Turn your chin a little to the right."

Lizzie made a face, fidgeted, pushed her hair behind her left ear, and kicked her legs back and forth. Then, as if a switch was thrown, she straightened and sat perfectly still.

Looking into her daughter's face, Megan again saw how much it was like her own: straight brows, brown eyes, small nose, all in the shape of a heart. Lizzie was such a miracle. If there was such a thing as heartstrings, this child held hers in her warm little hands. She began to click the shutter. "Don't think about the camera. Just talk to me."

"What's that stuff on your face?"

"A masque. M-A-S-Q-U-E. Not a Halloween mask. A facial."

"Can I have one?"

"You don't need one."

"Why do you?"

"Because I'm getting old."

"You're only thirty-five."

"When you're thirty-five, you can have one."

"Your hair looks funny," Lizzie said. "It's sticking out."

Megan smoothed her hair. "When I cut it I didn't get all the lengths right."

"Why didn't you go to a hair place?"

"To save money. My hair isn't as important as it was when I was working."

"It *is* going to snow," Lizzie said.

"No it isn't. Move your chin up, just a little." *Click.*

Lizzie careened to another subject. "Nana didn't like me, did she?"

Megan looked over the camera at her daughter. "How can you think that? Nana just wished I didn't decide to become a mother right when I did, or the way that I did. I'll probably have those sorts of feelings about you. But it was my life, and it will be your life." She carefully scratched her temple where the drying masque was beginning to itch.

"Nana thought you liked living dangerous, and she wanted me to have a father."

"I don't live dangerously. I'm not a spy or a skydiver. And I certainly hope your children will have a father. But all you've got is me. Am I good enough?"

The mischief in the elfin face gave way to a grin. "Yeah. You're enough. Except . . ." Lizzie wriggled. "Why do we always have to take pictures?"

"So I can become a famous photographer. Or at least make a living."

15

Lizzie gave a mock groan. "Your face looks funny. Why is it that icky yellow?"

"It's a mustard masque."

"Mustard?"

The doorbell rang. Lizzie leaped up. "I'll get it."

"Wait a sec! Don't you dare open that door," Megan yelled, dashing for the bathroom. She spun the knob on the faucet, bent over the sink, and began scraping the plasterlike mess from her face.

"It's some guy, Mom," Lizzie called. "I don't think he laughs very much."

Straightening, Megan glanced in the mirror. Blobs of yellow still clung to her cheeks. The doorbell gave out another insistent ring.

"Okay, okay!" Holding a towel to her face, she headed for the living room.

Lizzie had opened the door. The man standing just inside was clad in the sort of uniform worn by delivery people, but he wasn't carrying a package.

"Yes?" Megan hoped the light was dim enough that he wouldn't notice the few bits of masque still stuck to her face.

The man was darkly good-looking and had an intensity that seemed to send out little shock waves as his gaze flitted about the room. Thick black-brown hair curled at his temples. Traces of gray in his nicely shaped beard made him look older than he probably was. She thought he should be modeling for Calvin Klein and wondered what he would think if she asked him to pose. Stitched across the pocket of his shirt was a name, but she couldn't read it.

"I am . . ." His eyes fixed on Megan's face, his voice died.

"It's a facial," Lizzie piped.

Avoiding Megan's face, the man began again. "I am from the electric." He looked Hispanic, but his words had a different lilt from that of her neighbors. Lamplight reflected dully from the metal back of a clipboard he was tapping against his leg. "We will do some work tomorrow.

It may be needed to stop the electricity one hour or two." Earnest dark eyes gazed about the room, pausing here and there as if he were checking the number of items that required electricity.

Megan felt the remains of the masque crack across her chin. "Okay," she said, clinging to her last shred of composure. "Thank you...." Her voice faded as she stared past him.

Fat flakes of snow were drifting lazily in the air.

Chapter Four

In downtown Santa Fe, the streets were little more than twisting lanes. Every house, office building, hotel appeared to be sculpted from the same salmon-colored clay. The gallery's exterior was carefully aged to look like old adobe.

Megan already had visited six art dealers on Canyon Road. The artwork was world-class, the galleries rustic counterparts of their cousins in New York. And the answer was always the same. A polite—sometimes barely polite—brush-off. She hated the whole awful process, but there was no other way.

This was her first stop in town near the plaza. *You couldn't sell Girl Scout cookies when you were a kid. What made you think you could sell your own photography?* But maybe the seventh time would be the charm.

A bell tinkled as she pushed the door open. The floor inside was treated to look like the wood was so old the finish had worn off. A man with dainty hands, soulful eyes behind fashionably small eyeglasses, a small oval face, and well-styled faded-blond hair—a sort of male Dresden doll—appeared from an inner room. "May I help you?"

Megan forced a smile. "Do you handle photography?"

"Of course." Then he caught sight of her portfolio case. "We'd be pleased to look at what you have, but we're full up on photography just now."

She willed her fingers to stop shaking as she started to unzip the leather case. "Shall I just put it on the floor?"

"No." He drew out the word with obvious resignation and gestured toward a hall.

Trailing him, she passed a series of paintings that mimicked van Gogh's style. They arrived in a small, windowless office, where the walls seemed to have molted and cluttered the floor with artwork. A faint odor of linseed oil hung in the air. Amid the hodgepodge, the desk was a naked oasis. A chrome lamp, the shape of an inverted funnel, hung over it, bathing the desk in a bluish glow that made her think of an operating table.

She hoisted the portfolio to the desktop and watched his manicured fingers flip through the samples of her work, stopping once or twice, then moving on.

When he reached the last he sat down in the big black-leather, high-back chair behind the desk. Megan wondered if his feet reached the floor. He took off his glasses and, holding them as some men hold a pipe, looked up at her. "May I give you some advice?"

Megan steeled herself. "Please."

"First, there's more competition in photography than almost any other art. And less of it sold. Any fool thinks he can take pictures. People go on vacation, shoot some scenes, and wow, there's a photo as good as any professional's. Never mind that they couldn't produce another that good in a year, and they certainly can't do it day in and day out."

The unctuous, professional voice was gone, his tone frank. "You have a good eye."

"Thank you." *Go on. Tell me a good eye and a quarter will get me a nice parking place.*

"A good eye can make a talented amateur. But you also show a certain command of the technical. Both of these will improve as you gain experience." His eyes moved to her face. "Your best work is in black and white, but you are no Ansel Adams. Stop me if I'm being too candid."

"No." She smoothed a runaway strand of hair. "Please go on."

"Your faces are good. Very good." He went back to a shot of Lizzie sitting on a limb of a tree in their backyard, the shadows of cottonwood leaves making patterns around her. "But tourists don't buy black-and-white, and they don't buy faces. They buy classic, quaint scenery. In color. Big postcards, actually."

"So who does buy faces?"

His narrow shoulders lifted eloquently. "A few book publishers, a few art lovers, a few museums, perhaps. The money ranges from zero to minimal. Even if you perfect what you do best, you're talking critical acclaim, which is nice but doesn't put much food on the table. And that's a very dim maybe. Art critics are more likely to rave about a stack of dirty diapers than a good photograph."

"You're saying I should forget this."

"I'm not God. I don't—" The sudden death of the funnel-shaped lamp made both of them jump.

Megan squinted, trying to see through the cavelike murk.

"Another power failure," he muttered. "It's just a matter of time. I'd lay money on it."

"What's a matter of time?" she asked nervously.

An annoyed sigh came from the darkness across from her. "Most of our electricity comes into New Mexico through one place near the Four Corners. All in one place before the power is stepped down and distributed. One of these days there will be an earthquake or a tornado or some other disaster, and the whole state will be without power. Probably for a long time. An event no doubt accompanied by riots, looting, and general all-around chaos."

Eyes adjusting to the dark, Megan could see the man's outline as he sat forward in the chair, elbows on the desk. "Well, that can't be very likely," she murmured, trying to seem interested.

"My father was one of the engineers on the project. It's part of a gigantic power 'doughnut' that circles the Southwest. Our beloved New Mexico has no other source. Classic bad planning." The funnel above his head pulsed back to life. "Ah. Now, where were we?"

"You were saying you weren't God."

"Of course." He glanced at the spectacles that were still in his hand, then went on as though the interruption was staged for theatrical effect. "I don't know anything for certain. Maybe someone at the Getty takes a liking to your work."

"Right. I might also discover diamonds in a box of Cracker Jacks." She began slipping her prints back into the leather case.

"Tell you what." He carefully fit the eyeglass temples back over his ears and rose from his chair. "Do some more faces. In a few weeks, bring me a dozen of your best. I'll pick a few, hang them for the summer, and we'll see what happens."

For a moment, she could only stare at him. He seemed taller than before. "Thank you."

"Keep in mind: I am very fussy about cropping—and dust if it's real film. Don't bring me anything until you're sure it's the best you can do. And I will set the price, not you. I'm in a better position to know what people will pay. And I should warn you that we charge fifty percent of the sales price. I know that's steep, but this is a high-rent district."

Megan restrained an urge to hug him.

"Even if they all sell, which they won't, you won't average minimum wage for your efforts." He picked up a business card from a stack on the desk and handed it to her. "See you in a couple of weeks. Or if you have something really spectacular before that, drop by."

His card read W. BREWSTER GILLETTE. Certain that before the lights went out he was about to turn her down, she was giddily grateful to whatever caused the power failure.

Portfolio safe in the trunk of her car, she glanced at her watch. The jewelry store should be only a few blocks. Walking might be faster than braving the tiny one-way streets and hunting for another impossible-to-find parking place.

*   *   *

The store smelled of a nicely spicy lemon potpourri.

Byron Spitz had a round baby face below a forehead that reflected light. A few very long hairs were combed from just above his left ear across the otherwise vacant top of his head. He owned, according to the sign outside, the oldest jewelry store in Santa Fe. His eyebrows edged toward his nonexistent hairline when Megan held out the plastic bag of stones to him.

"Sorry to bother you, but can you tell me what these are?"

He gazed at her for a moment, as if trying to decide if she was sane and not a felon, then ducked his chin in a slow nod. Long pale fingers with knobby knuckles and very clean nails took the bag from her hand. Without a word he walked along the lit counter and disappeared through blue velvet curtains.

While trying to kill time examining the glassed-in displays of wedding bands, necklaces, and elegant wristwatches, Megan couldn't keep her eyes from flicking between the blue curtains and the street door. Part of her expected a cop to appear, jingling a pair of handcuffs.

When Spitz placed a small white box on the counter behind her, she jumped.

"These," he said, in a voice that sounded like it was passing state secrets, "are emerald."

"Emerald?"

The jeweler gave a small nod. "Yes."

Megan stared at him. "They are . . . valuable?"

"Quite."

"Like how . . . ?"

He raised his eyes to study the ceiling before bringing his gaze back

22

to her. "These appear to be nonoiled fine, possibly even extra-fine, emeralds." He stopped and considered the ceiling again. "They may even be 'old mine.' Three are more than a hundred carats each, two a bit less. I know nothing of archeological value, but that would be a factor as well. Roughly, very roughly, I would guess a million, perhaps a bit more."

"Two hundred thousand dollars each?" Megan's voice sounded hoarse.

"No." The man's chin moved two inches to the left then two inches to the right, "a million dollars each."

Chapter Five

Miguel Estevan pinched a bit of soil between thumb and forefinger, held it up, and let it go. The wind carried it away.

Estevan was not his real name. Miguel selected it when he learned to write because he liked the way the capital *E* looked.

He was sitting with his back against a rock, in a pinto-bean field. He pressed the heels of his hands hard into his eyes, then shook his head until the thoughts ran into one another.

Miguel wasn't fond of farm fields. He had seen far too many of them, was in fact born in a strawberry field.

He knew the story, although he wasn't told it until he was nearly twelve.

In one of the wealthiest areas of the world—Orange County, California—his mother had crouched until noon, picking the berries no Anglo would bend down that far to harvest. Then she quietly lay down, without even a tree to shelter her from the blazing midday sun, and brought him into the hateful world.

She never got up again.

Tía María, whose own *niño* was born under similar circumstances and died a few hours later, did not know what became of his mother's body, or who or where his father was. She took Miguel from between his mother's bloody knees and cared for him as her own.

When he was three she made him a cross with a pair of small twigs bound together with yarn, white at the center, then blue where the threads became squarish with the twigs as ribs. This, she told him solemnly, was the *ojo*, the eye, of the Mountain God. It would make him strong. It would make him manly and fearless, and able to lead their people from misery.

Shy and introverted, Miguel did not think that was very likely.

Tía María held the Mountain God's eye to his ear. "Listen," she said, and he watched her, his eyes round and silent. "It is an eye, because it must see. But one day it will speak." She nodded solemnly. "It will tell you what to do."

From that day on, Miguel was certain Tía María was a saint.

The first eight years of his life were spent following the crops and hiding in arroyos and caves, even in outhouses, from the Immigration and Naturalization Service. If Tía María was a saint, the INS was Satan.

He watched the joints of Tía María's hands become huge and painful, and her back become twisted. When she could no longer pick, he did the picking for both of them, and tried to take care of her with the few dollars earned.

"School" was just a word he had heard. Tía María was his only teacher.

"You and I are the *herederos*," she intoned, in the sort of voice a priest uses for Communion, "the rightful heirs to Aztlán," which seemed to include everywhere they had picked crops. In Aztlán, she told him, his forefathers were born.

He was eleven when he began to formulate his plan, although he didn't realize until later that it was a plan.

Tía María became bone thin and began coughing so much she could barely talk. Miguel became very proficient at stealing. He found he could steal more in one morning than he could earn in a full week of picking. After that, life was a little easier.

Until the night he was arrested for breaking into a gas station.

He was forced to leave Tía María on the banks of the New River, a stream of sewage and disease that ran from Mexico through the lowest reaches of California's Imperial Valley.

In jail, he met Luis, who had been to school in Mexico and in Texas. Luis knew many things, including how to forge permits, passports, birth certificates, even driver's licenses. But he was caught, so he was maybe not yet quite good enough at forgery. Luis taught Miguel how to speak and read and write English. Their hatred of the Anglo world that put them in that filthy jail grew.

Miguel worried about Tía María. Without him, she could not live long. She might even be dead already. He began giving serious thought to his plan. Perhaps she was right. Perhaps he *would* be the one to lead his people out of misery.

Eventually he and Luis were put on a truck and sent to Mexico. Miguel was born in California, but he had no papers. He was not yet fifteen.

In Mexico, the authorities were no more pleased to see him than he was to see them. For some reason they let Luis go free but locked Miguel up and laughed when he asked why. This jail was worse than the first. It did not even provide prisoners with meals. The guards paid almost no attention to the convicts at all. Luis brought Miguel food and taught him forgery.

Sometimes, in the nights, Miguel dreamed of Tía María. He was certain she was dead. She could not have lived more than a few months, as sick as she was the last time he saw her. She probably did not live more than a few weeks, with no one to care for her after they put him in jail.

Luis was there when word came of the airplanes, the Twin Towers, and a place called the Pentagon. Luis pumped his fist in the air and said it was good. He told of American corporations that robbed many lands of their oil, their copper, their farmland, anything in the ground or under it. Miguel was not sure this was true. How could a company be so powerful?

Luis filled Miguel's head with stories of men like Fidel Castro, Benito Juarez, Simon Bolivar, Che Guevara, even Karl Marx. And last, with excitement lighting his eyes, he told of the new leaders, Hugo Chavez and Evo Morales.

Miguel wasn't sure exactly when he decided that the people of Aztlán must reclaim the land of their birth. One day he just knew it. *The call of our blood is our power, our duty, our fate.*

By the time the Mexican authorities tired of his presence and released him, Miguel's forgery skills far surpassed Luis's. The two headed for Ciudad Juárez, on the border. There Miguel plied his new trade. He learned everything he could about his new country, Mexico, and about the country north of the Rio Grande, which had treated him and Tía María like refuse to be tossed away when no longer useful.

On a dark night a few years later, he took the considerable sum he had earned falsifying papers and silently made his way into Texas. He told no one except Luis where he was going.

While he was picking his way north on foot, Miguel devised *El Plan Espiritual de Aztlán.*

Months before, after much studying of books and maps, he had carefully selected the site. Nuevo México was nearly perfect. There was much land, and except for Albuquerque, Santa Fe, and Las Cruces, not many people. Only three big highways crossed the state, two east/west, one north/south. And there were only a few airports of any size: one in Albuquerque, the others on Air Force bases. Much of the land was not even American, belonging instead to the *indios*. Barely half the population was Anglo; the rest was Mexican, Hispanic, and Indian.

In Albuquerque, Miguel found a small apartment near the main library, where he read everything he could find about New Mexico's history.

He loved the library so much he wanted to live there. He read about the Treaty of Guadalupe Hidalgo and the question of the national forest land that covered more than a third of the state. Much of this was *ejido* land—communal acreage where villagers once grazed their animals and gathered timber.

The Mexicans were mostly in the south. Miguel read how the Navajos were forced into the northwest part of the state by the Anglos. Most of the other *indios* lived in *pueblos*—tribal towns where their families had lived for hundreds of years. They built casinos where Anglos, whose laws forbid gambling on their own land, left huge amounts of money in the slot machines and on the gaming tables. This made the *indios* laugh, but Miguel could tell from some of the things they said that many were still bitter.

Miguel taught himself how to use the library's free computers by watching others. When he did his first Internet search it was as though the Mountain God had finally spoken—all that knowledge right there with a few taps of the fingers.

According to Hispano-Mexican law, this land was to be held "in common" for the people. The Treaty of Guadalupe Hidalgo committed the United States government to protect these rights. Instead, early in the twentieth century the Anglos stole nearly four million acres of private and communal land—in the name of conservation—to establish New Mexico's national forests.

The Hispanics were bonded by blood or language or anger at the Anglos, or by all three. It was as he thought. New Mexico belonged to them. It had been stolen.

He studied, scowled, and reworked his Plan.

Now it was a plan with a capital P, he thought, feeling clever. In Mexico, a plan of action spelling out grievances and explaining how injustices would be eliminated was issued before a revolution. Mexico had known many revolutions.

Miguel decided Luis was probably right. The Anglos and their corporations were the reason for the 9/11 disaster. The time had come for his people to free themselves from the *gabacho* who exploited their riches and destroyed their culture.

Now he understood the meaning of Aztlán. It was the stolen land. Aztlán should belong to those who plant the seeds, water the fields, and gather the crops, not to the greedy Anglos whose corporations were raping the world.

The idea was not new. He had read about how Chicanos had tried to escape the oppression. But whenever American prosperity slumped, Anglos would cast about for a scapegoat. Calls rose to rid the country of what they called "illegal aliens." In fact, since 9/11, people talked about this endlessly. He was reading more and more now on Internet blogs.

Miguel absolutely agreed. He just had a different idea about who the illegal aliens were.

How he would accomplish his plan was not new either.

The librarian, a prim woman with frizzy blonde hair, was condescending, but Miguel pretended great respect and she helped him gain access to information about the power grid.

Earlier Chicano efforts had failed. *This plan will not.*

Before, they had asked.

This time, they would take.

This country was too big for the tactics of Hugo or Evo. But Miguel would do at least as much for his people as Che. Maybe more. He needed only four things: someone near the border or in Mexico to recruit men, someone who could speak to the hearts of people as he could not, a job with the electric company, and money—a lot of money—enough to train and feed an army.

He wrote to Luis with instructions on how to set up a free e-mail account that he could use on a library computer.

At a fiesta he saw a woman who played her audience as though each listener was a strand on a thousand-string guitar.

And the Mountain God began to whisper.

Miguel explained parts of the plan to her, and she was clever in helping him prepare.

He shook his head as if to clear it. He always felt that way when he thought of Corazón. She was not an easy woman. Sometimes, when things went wrong, she screamed at him, her anger like molten metal. Did she think it would all be parades and singing?

She must be made to see that the people who died—and some would—were brought home by the Mountain God so their people could shed their chains, stop begging for crumbs, and become a free nation.

Maybe he should explain that part soon. Especially since the money part, which at first seemed a miracle, was now not good. They would have to do some things, maybe not very nice things. Corazón would have to understand and stop getting so angry.

Miguel was never angry. Or perhaps he was always angry, but his anger was cold, like the ocean, unceasingly grinding away until it swallowed whatever problem it found in its path.

The hot sun was dipping toward the west, and the soil was dry in the field where Miguel now sat staring over the rows of bean plants. He tossed another pinch of soil into the air and watched the grains disappear. *This is our land.*

And that is how our land disappeared under the feet of the foreigners.

It was too late for Tía María. He knew in his gut she had died there on that riverbank waiting for him. But it was not too late for others. She was right: Miguel would be the one to show them the way.

From his pocket he took a small pair of twigs bound with yarn and stared deep into the eye of the Mountain God.

Chapter Six

Megan stood outside the jewelry store trying to string together a few intelligent thoughts. Whatever she had expected, it wasn't emeralds.

And maybe these weren't even ordinary emeralds. The jeweler thought they might be ancient ceremonial arrowheads. He had handed the box to her with a seriousness worthy of a sacred ritual.

She walked back to the aging Honda Civic that had replaced the dead Nova. Getting in, she locked the door and opened her purse. She tilted the box lid and pushed back the cotton batting. The stones didn't look much like emeralds. But they did resemble the arrowheads she and Lizzie saw at the museum a few weeks ago.

Should she tell someone? The sheriff? Maybe go to the museum and talk to the curator? There was no safe place to lock up the stones at home. Her house had already been ransacked.

On Cerillos Road, along the ugly parade of fast-food restaurants that led south, she spotted a McDonald's sign and pulled into the parking lot. In a trash container she found a crumpled carryout bag and a cup with a straw jutting through the lid.

She filled the cup with sand from the little playground behind the restaurant. Back in the car, she pushed the stones into the sand, put the lid on the cup, tucked it into the bag, wadded up the bag until it looked like some forgotten piece of trash, and pushed it under the passenger seat.

*　　*　　*

Alma Peters was trying to find the right shade of yellow.

The narrow room was flanked by three walls of windows, but she was so intent on her painting she didn't realize the sky was going a blotchy, sullen gray. She stared at the Masonite board propped on her homemade easel. Masonite was cheap and held up better than canvas. The brush strokes were wrong, the colors didn't work. Had she lost it? The gift of seeing something beyond the ordinary? Alma had been through these dry spells before, but back then she had more time. Now, hard as it was for her to believe, she was pushing toward ninety. That bald fact rolled about in her mind like a marble in a metal bowl.

Maybe her painting days were over. That possibility raised a chill along her arms as she dipped her brush into a jar of linseed oil. Flinching, she dabbed the brush on a paint-smeared cloth. The arthritis was flaring up again. Well, she had to expect that at her age.

Her eyes moved back to the painting. Once the images fairly exploded from her brush. She could hardly paint fast enough. And with that came the joy, the drive, the reason for living. Today's work seemed contrived, artificial, just plain awful.

Beyond the windows a stand of juniper and piñon was bucking the wind, the trees' resistance written in their limbs. The sight reminded her that she needed firewood. A puff of wind, chill with an uncommon damp, blew the door toward her when she unlatched it. A large bird scurried around the corner of the cabin, lowered its head, and stared at her. "It's going to be a cold night, Rodolfo," she told the roadrunner.

The animals were shuffling about in the tin-roofed mud structure she called a barn. It was little more than a ramshackle shed, but it was good enough to shelter the few head of sheep and goats and the half dozen chickens she kept, as much for pets as for food. The barn needed a new coat of mud. She'd have to see to that before the weather got too hot.

Ducking her head against the wind, she strode to the woodpile, scooped up three logs, and headed back to the cabin. Plunking the logs into the fireplace, she added some wood chips for kindling. She had built that fireplace herself, made the adobe bricks with her own hands and dried them in the sun. They hoarded heat, warming the cabin long after the wood burned out.

She struck a wooden match. The flame sputtered about the chips, then grasped the logs in lengthening fingers of orange and yellow, slowly filling the room with a thick, spicy odor. Alma's face began to relax. Not much in the world smelled better than a piñon fire.

She had built the cabin herself, too. And after sixty-odd years it was still solid enough to last another sixty. Who would have thought she had such nerve? Especially after what she had been.

You fooled everyone. Maybe yourself most of all.

A pain shot down her right leg. Sciatica. She was really coming apart. Limping to the narrow table that stood against the wall, she sat in one of the old captain's chairs she had found at the dump and restored. The time just might be coming soon. Time to use the little package that lay beneath the roots of the weather-beaten scrub oak near the arroyo that ran across her land.

Maybe they weren't worth anything. Alma had never tried to find out, because if they were really valuable, just knowing that would change things. And if they were worthless, that would change things, too. She preferred not to know.

By the time she figured out how to live off the land, most of the money earned in San Francisco was gone.

She found them that first year after staking out her homestead after the war, back when she was sleeping in the open, still digging the foundation for the cabin. Her clothes were damp from rain when her spade brought two of them up. Careful searching unearthed the others. Every year after that, she dug them up again just to reassure herself that a storm hadn't washed them away. She would gaze at them awhile, feel the blunted edges and the places where some handheld stone had chipped away at their surface. But she always wrapped them up and put them back.

This time, maybe she wouldn't.

Something not quite a smile plucked at her mouth. She might have a little trouble collecting Social Security on the work she had done in San Francisco.

Chapter Seven

*F*ive million dollars!

Megan tried not to think that just one of those emeralds could give her all the time she wanted to build a career in photography.

There was a rightful owner. There must be.

If she turned the stones over to the cops, they might lose them, or steal them, or accuse her of stealing them. Who would believe they had just shown up wrapped in her newspaper? She wondered if the paperboy was still missing.

She was loading clothes into the washer when something slipped out of a shirt pocket. A camera memory chip. In her excitement over the stones she had forgotten the frames she shot that day. When she transferred the images to her computer, the woman with the roadrunner and the goat that appeared on her monitor were accompanied by a little thrill of triumph.

This was more than just a great face—it was an eloquent face, a part of a fluid landscape. Megan sent a few frames to the printer, then found a photo release form on the Internet and printed that, too.

By early afternoon she was heading back out to the mesa. On the passenger seat, a brown envelope of photos bounced with each chuck-hole. She spotted a pair of ruts on the gravel road that led through the brush. A driveway to the woman's cabin? Unwilling to risk the Honda's tires, she pulled off the road and set the emergency brake.

"Some folks think she's crazy." Here's hoping they were wrong.

The car door rattled when she closed it. Damn. She couldn't afford car repairs. Unless . . . But she didn't want to think about the emeralds that way.

A few minutes' walk along the ruts brought her to a clump of juni-pers and piñons and an ancient blue pickup. The little adobe house be-yond the truck looked sturdy despite walls scarred by the strafing of sandstorms.

In front of the open door, a woman was standing on a semicircle of chipped brick patio. She moved into the shade cast by a cluster of fruit trees. When her eyes found the stranger in her driveway, she stiffened and slowly folded her arms across her chest.

"Mrs. Peters?" Megan called.

"Alma's good enough."

"I'm Megan Montoya. I'm a photographer. I wonder if you would do me a favor."

"If your car broke down, I don't have a phone."

"No, no. My car is fine." Megan waved toward the arroyo. "I was tak-ing pictures over there and happened to get you in some of them. They turned out to be really good and . . . I'd like to use one or two. Would you be willing to sign a release?"

"Use them how?"

"Hang them in a gallery. And sell them." *I hope.*

Alma took her time appraising her visitor. Then, "Would you like some tea?"

"I'd love some." Megan followed her into a narrow sunroom. The second room was wider, darker, cooler, and a remarkable combination of bedroom, kitchen, dining room, living room. It smelled of cinnamon. A small pockmarked maple table sat against a bright yellow wall. Alma pointed to one of the captain's chairs next to it. Long dusky braids swayed across her back as she moved into the small kitchen, which was separated from the rest of the space by a half wall that also served as the headboard of a bed in the main room.

"What a nice place you have," Megan said. The rooms were not only spotless, the walls were hung with oil paintings, watercolors, and sketches.

Alma gave her an amused smile. "It's comfortable enough. No electricity or running water, though." She pointed at a neat stack of gallon jugs that had begun life as milk containers. "Tommy Ruiz lets me fill those at his gas station." She uncapped one and picked up a copper teakettle. "I irrigate the garden from an old well, but the water's not fit to drink."

A painting caught Megan's eye: an adobe wall, a dusty window, a Coke bottle holding a solitary rose. "That's beautiful," she said pointing. "Who's the artist?"

Alma brought two ceramic mugs to the table. "A friend."

Megan studied the other paintings. "Your friend did all of them, didn't she? Or is it a he?"

"Yes," Alma said. "May I see the pictures you mentioned?"

Megan slid them from the envelope.

Alma examined them for a long moment. "Yes, these are quite good. What do you want me to sign?"

Megan handed her the release form. "You can keep those prints if you want."

"Thank you," Alma said, and signed.

Fascinated by the woman's face, the high, broad cheekbones, the piercing eyes of some Greek or Roman warrior queen, Megan said, "I wonder . . . Just say no if you aren't interested."

" 'No' is one of the easiest words for me."

"Could I do some informal portraits of you?"

For a moment, Alma didn't answer, then: "You know, I just might be able to do that. Are you willing to get dirty?"

"Excuse me?" Megan wondered if this was the crazy part she'd been told about.

"I need to get a coat of mud on the barn. It isn't a hard job, especially not for two, but the mud does make a mess of your clothes. I'll let you take pictures if you'll help with that."

"You got it," Megan said, delighted, and they set a date. As she was leaving, the linseed odor, the several boards stacked against the wall in the sunroom, made her think of the art dealer's office. "Are those paintings?"

Alma gave her a small smile and began to draw the door closed. "Thanks for stopping by. It will be good to get that barn done."

Chapter Eight

The sun was beginning its slide west, deepening the colors of the landscape as Megan made her way back to her car. A quarter-mile drive down the road, the views became irresistible.

Remembering the guy at the gallery saying tourists buy local scenery, and knowing every extra dollar would help, she stopped and reached into the Honda's backseat for her camera. As she got out of the car an old van barreled along the road, trailed by a thick, orange cloud.

An easy walk brought her to a landscape dotted with several distant cabins. In the other direction, an ancient scrub oak, its branches spread wide, seemed poised like an ancient worshiper stiffly preparing to kneel on the edge of an arroyo. The tree, so solitary, so fiercely proud of its survival, was a compelling image. Megan forgot about postcard landscapes.

As she drew closer she saw a figure hunched over the ground just beyond the tree.

Intent on whatever he was doing, he didn't look up. But she recognized the shapeless hat.

"Hello!" she called.

Still not bothering to look up, he called back, "Taking more pictures?"

"Yes. Nice to see you again." She waited, but he didn't respond. "Would it be rude of me to ask what you're doing?"

At length, he tilted his face toward her. "Digging."

"What are you digging for?"

"Don't know." He returned to the careful scraping. "Whatever's here."

"Are you a detective?"

"You could call it that, I guess." He went on probing the sun-dried ground with a small tool.

"Would you mind if I took your picture?"

His head shot up, unseating his sunglasses from his nose. Startled hazel eyes stared into hers as if she had offered to chop off his foot. "Of me?"

"Just while you work. You don't have to pose or anything."

His face grew lines of discomfort, and he put the sunglasses back in place.

"It's quite painless. Really."

After a moment he shrugged.

Taking that to mean okay, she backed up a few feet, squatted in the brush, and raised the camera. "Just ignore me. Go on with what you're doing."

For a while, his posture remained tense, but gradually his face took on a gentle look as he explored the soil. Lying prone on the ground to catch more of his expression, she marveled at how a group of relatively unattractive features could combine to make a curiously appealing face.

"You always take pictures lying down?" The straight line of his mouth seemed to argue with a grin.

"Sometimes. What do you find when you dig?"

"Pottery shards. Maybe an arrowhead or two, pieces of tools, bones. But mostly just pottery." It was his longest statement yet.

"So you're an archeologist."

"Ayah."

"What do you learn from the things you find?"

"How the Ancestral Pueblo people lived."

"How did they live?" she asked, more interested in his expression than his answer.

"Pretty rigorous lives, but more civilized than you might expect. They built themselves a fine city on a cliff over there. A sort of huge apartment complex. They farmed, they cooked, they hauled water from more than a mile away, worshiped their gods, buried their dead, thatched their roofs. And they were visited by traveling salesmen from the Gulf of California."

Megan sat cross-legged in the dirt, forgetting the camera for the moment. This guy was downright talkative once he got started. "When was that?"

"Eight hundred, a thousand years ago."

Megan held the camera up again. "Why are you looking for things down here if they lived up there?"

"Oh, this is something else. This is just a wild hare, probably a wild goose chase, too." He sat back on his heels. "Spanish explorers came through here in the 1530s, you know, looking for what they called the Seven Cities of Cibola. We know that somewhere southwest of here, the Pima Indians gave some Spaniards five emerald arrowheads."

For five whole seconds, Megan didn't move. Then she lowered the camera and gaped at him.

"The Pimas told the Spaniards the emeralds came from up north." Oblivious to her stunned look, he went back to scratching the ground. "They didn't, of course. No emerald mines hereabouts. But I figure most stories have some basis in truth. Those stones just may be buried near here."

She struggled to keep her tone steady. "The Indians gave someone five emerald arrowheads?"

"That's the message the Spaniards sent back."

"Have you found anything like that?"

His eyes held a bittersweet look. "If I did, I wouldn't be scratching around in this dirt. But the Pueblo peoples in the 1500s had trading partners way to the south. And those partners had others. That's what gave me the wild hare that those arrowheads just might not be such a wild story."

Megan rose. "I'd better go. My daughter will be home from school early today. I . . . uh, I don't think I know your name."

He watched her solemnly. "Ben Corgan." He tilted his head toward her feet. "I see you got the boots. Now you need a hat."

She barely heard him. She was plodding back to her car with her head churning when some movement on a nearby craggy hillock caught her attention. A silhouetted figure stood there, hands on hips. The posture was both angry and female. Pants, vest, and a big-sleeved tunic or shirt were outlined against the sky. Something on one wrist caught the sun. A swirl of hair that might have been any color suggested the aspect of an avenging angel.

The sun forced Megan to blink. When she opened her eyes, the hill was empty.

Chapter Nine

A few days later, as soon as Lizzie was off to school, Megan took the route east of town into the mountains, hoping to find some interesting scenes to shoot.

Choosing a mountain road to explore, she slowed the car through the twists and turns.

A church stood in a narrow, flat-bottomed canyon. Surrounding walls gave it the look of an old fort. Two giant cottonwoods gave just enough space for the faithful to pass over a tiny plank bridge between them, and through a wooden gate to the heavy carved doors. On both sides of the bridge, enormous tree roots grasped the edges of the dry streambed. Leaves twinkled silver in the slight breeze.

A small funeral party was milling about in the tiny churchyard, where faded plastic flowers bedecked a pair of graves. Above the copper brown stucco of the church rose the peak of a mountain, its rocky face a nearly perfect pyramid criss-crossed by deep crevices that sliced out a jagged cross. In winter, the cross would gather snow, whitening it against the dark, gray rock. It was easy to believe that God himself chose this spot for a church.

Megan hunkered down beneath one of the cottonwoods and focused her camera on the mourners. Feeling like a paparazzo but unwilling to pass up the opportunity, she began clicking the shutter. Turning to reach for another lens from her camera bag, she was startled to find a child standing at her elbow.

He looked several years younger than Lizzie and much smaller. The grime of at least two or three days was smudged across one cheek and along the thin arm that led to the thumb jammed into his mouth. He was barefoot and wearing pants that once might have been lime green. The pant legs, hacked off unevenly, ended a good distance above the boy's mud-caked ankles.

Her cry of surprise didn't alter the steadiness of his searching gaze. Did he belong to one of the mourners? But surely no one would bring a child to a funeral dressed like this.

"Hello," she whispered. "How are you?"

Huge brown eyes gazed steadily at her from beneath tangled hair.

Noting the time on her watch, she decided she would have to come back another day to see the inside of the church. She stowed the camera in the bag and got to her feet. The little boy followed a few feet behind as she walked to the rutted, packed-dirt strip that probably held wagons long before it saw its first car.

"My name is Megan," she said, as she opened the trunk to stow the camera bag. "What's yours?"

He took his thumb from his mouth, and his eyes grew rounder, but no words were forthcoming.

"Are you with someone here?"

Still nothing.

She wondered if he understood English. "Mama?" she said. Wasn't the word the same in Spanish? "Where is your ma-ma?" The child blinked and put his thumb back in his mouth.

She hated to just drive off and leave him. A sign on a shop on the other side of the parking lot advertised *Religiosos*. She would ask the clerk if he or she knew who the child belonged to. But when she reached the entrance and looked back, he was gone.

A search of the parking lot produced no clue to his whereabouts. Deciding his mother must have found him, Megan slid behind the Honda's steering wheel. The bag with the big yellow M was sticking out from under the passenger seat. She pushed it back, wanting it out of sight—not just for safety, but also because the sight of it reminded her of the emeralds, and she did not want to think about them.

If the Indians gave them to the Spaniards more than four hundred years ago, who did they belong to now? The state? The nation? The finder? Who wrapped them in her newspaper, for God's sake? And why?

Turning the Honda onto the paved road, she glanced in the rearview mirror. The little boy was standing on the edge of the dirt road, one thin elbow sticking out, still sucking his thumb. But by the time she pulled the car to the side and got out, he again had disappeared.

*　　*　　*

On their way home from school, Lizzie and her new friend, Maria, bounced over the sidewalks—and over the road when there were no sidewalks—in sheer high spirits.

"Why are you in special ed?" Maria asked, when they ran out of breath and had to slow down.

"I have a learning dis-a-bility," Lizzie said.

"Is that what that thing is in your ear?" Maria pointed. "A learning dis-a-bility?"

"No." Lizzie giggled. "That's just to help me hear better."

Maria grabbed at the hearing aid. "Can I try it?"

"I guess." Lizzie removed the device and held it to Maria's ear.

The little girl frowned. "I don't hear anything."

"That's because there isn't much to hear," Lizzie shouted.

"Oooh," Maria squealed. "You are loud."

"Okay, give it back." Lizzie reached for the buttonlike bit of plastic.

"No," Maria yelled, dodging and dancing away down the street.

The world felt strange without the hearing aid. Lizzie never took it off except when she went to bed, or when her mother changed the batteries, or once when she had an earache. The rush of noises, the birds, the sound of traffic from the busy street a few blocks over, the sound of her own shoes scuffing along the road all faded to a sort of faint hissing sound.

But maybe it was nicer to have a friend than a lot of noise.

A tall purple flower on a slender stem waved at her from the other side of the road. It couldn't belong to anybody, just growing there all by itself. Her mom would like that color. Darting toward the flower, she didn't see Maria jumping up and down and waving her arms.

Even Lizzie heard the wrenching, screeching sound as she neared the center of the road. A cold chill, like a damp wind, swept through her—something nudged her just enough to make her stumble as she twisted to see the nose of a blue car poking her leg.

A woman got out of the car looking pale and frightened, like she was going to be sick. "Are you all right?"

Lizzie knew that's what the woman's mouth was saying, even though she couldn't really hear the words. "Yes," she said, her voice high and a little shrill. "I'm fine."

"Thank God." The woman got back in the car. "Don't you know not to run out in the street like that?"

By the time the blue car drove off, Maria, hand shaking, had handed the hearing aid to Lizzie.

"It's okay." Lizzie twirled it into her ear. The two girls walked slowly, not saying much, to the corner, where they parted.

Her mother's car was in the driveway, but when Lizzie opened the front door and shouted, there was no response. She took off her jacket, put her workbook on the table, and headed for the refrigerator.

The back door was open. Maybe Mom was out there. She stepped out onto the concrete stoop. Nope. The yard was empty. But the side door to the garage was open an inch or so.

Lizzie was about to pull it shut when she saw movement in the corner of the garage.

Sunlight slanting through the dusty window lit two hands that were grasping the garden hose. Her mother's hands. They seemed to be pushing something into the hose. Several things.

Something told Lizzie not to interrupt. Backing away, she retreated to the kitchen, found an open box of apricot cookies in the refrigerator, and ate three.

Chapter Ten

Corazón Luz was doing her last haircut of the day. Her own hair, shoulder length and highlighted dramatically, hung wild and curling, seemingly unkempt but oddly attractive, about her face. Her features should have seemed too large, the chin too small. Instead the blend was striking. The color in the cheeks was high, and her own.

"You think it is right?" she said to the scrawny woman with tired eyes who sat patiently under a purple plastic bib. Damp snippets of dark hair cascaded to the floor as Corazón's scissors moved quickly around her client's head.

"Not too short," the woman said plaintively. "He wants it long."

Corazón spun the chair until she could look her client in the eye. "But this is your hair. How do *you* want it?"

The woman looked at her purple plastic–covered lap and gave an almost invisible shrug.

"Okay," Corazón said. "A little shorter maybe, but not too short." Long tangerine-lacquered fingernails tapped the woman's shoulder as the chair spun back into position. "Tell me the truth, Josefina," she said, scissors going back to work, "You think it is right?"

Josefina brought a nervous hand to her temple, then dropped it again. "What is right? This? That? Right is *nada*."

"It is not nothing," Corazón growled, scissors snipping even faster. She was a tall woman and the tights and black boots below a smock of electric orange made her seem even taller. A wide metal bracelet on her left wrist caught the light, reflecting it into the mirror in laserlike bursts. Anywhere she went, she would be noticed. And her voice, with its barely restrained energy, more than equaled her appearance. She seldom raised that voice, speaking instead with a sort of conspiratorial intensity that tended to rivet a listener's attention on every word.

"We have two very big problems," she said in that tone now, as she snatched a sideways glance at her own reflection in the wide mirror. Bringing her face close to the woman's head, she pinned Josefina's eyes in the mirror with her own. "First, we Hispanics are second-class citizens in our own land. Our own land! Second, we women are third-class citizens in our own homes. Look at you. You still have marks here, and here."

The woman shrank under Corazón's pointing finger.

"He's drinking again, isn't he?"

Josefina closed her eyes for a long moment. "*Sí*, Corazón, of course he is drinking."

"And why is he drinking? Because he cannot be a man. Because the only work he can find is mowing the grass at the Anglos' country club in Santa Fe. Because he is not wanted. Here. In his own land. He is not wanted."

"I don't know," the woman protested wearily. "I don't know."

"That is the main reason men become bums. No?"

Josefina sighed. "*Quién sabe.*"

"So you, Josefina, you have two very big problems. You are not wanted here, where your father, and your grandfather, and many grandfathers before him, grew *frijoles* and *maíz* and looked after sheep, and sang and made love in the cool evening. You are not wanted here."

49

Corazón brought her mouth close to Josefina's ear. "*And* your husband is a bum who gets drunk and hits you."

"*Sí,*" the woman nodded, her voice barely audible.

Corazón's finger touched Josefina's cheek lightly. "Three months ago, he broke your jaw."

The woman twisted the edge of the plastic bib between her fingers.

"Next it will be your neck." Corazón opened a drawer in the cabinet beneath the sink. Under the hairbrushes and combs was a stack of small cards. She withdrew one and pressed it into the woman's hand. "This is a place for what they call 'battered women.'"

Josefina looked at the card as if it were a spider.

"It is called a shelter." Corazón dusted the clipped hairs from the woman's neck with a soft shaving brush. "You are a battered woman, Josefina," she said. "They will keep him away. Call them. Tell them. Trust me."

"But . . ." The woman's eyes darted away, and her voice trailed off.

Corazón swiveled the chair again, bent down, and looked directly into Josefina's face. A scent of rose petals and something else, cloves perhaps, hovered about the highlighted hair like an aura.

"How many children do you have still at home?

Josefina's eyes dropped again to her lap. "*Cuatro.*"

Her fiery eyes were pinned to the woman's face, but Corazón's voice was soft. "Do it for them. You are stronger than you think. Yes, you are, Josefina. Where is your pride?"

Corazón drew herself up. "Your pride is in there somewhere. We will find it. It is time you stop sitting there waiting for the next bad thing to happen. It is time you stand up for yourself. It is time you stand up for us. Look at me."

She held the woman's eyes for a long moment before untying the purple bib and folding it. "We need you, Josefina," she said quietly. "*We need you.* Will you be with us next Thursday?"

Slowly, eyes childlike wide, Josefina nodded.

When the woman had crept out, Corazón locked the door and sat down at the small reception desk to fill out an order for supplies and finish the day's bookkeeping. She was twenty-nine. She had managed to buy the shop two years before with savings squeezed from fourteen-hour workdays.

She was never tired. She slept only four hours a night, and it was unlikely that her mind stopped even then. She had redecorated the shop in her own inimitable style. Huge tiles of black and white covered the floor, abutting textured black paneling on the lower walls. The rest of the walls, and the ceiling, were stark white. The furniture was vibrant greens and purples.

She finished the paperwork, put her feet on the desk, thrust her chin up, and was staring at the ceiling through narrowed eyes when three taps sounded on the storefront window.

"*Bueno*," she said when she saw him. He was looking away from her, toward the street, his back to the window. She swung her feet down and sidled to the door as sure as a jaguar that knows its own strength and reserves it for the proper time.

Barely as tall as she, with a solid medium build, the man who stepped inside had an intensity about the eyes and a pent-up energy that crackled like a lightning bolt on the loose.

"How did it go?" she asked.

He pulled her to him, kissed her hard. "*Mal*. Not good. But it is now much improvement."

Corazón returned his smile. "Better," she said. "The day is now better. Not 'much improvement.'" He had asked her to correct him, saying poor use of English tied their people to poverty, and that the leaders, especially, must speak well.

His name was written on a white oval above the left breast pocket of his dark blue uniform. Miguel worked for New Mexico Power and Light. Corazón's cousin, who worked for a man who worked for the governor, traded countless favors up and down the state bureaucracy to secure the job for him.

When Corazón spoke at the Hispanic Arts Council, Miguel was in the audience. He waited for her afterward, invited her to lunch. He said he had come from Mexico to do graduate work at the university. He talked passionately about *la raza*, the need to liberate women and all of their people from poverty.

She knew immediately that he was the perfect track for her engine.

Now she watched him stride into the back room. When he opened the small refrigerator the light illuminated his features. He was the handsomest man she had ever seen. And his thick, dark hair was perfection. She saw to that herself.

"No *cerveza*?" he called.

"You know I don't like you to keep beer here." Corazón's father had managed to drink himself to death eight years ago. In her entire life she had drunk only two cans of Coors, both during her sophomore year in high school.

"Come, sit." She pointed to a bright green chair. "I will massage your neck. I am better than beer."

Miguel slumped into the chair. "We must find them, pronto," he said as Corazón began to work on his shoulders and neck. "These *hombres* will not wait more time for their money. The woman knows nothing. She is stupid." Scowling, he pushed her hands away and sat up. "*¡Dios!* That hurt."

"Sometimes pain is necessary to end pain. Those are your own words." She went on massaging his shoulders. "We will find them."

Miguel closed his eyes. "The people look to us. They need so much. They hurt so much." His eyelids flickered open and the somber brown eyes swam with anguish. "They do not even remember how to hope."

"We will show them," she said.

Chapter Eleven

Striped serapes hung at the windows of the Mesquite Grill. Megan sat in a booth drumming her fingers on a scarred table. *Did he forget? Change his mind about meeting her?*

In five minutes that seemed like ten, Ben, dubious hat in place, slid into the booth across from her. She wondered if he slept in the hat. He took a menu from the napkin holder. "Lunch?"

"Yes," Megan said quickly. "But could we get some takeout? Go where we could walk around? I don't want to talk here," she said to his raised eyebrows. "I'll explain later."

They bought hamburgers, and Ben headed his pickup out of town. She fell silent until he pulled the truck off the road near the riverbank and they got out. "You probably think this is a little odd," she said, avoiding his eyes.

"Not at all." He leaned against a fender oxidized to the color of rust and bearing the marks of more than one minor collision. "People call all the time with a sudden urgent interest in artifacts, then refuse to come to the lab and insist on meeting at a café where they don't want to eat." He righted himself and beckoned. "Never mind. Let's have lunch."

They found a big cottonwood on the river's edge. Megan sat down under it. "Something weird happened," she began.

He peered into the takeout bag and handed her a burger. "Okay. Shoot."

"It's crazy, my telling you about it, but I think you'll understand why."

When she finished he blew a soundless whistle. "The stones just turned up in your paper? And you think they're emeralds?"

"I *know* they're emeralds, the jeweler said so. And he thinks they're some sort of ancient ritualistic arrowheads." She did not mention what the jeweler thought they might be worth.

"And the kid who used to deliver your papers is still missing?"

"Far as I know. There's someone else on the route now. How would a kid like that get hold of five pieces of emerald? I'm not saying he stole them, but they must have been stolen by someone. From where? A museum maybe? You're an archeologist. I was hoping you might have some ideas."

Ben thought about that. "That wouldn't explain why they were inside your newspaper."

"My guess is the thieves were about to be caught. So they hid them there."

"Caught by whom?"

"How would I know? The sheriff? The people they stole the arrowheads from? The Mexican drug lords? The Mafia? My point is, smugglers or thieves or whoever probably figured no one would suspect a single woman with a kid. They probably planned to come back later and get them." Her words slowed. "Actually, maybe they already tried to do that." She told him about the break-in.

"Shit," he said quietly.

"I put it out of my mind. Blocked it, whatever. And then you started talking about emerald arrowheads out there on the mesa."

Ben's eyes swept her face, examining each feature as if testing its integrity. "It's very hard to be certain about this sort of thing," he said carefully, measuring his words. "Some of the best museums in the world have been fooled by counterfeits. Where are the stones now?"

"I'd rather not say."

"Well . . ." He sat back against the tree trunk, pulled on the brim of his battered hat, and crossed his ankles. "Either you trust me or you don't. If you don't, there's not a lot I can explain—assuming I could explain anything."

Megan examined the ground in front of her. A lizard skittered over her shoe and into a tuft of dry grass. She wondered if Ben thought she was making it up. Turning, she looked straight into his eyes. "You want to see them?"

"That seems like the obvious next step."

"Okay." She slapped at an insect on her arm.

"Now?"

She shook her head. "Thursday evening? My house?"

Ben got to his feet. "Give me the address." He held out his hand and pulled her up beside him. "Let's walk."

She threw him a confused look.

"You said you wanted to go somewhere you could walk around," he said.

"I guess I did."

The air smelled of sage. Silvery green chamisa with remnants of last year's smoky yellow flowers dotted the bank of the muddy Rio Grande. Beyond the river, the land seemed to race to the edge of the world. They walked a hundred yards or so in silence. Their arms brushed lightly. She tossed a stone into the water. It hit with a plunk and sank.

Ben finally broke the silence. "You really a full-time photographer?"

Megan found a place where the earth dipped toward the water, sat down, and bent to untie her boot laces. "I work at it pretty much full time. But I haven't sold anything yet."

"You still haven't got yourself a hat."

She shaded her eyes to look up at him. "I will. I promise. You were right about the boots. Have you lived here a long time?"

Ben was gazing at the mountains the way people stare at burning logs in fireplaces. "Just about forever."

"You were born here?" Megan tossed the words over her shoulder as she dipped first a toe then both feet into the water. She pushed her hair behind her ears, wishing for the first time that she had gotten a real haircut rather than trying to trim it herself.

"Yeah. That rare breed. Anglo native. *Más o menos*, as they say. More or less. Born here anyhow." He glanced at the top of her head. "You Mexican or Hispanic?"

She looked up, frowning. "There's a difference?"

He sat down a foot or so away. "I reckon." For the first time she noticed three perpendicular lines above his nose. They deepened, giving him an earnest look.

"My mother never talked much about it. She figured it was more important to be American than to be Mexican or Chinese or German or whatever. I think she was right. Isn't that what the melting pot is all about?" She kicked her feet in the water and flicked a glance at him. "So what's the difference between Mexican and Hispanic?"

"The Spaniards didn't bring their wives when their army and their priests marched up here to stake claim to this corner of the world. So they married Indian women." He twisted a frondlike stem of the salt cedar next to him.

She frowned, not sure whether she was disconcerted by the topic or by its narrator. "They . . . we're . . . all half-breeds, is that what you mean? Or quarter breeds, in my case."

"No more so than a German Anglo, like me. Sorry. I didn't mean to pry. Guess I can't stop thinking like an anthropologist."

"I thought you were an archeologist."

"I found I liked bones better than people. My bachelor's was in anthropology." Ben stood, took out his pocket knife, and cut a branch from the salt cedar.

"So what's the difference between people here and in Mexico? They're all Spanish Indian."

"Most Hispanics here have never been to Mexico," he said, sitting down again. "They've been here hundreds of years longer than the United States has been a country. Second, strangers tend to think Indians all look alike, but they're no more alike than the Koreans are like the Cambodians or the Italians are like the Swedes. Here, the Spaniards married Pueblo women. They didn't look like the Navajo or the Apaches, or the Aztecs, for that matter. The cultures weren't alike either."

A scruffy jay landed near her feet. She watched it peck quickly at the earth, then fly off again. "You call them Indians, not Native Americans?"

"We called them Indians for centuries. It seems kind of silly to start calling them Native Americans." Ben was idly stripping the green from the salt cedar's red stem.

"The . . . Indians probably care what they're called."

"I doubt it. But they probably enjoy our discomfort about what to call them."

She glanced over to see if he was joking and decided he wasn't. "New Mexico isn't simple, is it?"

"And all that is before you get to *la Causa*."

"What's that?"

"Oh, it comes in waves, the rumbles about taking back the land the Anglos stole." He looked out across the valley flatland toward the mountains. "Every so often someone dusts off the Treaty of Guadalupe Hidalgo and decides the national forestland here was stolen from the Hispanics. In a way, it was. They used it for centuries, grazing their flocks on it, cutting its timber for their homes. Back in the sixties a guy raised a sort of ragtag army, took over a national forest campground, and raided a courthouse."

A distracted smile gave Ben a rueful look. "No, New Mexico is not a simple place."

Megan gazed at the horizon where clear blue mountains seemed to be receding into another dimension. "Maybe that's part of its charm."

"I guess." He scratched at the ground with the salt cedar wand. "I've hardly been anywhere else. Colorado a few times. Arizona. Texas."

"Where would you rather live?"

"Oh, North Africa, maybe." Wistfulness crept into his voice. "Turkey—but not right now, with the god-awful mess in the Mideast. Peru, maybe. Even Mexico."

"Not me." Megan was examining his profile against the sun, the dominant nose, the strong jawline. The hat looked better in silhouette than in full light. "I might like to visit those places, though. You really think you could live there?"

"If I made a big discovery, I could live anywhere. But," Ben drew in a sharp breath, "I'm here. The early Pueblos became my specialty. As time goes by, it gets harder to switch to another group."

Megan made a half smile. "The moment I saw those mountains, I knew this was where I belonged."

"The Sangres have ways of doing that to people. Not just the Sangres. The whole range, down to Texas, for that matter. At least, that's what a lot of people say."

"Luckily, at least for now, I have time to do what I like, live where I like. Until we starve, anyway."

From beneath the crumpled brim of his hat, Ben's gaze flicked from the mountains to her left hand and back. "We?"

"My daughter. Lizzie."

"Why did you tell me about the arrowheads? Why not the cops who are looking for the kid who delivered your papers?"

She watched a hawk circle. "You want the truth, or something pretty?"

"The truth will do," he said, watching her watch the hawk.

"Fear. Greed. All the good old-fashioned deadly sins. Or maybe you'd call it a good old-fashioned dream, like winning the lottery." She got to her feet and brushed herself off. "I'll bet anything those stones are hot. Probably smuggled, even. But I don't think showing them to the cops would help find that kid. Maybe they'd arrest me, maybe not. But they would sure enough grab those emeralds, and I'd never see them again. If they're worth anywhere near what the jeweler said, they could make Lizzie's life, and mine, a whole lot easier. I could even take the time to *learn* how to be a photographer. What if they don't belong to anyone? What if they just washed up in a rain?"

He helped her up the riverbank. "They sure as hell didn't wash right into your newspaper."

She didn't answer. The hand on her arm was large and strong. She moved away as soon as they reached the path. They spoke little on the ride back to the diner, where she had left her car.

"Thursday. Seven," he said, pulling into the parking lot.

She tore a scrap from the empty burger bag, wrote out the address for him, and got out of the truck. Driving home, she paid scant attention to the road. It had been a long time since a man had mattered to Megan. And she wasn't about to let that change now.

She was out of the car by the time she noticed the outlandish shape that was rounding the garage into the driveway.

The oval shell was a foot or so long and the color of cement. Scaly legs like small stumps came to a halt; the head rose on a stalk of a neck to stare at her, unblinking. A giant turtle?

Moving surprisingly quickly, it disappeared.

Chapter Twelve

Sitting on a box in the courtyard, if you could call the space between the cabin and shed a courtyard, Megan adjusted her camera while Alma leaned back against the shed wall. Curious sheep and goats watched from the shade near the piñon trees.

A sharp shadow cut across Alma's shoulder, but her face, despite the straw hat, caught the sun. The casual elegance in the tilt of her head made Megan wonder if the woman's class, her style, was genetic or if it came with age. She clicked the shutter. "Could you take off the hat?"

"You want a picture of me or someone else?"

"Is the hat important?"

"It's who I am these days. The doc took a little red bloom off my cheek. Melanoma. You ever see me outside without this hat, you'll know my mind is going." A faint breeze brought mingled scents of piñon, juniper, and earth still damp from a rain the night before.

Megan studied the pattern of light and dark that played across the wall of the shed. "Okay. I'll work with the hat."

"You might think about getting one yourself."

"I will. I've been nagged about it already. Now, try to ignore the camera. Tell me about how you came to live here."

"You saying you haven't heard?"

Megan snapped away. "Should I? I'm new here."

"This land was open for homesteading after the war. The last real war. World War II. All you had to do was build some sort of place to live in. So I did. The officials got a little excitable about a woman doing it, so I took title as Albert Peters."

"By yourself? You built the cabin yourself?"

"And the barn. All the cabins here were built by homesteaders, but I was the only one who stayed and lived on the land."

"You've been here since the forties?"

"Came here from San Francisco, in forty-nine. Of course, that's when everyone was going *to* California. I was never one to go with the crowd."

The worn-away mud exposed footwide bricks on the corner of the shed Alma called a barn. The bricks were a shade of dusty rose. Tiny bits of grass were sprouting in the crevices. Megan focused the lens again with Alma at the edge of the wall. "What made you decide to homestead?"

Alma shrugged. "I wanted a different life."

"That part I understand. I moved here from the East." Megan went back to clicking the shutter, talking just to keep her subject talking. "You wanted a different life from what?"

Alma's expression went as blank as a mannequin's. Then came a very small smile. "Well, dear, I was a hooker. In San Francisco, during the war. Damn good one, too."

Chapter Thirteen

The doorbell rang just as Megan finished washing the last plate. A hurried glance out the window showed a shabby red pickup sporting a dented fender.

She met Ben at the door, put out a hand, realized it was still wet from the dishes, and wiped it on her jeans. "Thanks for coming."

Lizzie, eyeglasses slightly askew, popped around the corner from her bedroom. "Who is it?"

"This is Ben, Lizzie. He's here to talk to me. Go on back to your homework. Did you copy those words I gave you?"

"Mom." Lizzie gave the word two syllables. "There are too many."

"Copy all of them," Megan said firmly. "You only have a few minutes left before bedtime."

With a theatrical sigh and a roll of her eyes, Lizzie disappeared.

Megan steered Ben to the dining room table. "Mind waiting till she goes to bed?"

"No problem." He took off his hat. It was the first time Megan had seen him without it.

His forehead was broad and high, hair receding from a widow's peak. The remaining hair was thick, dented where the hat had been, and the color of maple syrup, except for the flecks of gray in the sideburns. She thought of a dozen reasons she shouldn't have invited him here. "How about some tea?"

"Sure." Hat in hand, he followed her into the kitchen and watched while she boiled water and arranged some blueberry fig bars on a plate.

"So how did you become an archeologist?" she asked, trying to pick up the plate and two mugs of tea.

He took the plate from her and they sat at the table. "The summer I was twelve, a class from the college was doing some digging near where we lived. I started hanging around, more to get out of chores at home than anything else."

Megan watched his face as he talked. In another ten years it would be called craggy. The nose looked like it was broken some distant time ago. Thousands of days in the sun had etched lines in his cheeks. His chin had a slight cleft, and any five o'clock shadow would have lost itself in the burnished-copper hue of the skin. It was a very comfortable face, she decided, wishing she had the nerve to get out her camera.

"The instructor explained what they were doing," Ben was saying. "That's the first time I ever thought about people being there before us." He reached for a fig bar. His large hands looked capable of a brawl. Featherings of hair crossed the knuckles. His nails were remarkably clean for someone who rooted around in the soil for a living.

"Never much liked history in school," he went on, "but those guys poked around in what looked like plain, ordinary dirt and found history you could touch. They showed me how pieces of pottery fit together to make an *olla*, a big pot. Someone, maybe a thousand years ago—back then that seemed like right after God created the earth—maybe someone had cooked up a stew of antelope or jackrabbit in that pot."

"Your family still in the same area?"

"Sure. They believe the entire world is about fifty miles by fifty miles."

"What's it like when you go back?"

"I don't go back."

"Never?" she asked.

"Not much," he said to a spot above her right shoulder. "The equation changes. You remember the good things, but they get spoiled if you go back."

Lizzie poked a freshly washed face between them. "What're you guys talking about?"

"Math," Megan said.

Lizzie pulled a face. "Ugh."

Megan rose to go tuck her daughter into bed. When she returned Ben had moved to the big easy chair and propped his feet on the foot stool. The flowered upholstery should have seemed incongruous with his lanky frame, but somehow it didn't. She beckoned.

He followed her through the kitchen and into the garage. She shook a stone from the garden hose. Suddenly wary of showing him where she kept them, she drew in a sharp breath. Too late now. She shook the other four stones into her hand.

He took them from her palm and moved toward the door.

"Hey!" she said.

"Maybe you can see in the dark. I can't."

In the kitchen he held one of the stones up to the light and gave a low whistle. "They're arrowheads all right. You sure he said emerald, not malachite?"

"Yes. I already told you that."

"Just asking." Ben handed them back to her. The perpendicular lines above his nose deepened. "You sure found an ingenious hiding place."

She left him there to fidget while she returned the stones to the garden hose. When she reappeared, she asked, "What do you think?"

"They're valuable all right. Not just because they're emerald. A lot of archeologists would give an arm and a leg, maybe even ten years off their lives, to have found them. Including me."

"I wonder how the paperboy got them, why he wrapped them in my paper. Or maybe someone else put them there after the paper was delivered."

"No idea on that."

"Out there on the mesa, you mentioned five emerald arrowheads."

"Aside from historians, few people have ever heard of them," he said, hoisting himself to the kitchen countertop as if he was accustomed to sitting there. "It was probably sometime in the autumn of 1535 that the first Spaniards reached the Rio Grande. Hundreds of men were lost along the way. Only four were left when they met the Pimas. The Indians apparently showed them five emerald arrowheads they said came from rich cities in the mountains to the north, where such stones were so common they made arrowheads of them."

"The Seven Cities of Cibola?"

"Maybe. One of the Spaniards recorded the encounter in his journal. Someone mentioned it in a report to Spain. Most historians suspect the arrowheads were malachite, not emerald."

"But the ones I have are definitely emerald." The sink faucet was dripping. Megan turned it off. "What's your take?"

He shrugged. "The Spanish were intrigued enough by the tale to send another explorer, a Franciscan friar, Fray Marcos, to the same area. The good friar dispatched an advance scout who was to send back a cross each time he found something worthy. The bigger the cross, the more important the find. The scout sent crosses back, all right, a whole series, each larger than the last, but he never came back himself, so no one was ever sure what he found."

She gestured in the direction of the garage. "You think those are . . . ?"

"Either that or one hell of a coincidence. A lot of people think the cities of Cibola were somewhere in northern New Mexico. Fray Marcos came back a few years later with Coronado. Near what's now Albuquerque, they met an Indian they called the Turk, who told them of a place called 'Quivera,' a land of vast riches to the northeast. He offered to escort them."

"Why were the Indians so helpful?"

Ben gave a sardonic laugh. "They weren't. They wanted the white men out of there. There are ruins of a large village near Santa Fe. Gran Quivera. People there led pretty decent lives farming; we've never found any sign of great wealth. The Turk, however, had no intention of taking the Spaniards to any village. He was very clever and as devoted to his cause as a kamikaze. Every so often he 'discovered' a few gems or precious metals and showed them to the Spaniards, saying they came from a place just a little farther on." Ben squinted at his fingernails, took a penknife from his pocket, and removed a grain of dirt.

"Avaricious fellows that they were—gullible, too, obviously—the white men followed the Turk, expecting to reach the promised riches. Apparently he kept up the scam all the way to what's now Wichita, Kansas. When the Spaniards realized it was all a hoax, they killed him."

Megan eyed Ben thoughtfully. "You think he carried the gems and metals with him?"

Ben shook his head. "If he dropped something or was searched and found out, they would have killed him on the spot."

"So an advance party of Indians must have buried those things along the path. That's what you're looking for, isn't it?"

"Been looking for something like that for ten, twelve years off and on." Ben rubbed his thumb across a dent on the countertop. "Probably just wishful thinking. A find like that would be my ticket out of here."

"But someone did find them. The arrowheads are in my garage."

"Not necessarily." Ben got down from his seat on the counter as though suddenly remembering he didn't belong there. "All I know is the legend. Most historians think the Turk's emeralds were really malachite. Maybe yours were stolen from a museum. Maybe they aren't even from here, have nothing to do with the legend. Yours could be from Africa."

"Is there any way to find out?"

He strode toward the front door. "I guess I could do some checking. If some museum is missing five emerald arrowheads, they would make a pretty big noise about it."

Chapter Fourteen

The scent of lavender soap mingled with a hint of photographic chemicals. Megan lay back in the bubble-filled bathtub. When she shot regular film the bathroom doubled as a darkroom.

A sort of free-floating anxiety had been haunting her ever since she showed the arrowheads to Ben. He seemed a decent sort. She trusted him, but . . .

In her head, she replayed the scene from that afternoon in Alma's cabin, when the woman she was beginning to admire very much said, "I'm no traditionalist, but deep in my gut part of me has wanted something as traditional as apple pie. I always wanted a child, a daughter."

Megan had never told anyone the whole truth. Not even her mother. Alma was the first. "You're probably the only person who wouldn't be shocked to know how I came to have Lizzie," she began.

"I doubt you were a hooker who forgot the precautions."

"Not exactly." A smile that was both wry and shy played about Megan's mouth. "I didn't want to get married, but I wanted a child. So I found a guy I sort of liked, but not too much, and . . . Lizzie came along nine months later."

Alma laughed. "And what did he have to say about that?"

"He never knew." Megan examined a thumbnail until her discomfort subsided. "Lizzie is an unusual child. She's autistic. Luckily it's very mild. One doctor suggested medication to control the symptoms, but I decided too many drugs have too many side effects. The M.D.s think her brain is structured a little differently from most people's, but they expect her to have a normal life."

"What are the symptoms?"

"Kind of like attention deficit, I guess. She's not your average kid, but she's not a problem." Megan looked away. "It was when her hearing tested way below normal that I began to wonder if I had broken some terrible rule, if I was being punished."

Alma's eyes fairly snapped. "Don't you ever even *think* such a thing! What kind of a god do you think would punish a child? No way in hell. Get it out of your head."

Now, in the bathtub, Megan smiled at Alma's lecture. For some reason it made her feel better. She was reaching lazily for one of the books on the hamper next to the bathtub when a muffled click came from somewhere in the house. A door closing? Or opening?

Water sloshed as she bolted to a sitting position, straining for a second sound. But there was only Lizzie's soft, even breathing in the next room. Just her imagination. Or the creaking of an old house. She settled back and opened the book.

A dull thud from somewhere in the direction of the backyard jolted her senses to red alert. Suds clinging to neck and shoulders, she leaped up, grabbed a towel, then froze, listening.

Water sloshed, breaking soap bubbles hissed, Lizzie's faint gurgling snore came from the next room, but nothing else broke the silence. Had she fallen asleep in the warm water? Did she dream the sound?

Suddenly the room went black. A paralyzing fear crawled up Megan's arms, raising goose bumps in its wake. She had no weapon, nothing, not even her clothes. She fumbled in the dark for a towel, ears straining, but there was just the sound of the bathwater talking to itself about her rapid departure.

A power failure? Or did someone cut the electricity?

Jesus. Is someone in the house?

The only phone was in the living room. A cell phone was a luxury she thought she could do without, especially since she heard the reception out of town was spotty at best.

Something fell and broke. Glass. In the kitchen?

A pale glow showed at the pebbled-glass window above the tub. Then it, too, went dark. The carriage light in the driveway had a motion sensor.

Someone is out there. A stray cat, she tried to reassure herself. But neither a cat nor an innocent passing human outside could explain the sound of breaking glass.

Megan reached to close the bathroom door. If someone was inside the house, the lock might hold long enough for her to get out through the window. Her damp hand stopped on the doorknob. Lizzie! She couldn't escape without her daughter. She moved into the short hall that linked bedrooms and bath to the living room.

Somewhere in the distance—perhaps across the street?—came the faint sound of a door closing.

She made a headlong rush for Lizzie's room, swung the door shut behind her, and struggled to push the chest of drawers across it. Stuffed animals spilled from the top of the chest. A monkey landed on her shoulder as she bent to shove the base against the door.

"Mom?"

"Sssh! I'm right here," Megan whispered, holding her daughter's shoulders and exaggerating the words so Lizzie could read her lips. "Get down on the floor below the window and be very, very quiet."

Lizzie did as she was told, then piped, "What's going on, Mama?"

"I thought I heard someone in the house," Megan patted Lizzie's shoulder. "But we'll be okay." She edged along the wall to the window and moved the drape just enough to peer into the front yard: grass, a few shrubs, a broken flowerpot. Nothing seemed out of the ordinary.

But it wasn't ordinary.

She shouldn't be able to see these things so clearly. The streetlight was too far away. The carriage light, just out of sight by the driveway, must be on again.

Someone is out there!

Or was it just a cat, or a stray dog? An animal or even a gust of wind might open or close the side door to the garage if it was left ajar. Megan tried to remember if she had locked it.

The glow from the carriage light disappeared again.

Sitting on the edge of the bed, she fixed her eyes on the slit of space beneath the yellow curtains. Nothing moved. No sound betrayed some unseen presence.

Lizzie crawled into her lap and went to sleep. Endless minutes passed before Megan put her daughter back to bed and tugged the chest away from the door. In the hall, she flicked the switch. No light responded.

Were there electrical problems in the neighborhood? No light showed across the street, but perhaps the Gonzalezes were in back.

Almost as soon as she put down the telephone, Mr. Gonzalez was on her doorstep. Short and barrel-chested, in blue-striped pajamas and an old brown terry cloth robe, with sockless feet thrust into untied shoes, he was holding a flashlight in one hand, a hunting rifle, muzzle pointed at the welcome mat, in the other. Waggling his grizzled head back and forth, he told her again that no, the lights in his house across the street were fine. There was no problem with the *electricidad*.

Megan led him into the driveway to where the breaker box was fixed to the wall of the house opposite the garage. Her breath went to sandpaper in her throat when his flashlight beam revealed all the circuit breakers lined up to the right, the word "off" showing on their square red faces. The carriage light had a separate breaker box inside the garage.

The now irrefutable fact that minutes ago someone was standing here deliberately throwing the breakers, cutting off her electricity, was more eerie than the glass breaking.

Mr. Gonzalez flipped each switch to "on." "We must search in the house," he said sternly, as if he expected her to object.

Looking ready for a fight despite his bathrobe, he inspected every possible hiding place, from the closets to the little shower stall in the second bathroom. In the kitchen, the remains of a shattered coffee mug lay in the sink. A small mountain of dishes was stacked in the drainer. Perhaps the mug just picked that particular moment to fall off. Nothing else seemed out of place.

"Now we see the garage," he announced.

The faint sound of the closing door surged back into Megan's head. *The arrowheads.*

Chapter Fifteen

Across the street, Mrs. Gonzalez, wrapped in a shapeless bathrobe, stood peering toward them. With Mr. Gonzalez close behind, Megan opened the side door to the garage, switched on the light, and let out a breath she hadn't known she was holding. "Everything seems okay. Maybe it was just kids." She desperately hoped that was true. Just some silly prank.

Not to be deterred, he insisted on finishing his mission by poking about in the garage.

"We'll be okay now," she said when he finished. "Thank you for coming so quickly."

He waved to his wife and stepped out of one of his untied shoes. Megan held the rifle and flashlight while he put his foot back in the shoe and tied both sets of laces. When he had crossed the street, she quietly slipped back into the garage.

A frantic thought careening through her mind, she locked the door, found a dusty Maglite on a shelf, took a piece of cloth from the rag bag she kept in the corner, and with the flashlight bouncing in unsteady fingers, she shook the garden hose. It responded with a muffled rattle. She held the end of the hose over the cloth, shook the hose again, and the arrowheads bounced out. "Amen," she said softly, quickly knotting the cloth around them.

She was almost inside her kitchen when a scraping sound came from somewhere nearby. Soft, plodding footfalls were moving toward her. She slammed the door and locked it before lifting the ruffled curtain on its small, square, newly replaced window. A snakelike shadow was moving along the garage wall.

Blood thundering in her ears, Megan watched what seemed to be an enormous lizardlike head appear, cocked sideways so she could see only one of its eyes. She squeezed her own eyes shut, then opened them and looked again. It had lumbered a few steps farther. She saw a shell, and beneath it, legs. A tortoise. Probably the same one she saw before. Was the whole scare caused by a tortoise that wandered in from the desert?

But tortoises are even less likely than kids to throw circuit breakers.

In the house, Lizzie's breathing still had the even rhythm of sleep. Megan shoved the knotted cloth with the arrowheads into a pocket of the jeans Lizzie had worn that day, wadded up the pants, and buried them in the clothes hamper.

It wasn't until the next morning that she realized the corner of the kitchen cabinet, the space between the Mr. Coffee and the sink, was empty. She had left her handbag there.

*   *   *

The jittery redheaded deputy sheriff, who had come with his partner after the burglary, arrived alone this time to take the new report. Megan sensed suspicion when she said she had no idea who might have thrown the circuit breakers the night before and taken her handbag. He probably already thought she was a bit loony, so she didn't mention the tortoise.

"Why didn't you call the station last night? Why did you wait until this morning?" he asked.

"Last night I thought it was probably just kids pulling a prank. I didn't realize anything was missing until this morning."

Whoever it was left no sign of forcible entry. The deputy reminded her of his earlier warning that slipping the lock on her back door wouldn't be difficult for someone handy with a credit card. "My partner said he told you to get a lock with a bolt for that door."

"Locksmiths aren't cheap," she said, trying not to sound defensive. "And last time the window in the door was broken. The lock had nothing to do with it."

But now someone had apparently slipped the lock and taken her handbag, her wallet, and everything in it. Only about thirty dollars in cash, but replacing her credit cards, checks, and driver's license would take days. She called a locksmith and watched while he installed a dead bolt.

But would a dead bolt be enough? She was certain she knew exactly why someone was interested in her house. If they hadn't searched the garage this time, they would find a way to do that next. And they wouldn't stop until they got what they wanted.

A Wells Fargo branch was the only bank in town. Megan called and asked how much it would cost to rent a safety deposit box. The man she was referred to sounded like he had a bad cold. "Sorry, ma'am," he sniffled, "we don't have any boxes available. I could put you on the waiting list."

"Thanks anyway," she said, and hung up.

The banks she called in Santa Fe also had waiting lists.

Megan didn't know anyone well enough to even tell about the arrowheads, much less ask to keep them for her. Except Ben, and he already knew.

Would they be safe with him? An archeologist connected with the university wouldn't be a criminal, would he? Some artifacts must be valuable, and he must have a safe place to keep them. For that matter, the arrowheads were artifacts. They wouldn't look out of place in an archeology lab.

She phoned Ben and told him what had happened.

"I'm afraid to keep them here any longer," she said. "Is there any chance you could put them someplace safe?"

"Well . . . I guess so. It's pretty safe here in the lab."

Watching the rearview mirror as closely as the road ahead, Megan followed his directions to the archeology lab.

He met her in the parking lot, face lined with concern. She handed him the arrowheads still knotted in the cloth, and took a rain check on his invitation to tour the lab.

By the time she got back home, her thoughts had stalled on the realization that she had just handed Ben five million dollars.

Chapter Sixteen

A short, wide foot in a scuffed brown-leather boot pressed the pedal of the loom, and the wooden bar clacked another strand of nubby, wheat-colored yarn into place. Although the loom was indoors, a hat, the band rimmed with the sweat stains of many summers, shaded the eyes of the weaver. In his concentration, the tip of his tongue appeared under the heavy mustache.

Megan focused her camera, considered asking him to close his mouth, thought better of it, and moved instead to the side to catch him in profile. The tongue was still there. She focused on his foot. Then she noticed his hands. Thick-fingered, with black hair bristling at the knuckles, they were agile in a heavy, rhythmic way, like those of a heavyweight boxer. She shot a whole roll of the hands while the weaver stared at her, as if he couldn't believe it.

His name was Tenorio Clancy. The stray Irishman who apparently founded the clan sometime in the past had left no obvious mark on his descendant's features except for the eyes, which she now saw for the first time as he tilted back his head. The eyes were an amazingly clear blue.

She reached for her bag and changed cameras. For those eyes, she needed color.

This seemed to annoy Tenorio. He had nodded and shrugged when she asked to photograph him weaving in the back room of his little shop, had willingly scrawled his signature on the release form, but now his face took on a sullen cast and his jaw rose. "It is the custom to pay for pictures. *Veinte.* Twenty dollar." Perhaps owning two cameras made her out to be rich.

"I'm sorry, I must have misunderstood," Megan said, embarrassed. "I can't afford twenty dollars."

His eyes, now insolent, slid down to the camera, then back to her face. He stood up and stalked away from the loom.

She packed up the camera. She was finished shooting anyway. Never mind the eyes; the hands would be wonderful. "Thank you," she called to his retreating back. He didn't turn around.

Outside the air was cool; the sharp light, outlined in black, gave everything a hard edge, making a real-time Matisse painting.

She backed the Honda out of what passed for the shop's parking lot. The little church was just a few miles away. Maybe this time she could see the inside. She wanted to make the most of what would be her only shooting time this week.

After succeeding in putting the arrowheads out of her mind, now she could think of little else. Should she have mentioned them to the cops? Were they stolen from a museum or university? Could she wind up in jail for not reporting them? Did the paperboy mean to give them to her? Did he run away from home, or had something terrible happened to him? She had called the sheriff's station and asked for Deputy Córdova, the officer who had taken the report when her house was first ransacked, the one who had told her that the newsboy had gone missing.

She could almost see his pained expression when she asked if John Runyon had been found or returned home. "No," Córdova had told her. There was no news about the missing boy.

Maybe the boy had nothing to do with the emeralds. Maybe someone else came into her yard and wrapped the packet in the newspaper lying on the ground. But why?

This time there were no cars at all in the unpaved parking lot next to the church. Megan left the car there and made her way to the door. But when she grasped the handle, it would not open. She pushed, then pulled, but it didn't budge. Did they lock churches?

The mounded new grave was blanketed with plastic flowers already bleaching in the sun, giving it the look of something children might leave behind when called in to supper. She tried a couple of shots with the digital camera, but the light wasn't right.

Following a path along the outer wall, she was surprised to discover, in a hollow area directly behind the church, a small amphitheater. Benches circled a large cross on which a tormented Christ was laden with rosaries.

The scene seemed both eerie and forlorn. Here the light was good. She shot all the high-resolution images the memory card would hold. Then shot again with black-and-white film.

Searching for yet another angle, she stumbled and skidded down the rocky face of what she now realized was the shallow edge of a small canyon just behind the amphitheater. Barely managing to right herself in time, Megan gazed into the canyon and saw that it was deeper than it looked. Green canopies of full-grown trees floated ten feet below the rim.

She was climbing up on a flat boulder to get a better look when a light glittered below. Through the treetops and scrub, she caught a flash of something blue but couldn't make it out.

Using the camera's telephoto lens to bring the bottom of the canyon closer, she saw people—a lot of people—down there.

Something touched her elbow.

Megan whirled to find a small, grubby face—almost certainly the same little boy she'd seen there before. Wide brown eyes gazed into hers. He was wearing a yellow T-shirt and denim pants that must have been a hand-me-down from a child much larger and taller. The seat of the pants hung down almost to his knees. A rope that might once have been part of a clothesline held the waist of the oversized pants about his middle. He was holding one hand behind his back.

Megan said, "Hello," but the child only stared, no more communicative than he was before. "Do you live around here?" she asked, keeping her voice low so as not to frighten him.

His eyes slid off to the left then came back.

"May I take your picture?" Still he stared, motionless. She raised the camera.

Suddenly the hand behind his back snapped forward, pointing something straight at her head.

Knee-jerk instinct sent Megan's hands flying to cover her face as she backed away, almost dropping the camera. But when she finally got a good look, she saw the object in the child's hand was not a gun but some sort of icon, a religious figure of faded blue and worn-away gold paint.

"Bang!" the boy mouthed. "Bang." But no sound came from his lips. He turned and was quickly out of sight around the corner of the church.

When she looked again into the canyon, the people were gone.

Chapter Seventeen

Bernadette Ortega was pissed off. At God. And at the Virgin, too, for that matter. It was four in the morning, and she was not going back to bed. She would watch television, read the encyclopedia, knit, whatever. Maybe she'd dye her hair; it needed it, anyway. Anything that would keep her from falling asleep would do.

She was having dreams again.

Sometimes what she dreamed was too close to what turned out to be true. Maybe God thought this was a wonderful gift, but Bernie emphatically did not. She thought it was a rotten trick. Like getting racetrack tips that were accurate only 70 percent of the time. You might bet your entire life's savings and find out you were having an off day, or wager two dollars and learn that your gut feeling was dead-on. And that was nothing compared to other people believing your so-called insights and risking everything because they trusted you.

Where was the Virgin in all of this? Why didn't She do something? As Bernie saw it, God was a tremendously powerful but somewhat thickheaded male. It was the Virgin's job to guide Him and moderate His blunders.

She took a box of Clairol from the bathroom shelf. Hitching up the sleeves of her shapeless blue robe, she set about preparing the dye. She was fifty-eight and had long ago forgotten the real color of her hair. Lately it was a nice strong red, not carrottop, of course, but definitely red. She didn't give a damn how it looked; it was the *idea* of red hair she liked.

She snorted at the reflection of her broad face in the mirror. God only knew where she got that nose. Perhaps her mama's life was a little more interesting than anyone knew.

It broke her mother's heart when Bernie refused to become a *curandera*—a healer—what the Anglos sometimes called a white witch. Instead Bernie went to work with her father in the little market on Alameda. He didn't have any sons, but he never held that against her. And he didn't believe in all that hocus-pocus stuff.

After Papa died, she built an addition on the market. It was the only place people could get groceries on that end of town. She set fair prices, carried a little bit of everything, and her produce was better than Albertsons because she could threaten the produce suppliers with physical injury and Albertsons couldn't.

So if people didn't want to drive five miles to stand in a cashier's line for twenty minutes for a head of wilted lettuce, they could put up with her appearance. And her mouth. She didn't have to work the register and scales all that much anymore; the shop was doing well enough to pay a clerk. She hated to admit it, but she was a little bored. She needed something else to do.

Bernie's mouth had gradually filled up with four-letter words as she got older. She'd never even uttered the F word till she was well past thirty. If God didn't like it, she was ready and willing to give him the world's cleanest vocabulary as soon as he removed his heavy hand from her head and, with it, the damn dreams.

And not just the dreams. When the dreams started stuff began happening during her waking hours, too. The day stuff wasn't dreams, really; it was sort of knowing things she couldn't know.

A few months after Bernie's ninth birthday, La Grande—the ageless *curandera* who was her mother's friend, and her grandmother's before that—announced that Bernadette had "the sight."

La Grande began teaching her about plants and herbs and healing, how to hear what an animal said, and how to see something that happened last year or hadn't happened yet.

Never should have believed that stuff, she told herself for the hundredth or five hundredth time. What does a kid know? A kid gets a big head and thinks she's so special she knows everything. And other people start believing she knows more than she does, too. And then they go off and do something based on her overrated imagination. And they get hurt. She didn't mention any of that to anyone anymore. Now she just minded her own business.

She was named for Saint Bernadette, but for more than forty years she refused to answer to anything but Bernie. If God thought it was amusing to saddle her with idiot dreams, she'd be damned if she would carry around the three-syllable name of one of His saints.

Lately, every time she closed her eyes she was seeing three kids in danger. She didn't even know who they were or what the threat was, but she could see two of their faces—two boys—and *feel* the danger. What did God expect her to do about it? She ripped open the box of Clairol and attacked her roots.

Chapter Eighteen

Megan was making Lizzie's favorite dinner, macaroni and cheese. The pasta was going into the boiling water when the doorbell rang.

"I'll get it, Mom," Lizzie yelled, racing for the living room.

"Don't open the door until I get there," Megan called as she set the timer.

But Lizzie was already shouting, "It's a lady."

"Sweetheart, I asked you to wait to open the door," Megan said.

On the doorstep was a woman whose dark hair was swept tightly back from her face. Not a stray strand anywhere. She wore black tights and an egg-yolk yellow tunic. A wide black elastic belt nipped the waist of the dress and kept the hem about three inches above the knees.

Megan looked at her own faded jeans, which had threads beginning to show at the knees. "Can I help you?"

"Mrs. Montoya, my name is Corazón Luz. I have come to ask you a favor."

"Yes?"

"I am with an organization called Save the People."

Megan groaned inwardly. A fundraiser. The woman would probably camp on the doorstep until she got a donation, and the macaroni would be getting flabby any minute.

"I'm kind of broke but . . . She turned to look for her new handbag. At least it wasn't someone declaring the government was poisoning the water.

"No," Corazón broke in, "we are not asking for money. I have heard that you are a very good photographer."

Megan turned back. "You have?"

"I wonder if you would take some pictures for us. We could not afford to pay you, but you would be doing a great service."

The timer for the macaroni went off. "I'm sorry." Megan pointed toward the kitchen. "Would you like to come in?"

"Thank you."

"I'll be back in a minute," she called, as she dumped the potful of boiling macaroni into the colander in the sink. "Pictures of what?"

"People," Corazón said right behind her.

Megan whirled, startled, then gave her visitor an appraising look. "Like who, where, how?"

Corazón sat down on the step stool next to the sink. "Mostly the women and children of Aztlán. They are the ones who have suffered the most."

Megan reached for the packet of cheese to make the sauce. "Where is Aztlán?" She stumbled over the pronunciation. "Suffered from what?"

"From the fists of frustrated men." Corazón's voice filled the little kitchen. "From little or no education, health care, nutrition, decent housing. But mostly from no hope."

Megan—hands holding a wire whip above the bowl, eyes pinned by Corazón's piercing gaze—thought she looked like an Indian princess. One who became fierce without warning. The woman was positively stunning. The people she described—could this be a real chance for her career? "How would you use the pictures?"

"To tell our story."

Megan began mixing the ingredients in the still-warm pot. "Could I use the pictures, too?"

"For what?" Corazón asked, handing Megan the serving bowl she was pointing to.

"For art. To sell as art."

Corazón thought for a moment. "Okay, yes. Why not? That might even be better." She stood up as Megan finished pouring the cheese sauce over the macaroni.

"Where is Aztlán?" Megan asked again. "I have a little girl. I can't travel very far."

Big silver, disclike earrings swung at the sides of Corazón's smile. A slender, perfectly manicured finger with long, tangerine orange nails touched the center of her forehead. "You are a Montoya! It says that on the mailbox. You do not know?"

Megan turned to face her visitor. "I'm not from around here. My mother didn't believe in being anything but American."

"You don't speak Spanish?"

"No. My grandparents did, but I don't."

"Ah," Corazón took that in, nodding slowly. "Aztlán is no longer a place. Now it exists in the head." She tapped the perfect hairline that framed her face like a skullcap.

Megan frowned. "Then where do we shoot the photographs?"

"Mostly in the mountains." The silver earrings danced. "From Albuquerque to Taos there are little villages here and there. Not to worry, I will take you."

"How did you know I was a photographer?"

Corazón's smile was like a beam of light from another planet. "We hear things."

Megan eyed her guest. Was she from some weird cult? But even if she was, the people she spoke of had faces. Already Megan was imagining those faces, the textures, the light.

The gallery owner said she was good at faces. Did he somehow run

85

into this gorgeous, mesmerizing creature and mention Megan's name? Or maybe it was Mrs. Gonzalez across the street?

Whatever had brought this woman to her doorstep, Megan was hooked.

"Okay, I'll give it a shot."

*   *   *

The soil and water and cement Alma mixed with a hoe in the old wheelbarrow was the consistency of tomato sauce and oddly sensual to the touch. Having slathered the concoction over the shed walls and smoothed it with a broken piece of two-by-four, both she and Megan were covered with splashes of gray.

"This stuff really works?" Halfway up the ladder, Megan balanced a bucket on one of the rungs and used her fingers to spread the mixture over a place they missed near the roof. "It keeps out the rain?"

"Sure does. Adobe walls will last hundreds of years with no painting, just a new coat of stucco when it wears thin. Without the stucco, whole walls can disappear in a few years." Alma stepped back to appraise their work. "You hungry?"

"Starving." Each rung of the ladder creaked as Megan carefully descended.

In the tiny kitchen, Alma prepared lunch while Megan sat in the wooden chair by the table admiring the paintings on the wall across from her. "Lizzie would love that one," she pointed to a clown that hung below three balloons on a field of white.

Alma looked up from the bread she was slicing. "If you had it to do over, would you do it again? Become a mother in that particular way?"

Megan studied the straw place mat on the table in front of her. "If I was sure I'd get Lizzie, yes. Absolutely."

"And if you weren't sure what the child would be like?"

Megan didn't answer right away. "I don't know. I was twenty-seven.

Almost thirty. Maybe it was just the old ticktock of biology. I'd known a couple guys, but after a while I just didn't like them much. Not enough to live with forever and ever."

"But you wanted a child."

"So I had one." Megan's voice seemed to come from far away.

"By yourself." Alma arranged blueberry muffins on a plate.

Megan gave a small laugh. "I guess you'd have to say I had some help, but with no intention of it being a long-term thing."

"Why did you want a child?"

"I'm not sure. It made sense at the time. Maybe I just wanted someone to care about. I read somewhere that being loved is not as important as being able to love. It's probably true."

"My only regret is that I never raised a child." Alma leaned her elbows on the kitchen counter and pointed the bread knife at Megan. "I lied to you the last time we talked. I had one—a girl. In San Francisco in 1948. I gave her up for adoption. It wasn't that I didn't want her; I didn't have the guts to keep her."

Megan gave half a laugh. "That can't be true. I've never known anyone with half your guts."

"Of course. I managed to fool you. I'm good at that."

The roadrunner fluttered up to the outside sill and pecked at the window. In his beak was a very dead, limp lizard. Spokes of colors above his eye gave him the look of a medieval prince.

"He's just trying to prove he can take care of a family," Alma said. "Wouldn't it be nice to be taken care of?"

Megan eyed her friend for a moment. "Depends on the price."

"Ah, yes, there's always a price. So you had the guts to bear and raise a child alone. I know you're not going to tell me it's easy."

"The autism, the hearing, that part has been a little tough."

"You still think maybe God was punishing her because her mother wasn't married?"

"I don't know."

"If God is worthy of being a god," the bread knife in Alma's hand bobbed with each word, "he, or she, would not punish a child—or a mother, for that matter—who violated some artificial, man-made tradition." She paused, then gave a hearty laugh. "How many times do I have to say it? You know perfectly well I'm right. Old whores are very up on theology."

They feasted on apples, bread and cheese, and blueberry muffins, washing it down with cider. "How do you bake if you don't have electricity?" Megan asked.

"The stove is propane. So's the refrigerator. It's really not hard to live here once you get the hang of it. The apples are from the tree out back. They keep fairly well in the cellar—which is my euphemism for a hole in the ground. Peaches are not so accommodating. They have to be canned, and I've never acquired much enthusiasm for canning."

Megan's eyes went to the painting of the rose in a Coca-Cola bottle. "Can I see the rest of the paintings?"

Alma paused, glass of cider halfway to her lips. "Why?"

"Because these are really excellent. What's the painter's name? Maybe I've heard it."

"Nothing was ever sold," Alma put the tea glass down. "Or even shown." She began slicing an apple into very thin pieces. "I'd rather not get them out right now."

"Of course," Megan said quickly, wondering why a woman so frank about prostitution was so evasive about paintings.

Chapter Nineteen

The wind was spinning up dust devils when Megan set out again for the cabin a few days later. The sky looked like it was cooking up a storm, but on the high desert dark clouds usually blew over with little more than a few drops. She was anxious to show Alma the results of their photo session.

The digital images—even before touch-up—looked better on her computer screen than she dared to hope. She had printed a few of the best. And the contact prints from a full roll of black-and-white looked even more promising.

But when she reached the end of the ruts that served the cabin as a driveway, she saw that the rusty old Dodge pickup was gone from its berth. Disappointed, she put the Honda into reverse and, dodging rocks and scrub, backed all the way to the road.

The darkened sky was becoming purple, like a bruise. She had heard storms could be swift and harsh here, and unpaved roads quickly become impassable. As she headed for home, the sky blackened. One enormous, very white cloud welled up over the mountains as if to do battle with the advancing storm. The view was irresistible. Megan stopped the car, grabbed her camera, and climbed out.

Like good and evil, she thought, running to what looked like a good vantage point. Good and evil reduced to a common denominator: clouds. The small ridge to the east was a rich, deep blue in the cloud-filtered light. She could put that in the corner of the frame if she moved just a little to the left.

Dropping to her knees, she peered through the viewfinder, clicked the shutter twice, and was resetting for another exposure when the sky ruptured, spewing rain with fire-hose intensity. By the time she jammed the camera under her shirt and got to her feet, she was soaked, and it quickly was obvious she was farther from the road than she thought. The Honda was nowhere in sight.

Beyond a cluster of piñon and juniper, she saw what must have been one of the abandoned homestead cabins she had seen the day she took those pictures of Alma and made a dash for it, skidding on the wet caliche. Slick mud filled the treads of her boots and clung in clumps to the toes. Already water was puddling on the ground. Coming now in sheets, the rain plastered her hair to her head, and her collar funneled a stream of cold water down her back.

The cabin walls had turned a dark, dusty pink in the rain. She raced for the doorway, slipped, and sat down hard on the doorstep. Scooting back a few more inches into the shelter, she leaned her head against the door frame and tried to catch her breath.

"You okay?"

Startled, she swung around to peer into the cabin's murky interior.

Near the back wall, Ben was sitting on a bench made of two packing crates and a plank.

"You always hang out around here?" She tried to sound in control, but the words came out in a shivering stutter. At that particular moment, he was the last person she wanted to see, or be seen by.

"Sometimes. You look like a drowned rabbit."

"Thanks." She examined her camera. It was supposed to be waterproof, but she wiped it carefully with her shirt tail and hung it from a spike that protruded from one wall. Then she tried to squeeze some of the water from her hair so it would stop dripping down her neck.

Ben rose and unbuttoned his shirt. "Here," he said, holding it out but not moving toward her, "it's a lot drier than yours." A few feet from his shoulder was one of the open spaces in the wall intended for a window. The sky had brightened a little, casting half his face in shadow.

Wanting to say she didn't need the shirt, she felt her teeth begin to chatter and held out her hand for it instead.

Thunder crashed somewhere nearby. She darted a look out the window, half expecting to see a fork of lightning plunging into the ground. Water suddenly cascaded through a hole in the roof, splashing on what was left of the plank floor.

"I don't strip for just anyone I meet in a rainstorm. You mind facing the wall?" she asked.

He swung his feet obligingly to the other side of the improvised bench. The white of his T-shirt seemed bright in the dimness.

She struggled to undo the buttons of her drenched blouse, gave up, pulled it off over her head, and tossed it to the floor, where it landed with a waterlogged slosh. Ben's shirt was only damp about the shoulders. It smelled of wood smoke and something like mint. She tried to put it on, but her damp arms caught in the sleeves.

A few four-letter words jumped up and down on her tongue, but she kept her mouth shut as she wrestled the shirt off and tried again. Finally she managed to fasten two buttons and tie the shirttails around her waist. Rubbing her upper arms, she stared at his back, keeping her features neutral. "Thanks, this feels a lot better."

He turned back toward her. "Good."

She picked up her blouse and went to the doorway to wring it out. "How long is this likely to last?"

"These weather tantrums are usually pretty short, but there's no telling for sure."

Thunder cracked again, as if to give its own forecast. The cabin groaned and seemed to sway in the wind. Another loud crack brought debris spewing from what was left of the roof directly above Megan's head.

Ben lunged, yanking her toward him as a cross beam crashed floorward, grazing her head, then her shoulder. "You all right?"

She stood motionless, head against his shoulder, chest heaving. Finally, head ringing, eyes dazed, she drew back. "I'm okay." A small rivulet of blood was working its way toward her mouth from an ugly gash across her temple. Her tongue flicked across her lip, finding the metallic tang of the blood.

"Sit." Ben nudged her gently to the floor and went to the door, returning with something dripping and white. "The handkerchief's clean," he said, and began dabbing at her cheek.

He took the cloth back into the rain for a rinse, and dabbed again. "Nasty scrape, but I don't think it's deep." His thumb brushed her chin, then lifted it upward. He led her to the window and tilted her head back.

"What are you doing?" she asked

"I want to see if your pupils are dilated. Look at me."

"I don't think I have a concussion," she said, but did as he asked.

"Hard to tell," he said. "It's pretty dark in here. You're probably okay, but you look pale."

A tear, postfear or present pain, stung as it trickled across her cheek. "I'll live."

Rain pounded through the gap in the roof and splattered to the floor. Ben drew her down on the makeshift bench and gently gathered her toward him.

In spite of herself, she pressed closer, encircled by his warmth, drinking it in, soaking it up. Her head began to swim in it.

The stream spilling through the hole in the roof slowed to a drip. The room brightened as though someone flipped a switch. The effect was like a sudden brisk noon arriving after dusk.

Avoiding his eyes, Megan drew away and went to the doorway. Wind was pushing clouds across the sky as if opening a curtain after an intermission. The indescribable scent of a grateful desert after a rain made her feel light enough to float. "Does it always smell like this?"

"I guess so."

Megan turned back to him. Waiting. Willing.

He examined the toe of his boot. "I need to talk to you about something."

She waited.

"I sent the arrowheads to a lab in London."

Chapter Twenty

The gray Ford pickup was eleven years old, but the chrome gleamed and there wasn't a trace of dust on the dashboard. Corazón, hair loose and wild except for the part held by a bandanna that matched a shirt the color of hot-dog mustard, drove effortlessly. Long wooden-bead earrings hung just above her shawl-like collar. A wide metal band that ringed her wrist clanked against the steering wheel.

Feeling frumpy in jeans and a T-shirt, Megan sat quietly grinding her teeth as they sped out of town and up the steep slope that led into the mountains.

Anger at Ben still smoldered. How dare he do whatever he pleased with her arrowheads without so much as consulting her? And under that anger, *How dare he ruin the moment?* She wasn't sure how much of the rage that didn't abate after she stalked out of the cabin was directed at Ben and how much at herself. *This was not supposed to happen.* Nothing even remotely like this was supposed to happen.

In uncharacteristic bad spirits and flustered, to say nothing of being overwhelmed by her companion's apparent self-certainty and stellar style, Megan was now thinking the shoot probably would go sour as well. She tried to fix their route in her head so she could come back later without Corazón.

The woman glanced at her. "What happened to your face?"

Megan touched her cheek where the scrape was healing. "Nothing much. I was hiking and fell."

"It is good of you to do this." Corazón smiled at the road, apparently oblivious to her passenger's sour mood.

Megan struggled to be positive and courteous. "It's a good opportunity for me. Tell me again what you expect to do with the photographs, so I'll understand what kinds of shots to look for."

"We will use them to make known *la causa*. Our cause."

"And exactly what is your . . . cause?" Where had she heard that term before?

"We Hispanics have been here for hundreds of years. Many hundreds. But we are not welcome. In our own land we are outsiders." The earrings bobbed in time with Corazón's words.

"The black people in America are better off. We are last in line for everything. Our schools are hopeless. Some of the teachers are stupid, sent to us because they aren't fit to teach anywhere else. The few good ones are so shocked by how we are forced to live that they leave. And No Child Left Behind? That program should be taken up by *teatro campesino* as a comedy. It would be funny if it weren't so terrible. The doctors we get are *bufones*—alcoholics and drug addicts who would not be allowed to practice in any city."

Megan examined her companion's profile, unsure how much of this was true and how much was just Corazón's bombastic style. "I didn't realize . . ."

"How could you? You're new here."

Megan wanted to ask how she knew that but Corazón was into her tirade, tapping the top of the steering wheel for emphasis.

"Especially, it is very bad for our women. At fifteen, they are having babies; at twenty their husbands are so angry with life, they beat them. At thirty they are old, ugly, used up."

Watching the landscape slide by, Megan said thoughtfully, "Changing that—even a little—will be a very big job."

Corazón eyed her so long that Megan began to worry the truck would run off the road. Finally the woman swung her gaze back to the road. "We must organize. If we stick together, we can make things happen. If a tree becomes rotten, the stems must be cut off and rooted to grow a new and better tree." Her quick, sharp glance was like a pointer hitting a blackboard.

"We must make *la causa* more important than money, more important than our own little likes and dislikes, more important than anything, even our lives." She nodded at the road as if lecturing to it. "And we must have attention, from newspapers, from television, from Internet blogs."

Megan leaned her head back against the seat. "I hope you understand that I'm just an independent photographer. I don't have anything to do with the media, with TV or newspapers."

Corazón guided the pickup through a maze of dirt roads little wider than paths that Megan was sure did not appear on any map. "We will maybe send them to the press, maybe have posters, and I am checking how to post things on the Internet. Your pictures will help. Believe me, they will help."

Megan wondered if she could treat as art pictures that were in wide distribution. Maybe she should take two separate sets of photos. Just then the pickup lurched around a tree that was encroaching on the road. She grabbed at the dashboard to keep from hitting her head.

A tiny village appeared in a small valley below. When they reached it, Corazón parked beneath a bent and twisted cottonwood tree.

Megan slipped two cameras from the bag at her feet. The pickup door rattled loudly in the stillness when she closed it.

Dust was everywhere. The trees and a church gleaming with fresh whitewash were the only things in sight that were not the color of mud. A goat was watching them as if not sure what to make of their arrival.

An old man carving a small piece of wood sat in the doorway of a house that looked as though it would melt into the earth during the next storm. He stopped what he was doing and stared at them. Corazón spoke to him in rapid Spanish. His eyes flicked to Megan, then back to Corazón. He nodded and went into the house. The lower left corner of the front window was cracked. A Mason jar of canned peaches stood next to the crack, its bright yellow-orange the only color that didn't seem dusty.

He returned with a girl who was holding a naked baby. The girl's eyes held a nervous blankness. She didn't look more than twelve. Megan hoped this wasn't the infant's mother.

Corazón nodded to Megan and went on talking to the old man. The girl sat down on the ground, leaned against the side of the house, and stared at something in the distance.

Assuming the nod meant she was to take some pictures, Megan did so: the girl, the baby, the old man, the house, even the goat. At first the baby seemed content, but he soon began to howl convulsively, as if someone were jabbing him with a needle.

A man in a gleaming white sleeveless undershirt emerged from among a group of junipers that crouched near the corner of the house. Megan wondered if he had been watching them.

Ruthlessly intense eyes gazed at her from the shadow cast by a brown, small-brimmed straw hat. He didn't seem to fit with the rest of the village. Perhaps it was the eyes. But his face and the set of his jaw caught her interest. She was aiming her camera at him when Corazón tapped her arm and nodded toward the pickup. "In a minute," Megan murmured, resetting the f-stop.

"No," said Corazón, tapping Megan's arm again just as the shutter snapped. Already halfway back to the pickup, Corazón called over her shoulder, "Stop. It is enough here."

Annoyed, Megan reminded herself that the woman was her client, even if not a paying one. And there was a lot at stake here—a possible name for herself, a book even.

"Who cut your hair?" Corazón asked as she started the Ford's engine.

Megan bit her lower lip. "I did."

"You are good photographer. You are not a good hair stylist."

"I just thought I'd save some money."

"I think there is a way I can pay you for your pictures. You must come to my salon."

The next village was little more than a series of low mud huts with tomatoes and chilies growing on earth-covered roofs. The children were barefoot, their clothes crusted with grime, their rosy cheeks an odd counterpoint to apparently hopeless lives.

Corazón drove to two more villages, each interchangeable with the last. Megan photographed a crippled child who used two sticks for crutches, a toothless old woman whose knuckles were huge with what must have been rheumatoid arthritis, a toddler with a face badly scarred from some terrible burn.

On the downhill road toward home, Megan thought about the reporter who brought about prison reform by getting himself sent to jail and then writing about conditions there. She wondered if she was up to that sort of campaign. At length she turned to Corazón. "You really think you can raise the standard of living of these people?"

"Absolutely." The wide bracelet jangled against the steering wheel. "And you will help."

Megan half believed her.

*　　*　　*

Plumes of dust followed the old Dodge pickup as Alma swung it into the driveway and moved her foot to the brake pedal. The wheels didn't respond; the side of the shed was coming at her fast—the ancient little truck was about to tunnel right into the newly stuccoed wall.

She reached under the dash for the emergency brake. The truck lumbered to a halt just as the bumper grazed the stucco.

Getting out, braids swinging behind her, she repacked the two grocery sacks that had spilled in the truck bed. "Poor old thing," she said aloud to the front fender. "You're not going to last much longer." She wondered if she could afford to get it fixed. Even if she managed that, would something else send the pickup to the junkyard—a piece of scrap metal with brand-new brakes?

Preoccupied, she was almost to the cabin door before she saw it was standing ajar.

The floor inside was a well-churned sea of pots, pans, clothes, books. A grocery sack slipped from Alma's grasp and crashed to the floor. A can of tuna with a blue-and-white generic label rolled across the brick floor of the sunroom before it collided with a frying pan and fell over.

Chapter Twenty-one

W Brewster Gillette looked up from the small stack of eight-by-ten silver gelatin prints of the people in the mountain villages. Megan watched his face for some small sign of encouragement, but the pale blue eyes avoided hers, finding some compelling interest in the backs of the paintings stacked against the walls of the office behind his gallery.

Her shoulders sagged. "You don't like them. Okay. Can you explain what's wrong so I can work on it?"

He fanned the photos out on the desk, rested his chin in his hand, and studied them again. A gold and jade ring too large for his finger had turned sideways. Finally, he leaned back. Thoughtful creases appeared above his eyes. "It's not that something is wrong. . . . It's that something doesn't seem quite right."

She rubbed her forehead. "Stop pulling your punches. Just give it to me straight."

"I'm not quite sure. I think maybe you are telegraphing *your* punches, or pulling them."

"I guess I don't understand." But she was beginning to realize that a nebulous doubt had been nagging at her since she lifted the first enlargement from the fixer and examined it in the yellow light of her makeshift darkroom. She had chalked up the feeling to her own insecurity about her work.

Gillette waved his finger over the photos. "Are these staged?"

"How do you mean, staged?"

"Costumes, makeup, director."

"Good God, no!"

"Okay, maybe; maybe not that much. But accent the negative, show the worst?"

She shook her head. "I saw them, photographed them how they live, where they live."

He rubbed his thumb across his chin as if searching for signs of a beard. "In that case, I don't know what the problem is." He went through the stack again. "These could be really powerful. Maybe you're afraid of that much power?"

"Why would I be afraid?"

"Such scenes offer an opportunity to become this generation's Dorothea Lange. You're familiar with her work?"

"Of course." Lange's photography captured the human desolation of the Great Depression. Her poignant pictures moved the government to establish special camps for migrant workers. Lange, and what she accomplished, had crossed Megan's mind in connection with the mountain villages and Corazón's impassioned pleas.

"But these seem stilted." He gazed at her like a doctor forced to do something painful. "Even slightly artificial. I suspect something was bothering you about them, too."

"Maybe it's because these scenes are so depressing. Who would want to see them?" But she knew that wasn't it. Lange's work was depressing, but it was known as a great artistic and sociological achievement of its time and was still highly regarded today.

"Such photographs wouldn't make people happy. But when they are authentic, they have the power of genuine art."

"And you're right. These don't. Somehow I missed it." Megan was placing the prints in their slim box when she remembered something. "Did you tell someone about me? A woman named Corazón Luz? That I was a good people photographer or something?"

"Corazón Luz?" he said blankly. "I don't believe I've ever heard the name."

*   *   *

She stopped at the grocery store on her way home. The cart she took wobbled. A front wheel refused to turn. Megan peered at it. Finding nothing visibly wrong, she kicked it.

"That generally just encourages them to be even more perverse," said a voice behind her.

She spun around. She hadn't seen Ben since the storm.

He gave her a wry, half-apologetic look. "I guess you're still upset."

"I'm not *upset*, I'm mad. Pissed off. Furious. You had no right to do that."

A stony-faced woman in a navy blue pantsuit paused by the meat counter eyeing them disapprovingly. Her square jaw could have belonged to a prison guard or an IRS agent.

Megan lowered her voice, but now the words were hissing from between clenched teeth. "How could you do that? Just take things that belong to me and send them off somewhere?"

Ben blinked mournful eyes. "I said I was sorry. I just didn't think it would matter that much to you. I even thought you might be glad to get them clear out of town."

"Out of town, maybe, if I could have picked the place. But this is out of the country. And without so much as a phone call . . ."

"The London lab is in a better position to check with Egypt and other places in Africa. And maybe they'll recognize something about the way the arrowheads are shaped."

"You could have e-mailed them photographs, or sent a video." Realizing the woman in the navy suit was still watching, Megan lowered her voice. "You had no right to send them anywhere without even consulting me."

Ben made a valiant effort at a smile. "I don't suppose you'd like to have dinner."

"No, I don't suppose I would."

The smile slid off his face as she shoved past him to the checkout.

Still in a fit of temper when she got home, she stowed the canned goods and slammed the door of the cabinet next to the kitchen sink. It popped open again. She slammed it again. She hadn't bought even half the items on her list, and she'd forgotten to cash in the coupons carefully clipped from the Sunday paper. Being a lousy photographer wasn't enough; she had to be a lousy shopper, too.

"You're growling, Mom," Lizzie said after she got home from school and suggested that doing homework wasn't really urgent.

"My day was seriously awful. I'm going to lie down for a bit. You get that homework done. No ifs, no ands, no buts. I want to go over it right after dinner."

Trust someone, he takes your emeralds, and tries to buy you off with dinner. She went into the bedroom, threw herself on the bed, and tried to read a magazine, but she couldn't concentrate. If she wasn't a photographer, what was she? Alma knew exactly who she was. Alma had the strength of a Scythian Amazon warrior. Megan wished she had a little more of that herself.

And what about Ben? How could she forgive him? But he knew so much about the area. Who else could help her understand the people so her work wouldn't look artificial?

The room was dark when she awoke. She sat up and cocked her head. What was that funny sound? A sort of dull shuffling.

In the living room a dim babble came from the television. Near a stack of books still waiting to be put away, Lizzie was squatting, arms wrapped about her knees. "Yes," she was saying in a conversational tone, "I think so, too."

Speechless, Megan gaped at the scene.

Nudging at the books, its shell an etched, inverted, putty-colored bowl, was the tortoise.

"Lizzie!"

The child rose to her feet, careful not to disturb the animal. "She was in the backyard, Mom," Lizzie said plaintively, standing first on one foot, then on the other, in a mental effort to dodge a spanking. "She was lonesome. She's my friend."

"Get her out of here!" roared Megan. Lizzie was herding the creature to the door. "Him or her or it." She paused. "How do you know it's a female?"

"She told me," Lizzie wailed.

"That's all I need. A lonesome talking tortoise." Megan retreated to the kitchen to begin dinner. "I take a nap and you turn the place into an animal farm. Is your homework done?"

"Oh, Mom . . . I forgot. Mrs. Gonzalez said you could take some photographs later."

"Oh God, I was supposed to—" The phone rang, cutting off Megan's own wail.

"I'll get it," Lizzie said quickly, brightening at the good fortune of an interruption.

Megan banged a frying pan onto a burner and began punching hamburger into patties.

"It's somebody called Bernie," Lizzie shouted. "She says Mrs. Gonzalez told her you were looking for a babysitter. Mom, I'm not a baby!"

"Right." Megan took the phone. "You're ready to get married. And I'm ready for drugs."

*   *   *

104

Saturday's skies were cobalt blue, and the air was so clear that the few clouds seemed like three-dimensional fluffs suspended in space. Megan and Lizzie sat on the edges of a faded pink-and-white plaid blanket next to a gangly pine, licking the last of their picnic from their fingers.

The mountains, so dry before the rain, now seemed to glow with renewed life. Flowers Megan had never seen before were poking their heads around rocks, getting their growing in before the hot dry months ahead.

"I shouldn't have yelled at you last night," Megan said, looking through Lizzie's thick glasses into her daughter's eyes. "Or, at least, I shouldn't have yelled so loud."

Lizzie examined the edge of the blanket. "I shouldn't have let Tomasina in the house."

"Whatever possessed you to do that?"

"She asked me if she could come in."

"Sweetheart, please. I wish you wouldn't make things up."

A stubborn look tightened Lizzie's features. She tossed her head and examined the tree trunk as if the bark were utterly fascinating.

"Lizzie, is your hearing aid turned down?"

"No. Who's Bernie? Is she going to babysit me?"

"She sounds like a cross between Godzilla and the Flying Nun. I think you'll like her."

"Where are you going that I have to have a *baby*sitter?"

"Nowhere right now. But it would be good to have someone available. We can't expect Mrs. Gonzalez to be available every time we need her. Bernie will come by and meet us, and you can look her over. If you don't like her, we'll find someone else." A small, blue-gray bird with a touch of white at its throat landed at the edge of the blanket and pecked at the crumbs.

Lizzie made a face. "Are you gonna go out with that guy?"

"What guy?"

"The one who came over after dinner last week."

"No, I'm not going out with him."

"Why not?"

"What is this? An eHarmony checkup? Because he hasn't asked me. Because I don't want to. Because I'm . . . Why do I have to explain that to you?"

Lizzie shrugged. "I thought he was nice. And he likes you."

"That's a silly thing to say. How do you know?"

"I just know."

"No, Lizzie. You don't just know things like that. It seems like you 'just know' too many things lately. Like with that turtle."

"Tortoise. You said she was a tortoise."

"Okay. Tortoise. But you can't know that she's—it's—*lonely*, for God's sake! Or that it wants to come into the house. You've got to stop making things up."

"Mrs. Gonzalez doesn't think I'm making things up."

Knowing a losing battle when she saw one, Megan rolled over on the blanket and put her hand over her eyes against the sun. Did the neighbors think her daughter a bit touched in the head? "Want to go for a hike?"

Lizzie bounded to her feet. "Hug?"

Melting, Megan held her daughter close. Life wouldn't just be miserable without Lizzie, it would be boring.

The path was just a worn ribbon on the ground between the trees. In the rippling shadows, it snaked its way upward. "Where are we going?" Lizzie asked.

"Nowhere in particular."

The little girl danced along the path. "How come you don't like Tomasina?"

"It's not that I don't like her. But tortoises don't belong in the house. You know that. I don't know what tortoise poop looks like, but from the size of her, I don't want to find out. I don't know why she's hanging around. I thought they mostly steered clear of people."

"She's lonesome. Can I feed her in the yard?"

Megan sighed. She had moved her daughter across the country to an unfamiliar place, where she had to make new friends. Lizzie was probably projecting her own loneliness on the tortoise.

"I guess so. But she's probably perfectly happy with grass."

Lizzie's ponytail swished and bobbed. "She likes grass okay, but she likes spinach better."

"You didn't give that tortoise my fresh spinach, did you? It's expensive. I was going to fix it for dinner." They emerged on a ridge over a narrow valley.

"Just a little of it, Mom . . ." Lizzie was suddenly still. "What are they doing?"

"Who?"

"Those people down there."

Megan peered into the narrow canyon below. Sunlight glinted off white rocks. "What are you talking about? There's no one down there."

"Sure there is," Lizzie insisted. "Look." She pointed toward an outcropping of rock at the base. "They're going into a cave or something."

Megan stared into the patchwork of shade and brightness. In the shadow of the clifflike wall was a stream of flickering movement. She brought her camera to her eye and focused the telephoto lens. Now there were bits of blues and reds and yellows in the stream. She moved the camera in the direction the flow of colors was moving. The long line was disappearing into the mountain. "You're right, Lizzie."

Mostly men ahead, women toward the end, the stream seemed to fan out and thicken just before it disappeared into the valley wall. The steady movement seemed to indicate an earnest purpose. Megan snapped the shutter, afraid she would get little more than dark smudges of trees and bright rocks, but doing it twice more anyway.

"It's getting late," she told Lizzie. "Let's get back to the car."

Chapter Twenty-two

The cabin was dark and cool, but the noon sun made the light at the window almost white. Megan helped herself to one of Alma's bran muffins. It was still warm from the oven.

The two sat at the table, a pile of eight-by-ten black-and-white prints between them. "They're good," Alma said as she cored an apple. "So good they make me uncomfortable." She looked up. "You just may have a fine future in this new profession of yours."

"That's not what the guy at the gallery said."

"Did you show him these?"

"No, others. I took these at the carnival in Española."

"I've never had much use for people," Alma said. "These faces actually make me wonder whether I've missed something. Just wonder, mind you. I still seriously doubt people are worth the trouble. Present company probably excepted."

Megan laughed at the qualification. "Is that why you live out here, with no one around?"

"You bet. I wish I were farther out." Her jaw tightened. "The second year I was here, I met a woman I thought I liked and made the mistake of telling her the truth. Next thing I knew, there was a preacher on my doorstep telling me to give my heart to Jesus or I would burn forever in hell. I was courteous until it was obvious there was something else on his mind besides my soul. I told him to fuck off unless he wanted to spend the rest of his life as a soprano."

She fixed her eyes on the picture of the Coke-bottle rose. "Thirty-seven years ago this month, a crowd came out here and stoned this cabin."

"Good God!"

"They were Anglos, of course—the Hispanics were all Catholics then. The Catholics had stopped butting into other people's sins and weren't yet revving up that sanctimonious hard line again. Back then, if you weren't Catholic you were going to hell anyway, so it didn't much matter what you did. But those hard-shell Baptists convinced themselves that if I went on living here I would soon spend my spare time corrupting their children. That's when I learned to shoot."

"That's good advice. I should be careful who I confide in, too."

"Maybe," Alma agreed. "I'll wager there are still plenty of self-appointed and armed guardians of traditional marriage and family."

Megan selected another muffin. "So you built this place, you grow your own food, or most of it, manage without electricity or running water. That must be an awful lot of work. What do you do for entertainment?"

Alma was slicing her apple with the studied care of a surgeon. Finally she looked up and a hint of vulnerability crossed her face before it hardened into a tough serenity. "I painted."

"I thought the paintings were yours," Megan said. "I'd like to see the rest of them."

Alma's features went blank, as if a door had swung shut. "I've never shown them to anyone."

"But if no one sees them, what's the point of painting them?"

"If you don't know that, you're no artist." Alma's tone declared the subject dead, its burial overdue.

Megan gathered up the few dishes on the table and carried them to the kitchen.

Alma rose abruptly, jarring the table. Hands jammed hard into pockets, she said, "Please don't think I don't appreciate your interest." Her eyes bored into Megan's, and they must have found what they sought because she turned and disappeared into the sunroom.

The paintings she brought back she propped against the walls, the bed, the fireplace. Some were abstract, with vivid colors; some were impressionist; some expressionist. Most of the subjects could be seen no more than a mile from the cabin: A certain tree, one of the captain's chairs, a surprised goat, and several roadrunners. One scene depicted a mountain that when viewed more closely became a sleeping woman.

For Megan, the most arresting painting was of two women, one with attributes that suggested a large mouse, the other a small ox, yet they were neither comical nor unattractive. What to say escaped her. At length she said, "They are simply . . . Beautiful isn't a good enough word. They are elegant."

Alma moved to the kitchen, as if to put as much distance between herself and the paintings as possible while Megan examined them.

Leaning back in the chair and eyeing the older woman, Megan said, "I'm no art critic, but I believe these are more than just good. You really should show them."

In the shadows of the kitchen, Alma cleared her throat. "No. They are a very private bit of myself, done by myself, for myself. It's my one scrap of luxury."

"If I did anything even half so fine," Megan said, "I would be knocking on the door of every dealer in the country."

"I will not beg strangers for approval."

Megan recalled the cold knot in her innards every time she pushed open a gallery door. How she hated it. And no one had ever stoned her house.

"Still, I wish you would," she said, and helped Alma gather the paintings.

As she placed a stack carefully against the wall beneath the windows in the sunroom, a hand-painted blue and green teacup rolled away from the corner toward Megan's feet. "Hey," she said, picking it up. "Must've been one of those wild tea parties."

Alma was standing at the window. Finally she turned, wiping her hands on the tail of her shirt as if something was sticking to the fingers. "What?"

Megan held up the teacup. "This was on the floor in the corner."

"Oh, there was a small disturbance here a few days ago."

"A what?"

"Someone broke in. Made a mess."

"Surely not . . . ?"

"Like the stoning? No. I don't think they were after me, personally. Probably just a random burglary."

"Did they take anything?"

"Apparently not."

"My home was ransacked, too. They also left a mess but didn't take anything. Several of my neighbors' homes were broken into the same week. Same story. Nothing missing. Then, someone got into my house and stole my handbag. Is burglary a local pastime around here?"

Alma shrugged. "It's not uncommon. Illegal traffic from the border stops to rest about here. Not wetbacks—they're generally too scared to do much harm—but drug runners, fugitives, that sort of thing. And there are always meth addicts desperate for cash."

Megan followed her back into the main part of the cabin.

"Time before last," Alma said over her shoulder, "I lost a shirt, some cans of food, a nutcracker, of all things, and a cast-iron frying pan. I don't have much that anyone would want. My main worry is that someone will be clumsy, or just plain mean, and damage the paintings."

She began washing up the few dishes. Her sink was an old Thermos jug propped up on bricks, its spigot over a dishpan. "You can't run scared every time something unpleasant happens."

"Maybe that's why that horrid mob stoned this cabin. You refuse to be afraid. That scares some people."

"What a melodramatic thought!" Alma said. "I'm just a garden variety nonconformist."

Rinsing the last plate, a crooked smile skimmed across her mouth and vanished. "But there are times I wish I could be weak." The jug's spigot was dripping into the pan.

Megan stared at her. "I don't believe that."

"Don't kid yourself." Alma's eyes were brown agates. She rested one hip on the old iron cookstove that served as a shelf for the makeshift sink and crossed her arms over her chest. "Sometimes it would be damn nice to be taken care of. The weak are taken care of. Girls learn early to use helplessness to trap big strong males into taking care of them. That used to offend me, but I can see how it's very useful. I never got the hang of it, but it keeps them warm. That's more important than people like you and I think. Remember it."

"I'd rather be free than warm," Megan began, but Alma cut her off.

"Freedom!" the older woman hooted. "People love the word and loathe anyone who has it." Her eyes focused on something beyond the cabin walls. "Nonconformists threaten the established order. They are feared. And shunned. It's probably best to look and act just like everyone else."

"I don't think so."

Alma ignored the statement and eyed Megan thoughtfully. "I wonder if you would do me a favor."

"Sure."

"I have no family, no friends. I have not wanted any." Alma's smile was small but only slightly bitter. "If, or rather *when*, I die, would you take the paintings?" She paused. "Well, things do happen eventually," she said to Megan's surprised frown. "And I guess I just don't want them to be trashed. They are," she added quietly, "my only children."

*　　*　　*

The scissors seemed to be everywhere, sending bits of hair tumbling to the black-and-white tile floor. Corazón was clipping so quickly Megan wondered if she might end up with a punk 'do needing neon colors and a pound of wax.

She started to say something and stopped. Corazón was one of the most stunning women she had ever laid eyes on. The room they were in was a work of art in itself. And she had seen this woman's extraordinary feeling for the mountain village people. Trust didn't come easily to Megan, but she decided that if the cut was awful, it would grow out. "Tell me about the people we are photographing," she said.

The snipping stopped. Corazón's eyes caught Megan's in the mirror. "What do you want to know?"

"Nothing personal. Just sort of who they are generally, why they live there, what they want out of life. It might help me take better pictures. You said they are treated badly. Why do they stay? I pulled up stakes and moved across country. It isn't impossible."

Corazón's scissors began working again. "There is no comparison. You do not live on the same planet. If you were very poor, not dumb but badly educated, and every human you ever knew lived nearby, could you just pull up the stakes and go somewhere else?"

"I don't know."

"We are Hispanic, and many of us do not even know what that means. We are not Native Americans, we are Native New Mexicans—native to a place other people named. Hundreds of years ago our women lay down with the Spaniards. Some by choice. Many were raped. Men and women both were enslaved by the army, and also by priests. They were treated like animals. Worse than animals. You think that is a good beginning?"

"Of course not."

"That is a lot of the problem. We feel ashamed for being Hispanic. We have been told from the beginning that everything about us was worthless. Our religion was worthless. It had to be replaced. Our language was worthless. It had to be replaced. Our people had less value than a goat. The only land we have left, after the Anglos took what they wanted, is worthless for anything except a few bean fields."

"But that was long ago," Megan said. "You can't keep fighting what has already happened."

"It is still happening," Corazón said, stabbing the air with her scissors. "They took the land we used for grazing and made it national forest. Now they want to drill for oil on one of our mesas. To us the destruction of land is like a killing, a murder. But eventually they will have their way, because we have no money for lawyers to fight them. The *indios* have their casinos, and good for them. They have their reservations. We have nothing.

"And our women have less than nothing. They still lie down with murderous men, because they have no tools to fight for themselves. For husbands they have men who died years ago but still walk around." Corazón's scissors went back to work, but much more slowly.

Megan stopped paying attention to every amputated snippet of hair and watched the woman in the mirror. She couldn't help but admire the passion. "But can anything be done?" she asked. "You make it sound so hopeless."

"Maybe we can have something like the *indios* have. I don't mean the casinos. I mean a sort of nation within a nation where we can govern ourselves, where we who are all related to each other in one way or another can be recognized as a family, as real people who matter."

Corazón spun Megan around to face her. "It won't be easy. Already I know what the Anglos will say. They will say they cannot grant special status based on race."

Megan thought about that. "Racism with a reverse twist."

"Of course. But anything is possible." Corazón spun the chair back to face the mirror and held Megan's hair up and let it fall. "See? Anything *is* possible. Your bad haircut is gone."

Megan stared at her own image in the mirror. Impossibly, her hair looked longer, not shorter. There was much less of it, but not in length, and what was left curled gracefully about her heart-shaped face, giving her a youthful elegance she never imagined possible.

Chapter Twenty-three

With heavy black cloth taped around the window to keep the daylight out of the bathroom, Megan went about enlarging several black-and-white photos. She loved printing almost as much as shooting.

A dim light glowed very yellow, protecting the light-sensitive paper but making all skin tones look jaundiced. Clamped to a piece of plywood that was slung across the bathtub, the bulky enlarger was probably as old as she was, but since the principle was about as simple as a pinhole camera, it still made pretty good prints. An air cleaner hummed from a high shelf. Dust is a photo printer's worst enemy.

Black-and-white printing was at least as much art as science. One could sometimes make a great print from a mediocre shot, and somehow it seemed a lot more creative than computer enhancements of a digital-cam shoot.

As she prodded the sheet of Agfa double-weight paper, dim lines began to appear through the clear liquid in the first of three shallow pans of chemicals lined up in the tub.

There were several promising negatives, but this one she'd chosen out of curiosity. With long black pincers to prevent oily fingerprints she drew the paper from its bath and held it up to the light. The shadows and the play of light made a graphic pattern than might prove interesting. She returned the paper to the first pan, and when the image darkened to her satisfaction, she moved it to the next pan, then the next.

Lifting the print again, she placed it on the drying mat, checked to be sure all photo-sensitive materials were tightly wrapped, then carried it to the kitchen door and out into the sunlight. She had taken it during the picnic with Lizzie—the deep, narrow valley they saw. But it wasn't a great picture. Too much contrast, the people barely recognizable as human, the details lost in the shadows, except . . .

Along the rock wall just beyond where the stream of people bunched up, visible in a triangle of better light, was an opening in the mountain, apparently shored up with beams. Next to the opening was a delicate and perfect flower.

With dark petals, a white center, and a long stem, it emerged from what appeared to be solid rock. Megan's mind raced with possibilities. The focus in this shot was too soft. But given the right light, the right angle . . . to produce a sort of halo effect and sharpen the jagged shadows on the rock . . . this could be a truly arresting image—even a metaphor for . . . It made her think of Alma.

"Yes!" she said out loud. She would reshoot this afternoon.

She loved Alma in ways she had never loved her mother. Not more, perhaps, but differently.

*   *   *

The breeze riffling her newly styled hair, Megan edged her way down the steep hill. The sun was now high enough to reach the narrow basin. Unable to find a good path, she decided a rough and tumble scramble through the brush would have to do.

Her foot struck a loose rock and she slid, grasping at thorny branches that only tore at her hands, until she came to rest against a scrawny shrub a third of the way down the slope. Studying the hillside, she abandoned any notion of climbing back up this part of the canyon wall. But there were a lot of people down there. Unlikely they just skittered down the steep grade or leaped from the ridge. A good trail must be more obvious from below.

Her digital camera weighed only a few ounces. To do the best job she would need the single-lens reflex camera, with TriX film and a tripod, but she couldn't carry all that until she found a good trail.

Waiting to catch her breath, she examined the canyon bottom and wondered what brought so many people to such an unlikely place. The little she had seen of them somehow gave an impression of solemn, even religious intensity. An ancient ritual, maybe?

Megan knew little about religious traditions in these mountains beyond what Alma described as a "pungent mix of early Catholicism, with maybe a pinch of polytheism." Ben had mentioned that religion was a strong influence here at least since the sixteen hundreds.

Thanks to Corazón she understood more now. Starting cautiously downward again, her foot sent a cascade of loose rocks and dirt to the canyon floor. Finally nearing the bottom, she just sat down and, holding the camera above her head, slid the rest of the way.

A chipmunk sat up and cocked its head to peer at her. "Most humans do not use their backsides to get down hills," she told it. "But don't knock it. Sometimes it works," adding under her breath, "Lizzie would love to catch me talking to a chipmunk. Next it'll be a tortoise."

A trickle of water flowed along the narrow valley bottom, burbling over rocks, making more noise than its size warranted. Megan followed it in the direction the people had moved. Yes. There was the opening, next to a twisted, weathered tree. The timber that supported the entry looked as old as the rock and none too sturdy.

To the right of that was the flower. It was as exquisite as she had imagined. Marvelously, absolutely, perfect. Tough and sturdy, but also dainty and nonchalant, it posed on the massive rock. Its stem ended at a tiny crack, inside which somehow its roots found purchase.

She was already composing a title in her head. "Daring to Be Different, or Tenacity Can Crack Rock." She'd have to work on it. She was no poet. She snapped a dozen high-resolution images, changed memory cards, and glanced down the canyon wall. The entry to the cave, or mine, or whatever it was, looked shady and inviting. Maybe she could cool off there before trying to find a trail that would take her back to the canyon rim.

Reaching the opening in the rock, she found it even more comfortable than she had hoped, with cool air seeping from the cave's innards. She fumbled her key ring from her pocket and tested the miniature flashlight that hung from it.

Immediately beyond the entrance, the air turned even cooler. There was little hint of dampness, and a peppery odor of dust and mold made her want to sneeze. Her flashlight was limited but strong enough to pick out what appeared to be two hollow corridors that invited her deeper into the bowels of the mountain.

Chapter Twenty-four

She chose the larger opening and followed the thin beam of light down an uneven pathway that sloped into darkness. After a few dozen yards the passageway widened into a huge oval chamber, and Megan was astonished to see the beam of her light playing over a hodge-podge of folding chairs and camp stools surrounding a small wooden platform. This must be where all those people congregated.

The smell was different here—stale, a bit rotten, like a refrigerator that needed cleaning. The remnants of candles littered the floor, and eight or nine lanterns ringed the platform. An eerie feeling tingled its way up Megan's spine. A black mass? She quelled an urge to run back to the entrance. Don't be silly. Black masses, if they ever really existed, went out with the Inquisition. Didn't they?

Something fell across her sneaker and she very nearly screamed. Pointing the little flashlight, she saw what appeared to be two twigs bound together with many strands of bright-colored yarn. The center was white, giving it the look of a bull's-eye in a diamond-shaped target. She set it back against the platform.

Now she could see a low opening, not much more than five feet high, off to the left. She ducked and stepped through it. Intent on what was ahead, she almost missed the large low-ceilinged chamber to the right. The flashlight beam skipped across huge mounds of bulging plastic. Bits of yellow showed in a sea of greenish black that seemed to go on forever.

She poked the closest bulge with her toe. Something rattled. Touching it with her fingers, she wrinkled her nose. Garbage bags? Toxic waste? A trill of fear rippled up the back of her neck. *No. Not in plain garbage bags.* She fumbled at the bag's yellow tie. Inside were cans and bottles and paper wrappers. Ordinary trash. But no group of even a thousand made this much trash in one evening.

Turning back to the passageway, Megan crept farther along it. She didn't hear anything until she was suddenly aware of a dim babble. She crouched and doused the flashlight. The resulting deep darkness was disorienting.

All she wanted was some relief from the heat. She wasn't doing anything wrong. But the whole place seemed cloaked in secrecy. And she had violated it.

The voices were distant. She strained to make out the words but couldn't.

A hazy glow of light emerged from the gloom far ahead. Megan flattened herself against the floor of the passage, chest heaving despite efforts to calm herself. Her sinuses took note of the dust and mold and she held her breath, afraid of sneezing.

A man appeared in the faint, yellowish light twenty yards away. He wasn't large, but his posture was tense. He looked like the type who might face a knife bare-handed because he had nothing to lose. Legs planted apart, his sleeveless T-shirt a ghostly white in the darkness, he lifted his arm and Megan's throat nearly closed, sealing off the sound that was trying to escape.

Held high and ready to obey was a rifle.

She wanted to shout, *Please, I'm not armed. I just came in to cool off.*

He called out, his tone harsh, the words unintelligible. The murmur of voices ceased. Something was scuffed against the ground.

Megan's heart pitched itself against her ribs.

Had he seen her? Should she just stand up and say she was lost or something? He didn't seem the brutal type. But he did seem the sort inclined to regard questions as something you asked later. What if, seeing movement, he just pulled the trigger?

After an endless period of time, he lowered the rifle. Something clinked loudly and the spotlight went out, leaving circles of color exploding behind Megan's eyes. By the time she had adjusted again to the murky dimness, he had disappeared.

Gaze riveted to the place where the man had stood, she began to creep backward.

She hadn't realized how far she had come down the passageway. Crawling backward in the darkness was disorienting. She was no longer sure how her limbs would interpret her brain's commands. The camera case scraped the floor, and she swung it around to ride on her back.

Her hand brushed something sharp that stung her palm. Digging a fingernail into the flesh beside the cut stemmed the pain, and she continued her inch-by-inch retreat. The walls seemed to be receding.

She was thinking she must be nearing the large oval chamber when a sudden beam of light seared her eyes.

Blinded, she rolled against the wall. Had he seen her?

Her foot moved toward where the wall should have been but met a void. The opening to the trash room? Still hugging the ground, she slithered backward into the void just as the light began moving toward her.

The plastic stuck to her bare arms as she burrowed into the trash heap. The stench was awful. Her stomach began to roll. Footsteps were approaching. Too late now to declare herself. She was behaving like a criminal intruder, and no doubt she would be treated like one.

A light pierced the room, stabbed across the trash bags, and disappeared.

Had he gone back down the corridor or forward to the oval room?

Something fell across her leg. She jumped involuntarily. The footsteps were returning.

This time they passed on by and faded. Whoever it was, he was gone.

Megan scooted out from under the trash pile, stood, and felt her way along the wall to the opening. She heard no sound. Nothing. She slipped through the doorway and followed the wall to her right into the big, oval room. Should she turn on her flashlight now and run, or try to move slowly and quietly?

Slow, she decided, was not an option. One more minute of crouching and creeping and cringing at the slightest sound and she would be hysterical.

She ran. Stumbling over one of the camp stools, sending it careening into the rock wall, she didn't break stride, but ran on, camera thumping against her side. She raced through the large room and the tunnel-like hall.

Daylight should be visible any moment now. Maybe they would think the intruder was a stray coyote or bobcat. She didn't care what they thought. She only wanted out of there.

Suddenly the panel of daylight at the mouth of the cavern was there and growing larger as she pounded toward it: a bright entrance to a different, safer world. At last Megan darted through the opening and tripped over the roots of a twisted, stooping tree.

She staggered sideways, then raced toward the steep wall of the narrow valley. Where was the trail? Pretty unlikely the people she saw arrived there by helicopter. But she could see no access. She looked back.

The man was there, rifle propped against his shoulder, taking aim.

The camera strap caught on something, causing her to stumble back a step. Skirting a huge boulder, she clutched a shrub and pulled herself upward. Clinging to branches and rocks, she scrambled more than half the distance to the top before wrenching her ankle and hitting the ground hard in a broad space between two rocks.

The man had a clear shot. Why hadn't he fired?

Twisting sideways she could see him at the cave entrance. With the rifle at his side, pointed down, he just stood, his whole stance radiating anger.

Watching her.

Chapter Twenty-five

S he tried to get up but the pain in her ankle exploded up her right side, pierced her shoulder, and shot all the way to the top of her head. Breath coming in wrenching gasps, Megan tumbled backward, landing first on one shoulder, then the other, like a lopsided beanbag. Her slide accelerated, then slowed, then stopped.

Afraid to move, she lay still. A few feet away the branch of a bushy shrub bobbed as a jay landed on it, then took off again, the flutter of wings sounding very loud. She forced herself to turn her head enough to see if the man with the gun was still there.

He hadn't moved.

She tried to get to her knees but the pain flared again, and her vision darkened around the edges like a singed sheet of paper before it bursts into flame. She thought she heard at least one shot.

As the world went black she wondered if the pain was from a bullet.

*　　*　　*

The teacher was writing something on the blackboard. Lizzie squeezed her eyes shut, then opened them again and stared through smudged eyeglasses as the chalk in the teacher's stubby fingers continued to leave its yellow trail like a skywriter in a stormy green-gray sky, spelling IN DANGER.

A dry chill swept over her. The chalk smears on the blackboard wavered, like when the TV picture was bad. The blackboard began to develop shadows and depth, like a rock wall. It seemed close. It spun to the right, and she had the sensation of walking in a tunnel. Then the entire scene vanished.

Lizzie blinked and shook her head, but the blackboard was just a blackboard.

"Some of the early settlers in this country were young indentured servants," Mrs. Parsons was saying, pointing at the word she had written. "Now, what does indentured mean?"

*　　*　　*

Something was tapping Megan's elbow. She opened her eyes and found herself looking into a small, round face the color of caramel, except for the grime that streaked the cheeks and chin. The boy's small body was poised to run, but he eyed her inquisitively.

She slowly moved her head until she could see the opening of the cave. The man was gone.

Licking her lips, she raised her head a little and tried to turn toward the boy now crouched beside her. "I can't get up. I need help." He continued to stare. She wondered if he spoke English. "Please. *Por favor.* Get someone to help me." Sluggishly, her brain searched for the Spanish word for help.

She dropped her head back to the rocky soil. Her cheek burned, the skin apparently torn. She should wash the cut. There were reports of an odd virus lurking in the soil. Something from the droppings of mice. . . . She curled back into the darkness.

*　　*　　*

The sky was a powerful, intense blue. Rain had softened the soil. Alma scooped the dirt from between the oak's knobby, bleached roots.

The lines in her face deepened. Did she bury it that deep? She couldn't remember. Usually she dug it up once a year, just to reassure herself that it was safe, but this time it was only months. She wasn't sure how many. Was she that forgetful? That line of thinking was plaintive and weak. She tried to wipe it from her mind, but the thoughts kept nattering at her. Maybe it was time to cash one in.

This morning she had discovered a leak in the cabin roof. And the truck was twenty-odd years old and had more than 216,000 miles on it. Last year there were barely enough apples to sell to buy paints. And the paints she bought she had wasted.

Maybe that at least was changing. The awful months she could not coax anything worthy from the paint might be at an end. She had felt it deep in her bones since Megan's visit. And this morning, when the outline of the roadrunner, a drooping bit of straw in his beak, began to strut across the Masonite board, the old exhilaration had stirred again.

Alma stopped digging and wiped her hands on her jeans. Was she imagining things or was the hole much deeper than she'd ever dug before? Was this the right place?

Certainly it was the right tree. Only two roots, which reached across the top of the earth. But didn't she always bury the packet about a foot deep between those roots? The hole now was almost two feet deep. It wasn't large. Had she somehow missed it? She jammed the trowel into the earth again and began widening the hole.

*　　*　　*

Gentle hands were straightening Megan's body. Fingers probed along her leg. The hands rolled her over. A hot knife of pain stabbed her chest.

A face looked down at her. Questioning eyes, a beard dark above a Roman collar. "You have injured a bone or two," he said quietly, "but I do not think it is serious." He was about her own age. Megan had always thought of priests as at least in their fifties.

I guess they have to start somewhere, she thought stupidly, and tried to thank him, but the words came out in a dry croak.

*   *   *

Alma's dinner of apples, carrots, and pecans tasted like lead. It chewed like lead, too. One of her upper teeth was loose, and she had to gnaw at the carrots carefully. Could the piece of yellow oilcloth, salvaged years ago from an old table cover and used as wrapping, have rotted away? Could everything have been carried off by last week's flooding rains? A hard rain might erode the soil and wash up something buried even a foot deep.

Outside, the horizon was still a broad streak of garnet red, but already she could see the cool glitter of a few stars overhead. The air was turning crisp. The wind might be up tomorrow. The harsh spring winds made the worst weather of the year. She took two logs from the small stack next to the barn. Tomorrow she would have to split some more. Her forehead seemed so stiff she brought her fingers to it and realized a frown had set into her brow like concrete.

In all her adult life she had never asked God for anything except the courage and the means to make this place her home. Why now? Why now, when after such a long dry spell the paint was again dancing from her brush? It was like being at the end of one rope, and being rescued, only to find yourself at the end of another.

Was her insurance really gone? What she promised herself never to count on, she had counted on. She dumped the logs next to the fireplace. She shouldn't have buried it out there. She should have rented a safe-deposit box, she told herself for the hundredth time. But she thought paying thirty-five dollars a year to a bank for an eight-by-twenty-inch space was ridiculous. She was too clever for that. The tree on the edge of the arroyo didn't charge anything for its service.

Should she have kept the packet in the cabin? But then the people who broke in over the years would have found it. The burglaries were a nuisance but not really threatening. They always happened when she was in town, never when she was home. The thieves only made a mess; they didn't take much. Finally she had written an exasperated note and taped it to the cabin door: "Everything worth stealing has already been stolen." And amazingly, the break-ins had stopped.

Until now.

Suddenly needing fresh air, Alma opened the door. The roadrunner stopped its scurry across the courtyard. The fan of brilliant colors over his eyes seemed a comical but oddly touching mismatch with his heavy body and long tail. He tilted his head, then spread his wings and fluttered clumsily to the roof of the barn, where he gave a sort of dovelike coo. It was a very lonely sound.

She couldn't remember the last time she shed any tears. Probably when the old hound dog she called Romeo was killed by a coyote. That was twelve years ago. Through so many difficult times she never succumbed to tears. And she didn't weep this afternoon when she realized the packet was gone.

But now she could feel her eyes filling, like an arroyo fills even after a rain stops, when the water comes rushing down from the mountains.

Chapter Twenty-six

The room was a pale, ugly green, the foot of the bed an equally ugly gray brown tubular metal. A full-length drape of the same color made Megan's share of space very narrow, and the slight scent of disinfectant somehow made her feel irrevocably isolated, like a laboratory specimen in a jar.

A hand took hers. A strong hand, very tan. A few hairs sprouted above the middle knuckles. A small cough cleared a throat. "Are you awake?"

Megan's eyes moved up the arm to the face and stopped, puzzled. "Ben? What are you doing here?" She tried to frown, but her face felt stiff. "I fell."

"So I hear. They say it's a bruised rib, some lacerations, and a concussion. The ankle sprain isn't too bad. The concussion's the main thing. The others are painful but not serious."

Megan hesitated. The scrapes on her face made it hurt to talk. "Nothing else?"

"Like what?"

"Like a . . . a bullet?"

Ben gave a quiet laugh. "You must be having nightmares."

She stared at him. Did she imagine the gunshot? "Where am I?"

"Valle de Bravo. It's just a clinic, but it was closest."

"What are you doing here? How did you know?"

"José Rivera owns Las Gallinas bar in Española. They used his truck to bring you in. I was having a beer with him when he got the call, so I went along."

Megan tried to sit up. A sting lashed at her ribs like a whip. "What time is it?"

"Quarter after six. They probably gave you a sedative that put you out for a couple hours."

"Lizzie." She winced again. "Can you call the Gonzalezes and ask if they can keep her overnight?" She recited the number. "Tell them I'm sorry." Her gaze came to rest on the ugly green wall. She was very sleepy.

*　　*　　*

When she woke again Ben was standing at the end of the bed, framed by the brown plastic curtains, his face etched with concern. When he saw her eyes open again, his glance dropped to his hands, then back to Megan. "Lizzie is fine," he said. "She and the Gonzalezes were just terribly worried about you."

"Thanks." It came out a lisp. Her tongue wasn't working right.

"What happened to your hair?"

"A friend cut it," she pronounced carefully.

"It's awesome. As in beautiful. Even now, sort of messed up."

Her eyes began to close again.

"The lab in London," Ben began, but his voice ran down.

Megan's eyes flickered open. "Go on."

"The lab in London says the arrowheads are probably from South America, maybe Colombia. The world's best emeralds come from Colombia."

Megan watched his face, saying nothing.

"That's what I figured," he said. "During the Spanish conquest many emeralds were found among the Indians in Peru. But the Spaniards never found the mine the stones came from." He screwed his face into a lopsided frown. "Look, it was stupid of me to send them to London without talking to you. I apologize. I'm sorry. Really."

Megan bit her lower lip. And fell asleep.

*   *   *

Mrs. Gonzalez passed Lizzie a bowl. Eyeglasses a little askew, the child stared at the contents. Lumps of something in dark brown gravy. "What is it?" she asked cautiously.

They weren't in the kitchen where the Gonzalezes usually took their meals. They were seated on chairs—the backs of which were almost as tall as Lizzie—at the formal dining room table. Probably because her mother got hurt. Her mom was in a hospital. And Lizzie was scared.

"*Mole.*" Mr. Gonzalez nodded jovially. "*Muy bueno.* Very good."

Lizzie squinted into the bowl again. "Mo-lay?"

"*Sí.*" Mrs. Gonzalez's head bobbed. "*Mole. Chocolate con pollo y chile.* Chicken. *Para usted. Para ti.*" She substituted the form of the word "you" used for family and close friends. "*Especial.* For you."

Lizzie tried not to look shocked. The Gonzalezes were nice people. "Chicken and chocolate and chile?"

"*Sí.*" Mrs. Gonzalez nodded again.

Lizzie took the smallest lump, hoping she could get it down.

*   *   *

In the spare room off the Gonzalezes' kitchen, Lizzie sat down hard on the bed . The springs jounced so much her stomach began to feel funny. The murmur of the Gonzalezes' conversation in the living room sounded like the buzz of grasshoppers.

She stared at her schoolbooks on the dresser. She didn't like going to bed away from home. She didn't feel like doing homework, but Mrs. Gonzalez insisted.

Did she really see the words "in danger" on the blackboard that afternoon? Maybe her eyes were just playing tricks on her. Maybe she thought she saw the words because she was thinking about her grandmother. Nana thought Mama took too many risks. Risk and danger were the same thing, weren't they? And now Mama had got hurt.

*   *   *

Alma's voice echoed through the cabin. It was after midnight. She was singing an aria from *La Bohème*. Her voice was not what it had been; it broke on the high notes, but only the roadrunner, the sheep, and the goats could hear her anyway.

Her heavy braids swung as she swayed to her own music. She was tired, but it didn't matter. The painting was happening. It was beginning to move with a visual rhythm all its own.

She cleaned her brushes, tossed her clothes in a corner, slipped the oversize T-shirt she wore for sleep over her head, threw back the covers, and got into bed. God, it was good to be painting again.

But in the dark the beaten-down fear came back to life. She forced it away. It was just a fantasy, anyway. A safety net. She'd been walking a tightrope all these years and never needed it.

Something else prickled along the fringes of her mind. Something she had neglected to do. She always forgot things when she was painting. Remembering, she got up. Since she had pawned her pistol, she kept the ax next to the bed. She took it now and propped it against the door frame so she would see it in the morning and remember to split some logs. Fool idea anyway to keep an ax close by. Or a pistol, for that matter. All these years and the prowlers only came in the daytime, when she was gone. They never came at night.

A coyote howled in the distance. She thought about painting and was asleep in minutes.

*　　*　　*

The sedatives must have worn off. Megan couldn't sleep. She tried to turn on her side. Every time she moved a barb of pain grabbed at her ribs. No other patient shared the room, but the drape was drawn around her bed. She felt hemmed in, squeezed, almost claustrophobic.

Staring at the ceiling, she worried about Lizzie, and everything else as well. What was going on? First her paperboy went missing, then her house was burglarized, then she found arrowheads—*emerald* arrowheads, for God's sake—wrapped in her newspaper. Was that the right order?

The burglars must be thieves trying to get their stolen arrowheads back. Did that mean the missing newsboy was in on it? Her weary mind turned the incidents over and over but found nothing intelligible beneath them.

She and Lizzie saw a lot of people walk into the mountain. And in that cave or mine or whatever it was, she found a huge sort of meeting room, a ton of garbage, and a man with a gun.

Did he shoot at her? Yes. She was sure he had. Wasn't there the sound of a rifle barking in the canyon behind her? Was it a rifle or some kind of assault weapon? She wasn't sure she could tell the difference. An assault gun would make a burst of shots, wouldn't it? Or could you fire just one shot? Was he aiming at her and missed, or aiming at something else? What could the people and the cave and all that trash and the man who shot at her possibly have to do with her?

And Ben. How could he have the nerve to just up and send her arrowheads out of the country? Sure, he apologized, but talk was cheap. Was he trying to steal the emeralds? She must have been out of her mind to trust him.

After chewing on each of these notions, Megan finally found her way back to sleep.

*   *   *

Alma always slept like a rock. She never thrashed or turned or tossed.

She didn't hear a thing until the glass shattered.

Gasping, she sat up as if the top half of her body was on a spring. The light caught her full in the eyes, painful and white.

"A gun is pointed at your head." The voice came from behind the light. "You will please answer some questions."

Chapter Twenty-seven

Lizzie slouched, fingers picking at the veneer coming loose at the edge of the table.

Sitting at the other side of their dining table, Megan pronounced the word carefully. "Through." Her left cheek still hurt from the scraped skin. Both arms showed the purple of bruises. Maybe her rib was only bruised, but it sure hurt. The ankle still hurt a little, but she was feeling better.

"T-H-R-O-U-G-H." Lizzie spelled in a monotone.

"Laughter," Megan said. "Come on, Lizzie. As soon as we're done you can go play."

"I don't like all these 'G-H' words. Besides, there's no one to play with."

"We're still new here, sweetie. You'll meet some nice kids, make lots of friends."

"No, I won't."

"Yes, you will." Megan remembered what it was like to be a lonely eight-year-old and didn't know what else to say. "Laughter. Spell it."

"How come you stayed in the hospital so long?"

"I had to stay there because I fell and hurt myself. I'm sorry it was two nights. I thought it would only be one. What would you like for dinner?"

Lizzie tossed her head. "I'm not hungry. I had to eat chicken *mole*. They put chicken and chile—you're not gonna believe this, Mom—in chocolate." She paused, then rushed on in an uncommon whine, "I didn't think you were gonna be here when I got home from school."

"Well, I'm home now, and there's no need to worry anymore. But I still don't feel too shiny, so please help me out. Spell laughter. You can do it."

"L-A-G-H . . ."

"Nope. Start again."

The doorbell rang. Lizzie slid from her chair before it stopped.

"Don't you run off," Megan called after her.

The screen door sagged a bit in its frame. The woman on the other side had fire-red hair clipped short. The set of her head and shoulders, the determination written in her eyes, gave her the look of a pit bull.

Peering over small, round glasses that rather matched her body shape, she said, "Megan Montoya," as though she was assigning names and Megan happened to be next in line.

"Yes?"

"Bernie Ortiz."

The babysitter. Megan attempted a smile. "Oh, yes, of course. I'm sorry. I'd forgotten you were stopping by. Come in." She opened the door. "Lizzie, it's Mrs. Ortiz." She glanced at her caller. "Or is it Miss?"

"Well, dear, I've been a fool in my time, but never quite a big enough fool to get married."

Despite the pain in her cheek, Megan couldn't contain a lopsided smile. "Neither have I." It just slipped out.

The woman eyed Megan. "But you need a sitter."

"Yes." Megan offered no further information. Bernie Ortiz might make bold, joking statements about the unimportance of marriage but feel quite differently when it got down to motherhood without marriage.

The woman's eyes held hers and Megan had the uneasy feeling Bernie was examining her soul for pits and scratches.

"And the *niña*? Where is she?"

"Lizzie," Megan called again. *Where had the child gone?* "I'm afraid she's having a difficult day. Would you like some lemonade?"

Bernie said she would, so Megan left her in the living room to hastily toss some RealLemon and sugar into a pitcher in the kitchen.

"Looks like you've had better days yourself." Bernie stood in the kitchen doorway waggling a finger in the air. "What is all this? Bruises, scrapes . . ."

"I was doing some photography," Megan said, feeling oddly defensive. *Maybe the woman thought her boyfriend had beaten her up.* "I fell and—"

"Everyone has a right to a bad day now and then. I'm having one myself. A long one. Started about thirty-five years ago."

Megan set a blue pitcher, its side painted with a fat orange fish, on the counter and took a glass from the cabinet. "You mean it doesn't get better?"

"Nope. But there is some satisfaction in becoming meaner oneself."

Something in the carport knocked against the house. Megan went to the back door, stepped outside to see what it was, and stopped so fast she almost lost her balance. "Lizzie?"

Her daughter was sitting with her back to the wall of the house softly crooning a wordless tune. In her lap, its eyes squeezed shut, its chin held up to be scratched, was an ugly, scaly head.

Glazed eyes opened as Megan stared at the tortoise.

Behind her Bernie drew in a sharp breath. Lizzie seemed oblivious of the two women but the singing stopped.

"*Madre de Dios*," Bernie said softly. "She is one of them."

Lizzie looked up, eyes stubborn. "I heard you talking. I don't need a babysitter." The tortoise dropped its head back into her lap.

Opposing forces seemed to battle for control of Bernie's face. After a long moment she tossed one hand in the air and said to Lizzie, "This is a very fine *tortuga*. Would you like to know more about her?"

"Like what?" the child wanted to know.

"Like why she has come to you."

Bright eyes fixed on Bernie's for a long moment. "How do you know she's a she?"

One of Bernie's eyelids dropped slowly in a wink. "I know a thing or two, or six, or eight . . ."

Lizzie patted the tortoise's head, stood up, and came serenely into the house. "I'm hungry, Mama," she said as she passed Megan.

"Can you stay awhile?" Megan asked Bernie. "Would you join us for dinner?"

"Of course," the woman said, as if she had meant to do that from the start. "But if you will excuse me, you do not look so good, you are white like a ghost. Please, as a favor, go lie yourself down on the sofa and I will prepare the dinner."

"But you don't know where anything is."

Bernie gave her a bemused stare. "Not to worry, I will find what I need. The child will help."

And Lizzie was nodding.

So Megan did as she was told.

In no time Bernie was plunking dinner plates on the table. By seven o'clock she had persuaded Lizzie to help her with the dishes, and they ran through the whole list of spelling words while washing and drying.

Lizzie danced to the sofa to kiss her mother good night. "Can we keep her, Mama?"

Bernie insisted on tucking Lizzie in, returned to the living room, and picked up her canvas handbag. "This child of yours," she said, her voice little above a whisper, "is most special."

Megan smiled. "I know."

"No. I do not think you do."

Chapter Twenty-eight

Corazón Luz strode back and forth across the floor of her shop, face flushed, eyes bright. Her quick, staccato movements were accompanied by a sharp clank of metal when her bracelet brushed the brass chain belt that caught her deep turquoise tunic at the waist.

It wasn't yet 6:00 A.M. The odor of hair dye used the evening before still hung in the air.

Miguel sat in a lavender barber chair, swinging it side to side as he watched Corazón's pacing. His dark, almost black eyes flitted to the door, as if he yearned to be on the other side of it. Four fresh scratches were sprayed across his left cheek. One had narrowly missed his eye. His uniform looked like it had seen several days of hard labor.

"*¡Jesús, María, y José!* This cannot be," Corazón said between her teeth.

"It was not my idea!" Miguel growled. The woman was a wildcat. She didn't understand.

"And where are the—" Someone knocked on the shop window. She shook her head fiercely. "Closed," she shouted, pointing at the sign. "*¡Cerrado!* You think I am open all night?"

Grasping her own hair as if to rip it from her head, Corazón flung her head back. Anguish vied with the anger in her eyes. "Please, this is not good," she said. "We must talk."

"Our people are treated as *esclavos*, slaves!" Agitation ran Miguel's words together. "The only reason they are allowed to stay here is to do slave work. That is not freedom."

"My people are not the same as yours," Corazón said. "We are not *políticos*. We are not *mexicanos*. We are not really *chicanos* or *latinos*. We are *hispanos*. We have never had another land."

"Your people are stupid. They cannot do anything right!"

Corazón's eyes flashed. She lunged at him, grabbed his jacket, and tried to shake him.

Miguel leaped out of the chair and swung, his open hand stopping six inches from her cheek. Corazón didn't flinch. That made him angrier still. "We will find the goddamn stones!"

"You damn well better," Corazón shouted. "There was no need to do that. It was meaningless. Worse than meaningless. *Horrible.* Useless. You get more with sugar than with vinegar!" Suddenly calm, her hands fell slowly to her sides, her eyes narrowed. "Get Dolores."

"We don't need her hocus-pocus bullshit." Miguel kicked at the base of the salon chair. "We have more important things to worry about."

"Do it!" she spit at him. "Dolores will quiet the spirits. For *my* people." She bit off the words angrily. "*My* people do not take such a thing so easily. They have something your people maybe do not know. Honor. Go! What are you waiting for?"

Miguel eased himself to a standing position and edged toward the door like a lion keeper who wanted to believe he had the upper hand, because that was the natural order of things. But he knew the tables could turn in an instant.

"A la chingada . . . ," he muttered. But he went.

Chapter Twenty-nine

A flow of arms and legs coursed through the school halls, pushing toward the door. Lizzie was thinking that as much as she hated school and spelling stupid words, she hated recess even more. Someone bulldozed her shoulder. She caught the handle of the door to keep her balance.

Outside, the sun had burned the sky white and dulled the earth's colors. The light hurt her eyes. She let go of the door and walked slowly toward the cottonwood that stood near the adobe wall that divided the school yard from the rest of the world. Several wide cracks stood out on the wall like unhealed wounds.

The roots of the tree rose from the ground like knees. Between them was an ant hill. Lizzie bent down to watch the insects' determined march. She wondered if they thought about what they were doing or just marched because they were told to.

"Hey!" A hand rammed her arm. Denise, a girl with white-blonde hair said, "Hey! I'm talkin' to you."

Two more girls joined Denise. "Whatsa matter, you deaf?"

Lizzie shook her head stoically.

"Well, if you ain't deaf, you musta been spying on us."

"No," Lizzie said. An ant began to climb her leg and she swatted at it.

"Well, it's gotta be one or the other," Denise sneered, her face so close Lizzie could smell milk on her breath. "I think you came out here to spy on us."

"Why would I want to?" Lizzie muttered, thinking that if she wanted to spy she wouldn't get caught at it. "You don't know anything I want to know."

"Oh, is that right?" Denise poked Lizzie's shoulder. "You'd wanta know all right. But we were telling secrets. And nobody . . ." She pulled her arm back and started to poke again.

"What's that thing in her ear?" asked a girl in tight jeans and sweater.

Lizzie could see the third child now and felt better. It was her friend Maria, who piped up, a little worriedly, "It's a hearing aid, Brenda."

Brenda seized this information with glee. "Lemme see." She grabbed at Lizzie's ear. "I thought you said you wasn't deaf." Lizzie dodged backward, struggling to hide her anxiety, and hit her head on the trunk of the tree.

"She's not deaf," said Maria. "She can hear fine with the hearing aid. Leave her alone."

"If she can hear fine, she heard our secrets." Brenda's voice was shrill.

"So maybe she should tell a secret," Maria said. "That's what we said. Everyone has to tell a secret. Then they can't tell on the others or the others will tell on them."

Lizzie looked from one to the next. Her panic subsided. Maria was a good friend.

"Maybe she should give us the hearing aid. See what we can hear with it," said Brenda.

Maria ignored her. "Go on, Lizzie," she said gently. "Tell a secret."

"But I don't know any." Lizzie frowned. She wondered if she should make something up. But that didn't seem right. Maria was her friend. She couldn't let her down.

"Everybody has secrets. You must know at least one," Brenda pressed. "Or maybe you're too stupid. Maybe nobody trusts you with secrets."

Lizzie thought for a while. She didn't really know any important secrets. Except . . .

"Well?" snapped Brenda, taking a step forward.

"Okay," Lizzie said, looking at Maria, who brushed her dark, tangled hair away from her eyes and nodded expectantly.

"I don't even know what they are," Lizzie began. "They just look like green stones or little rocks to me. But they must be awful important, because Mama hid them in our garden hose . . ."

*   *   *

The air was warm and not a cloud was in sight. Megan hated running errands; as soon as she dropped the book off at the library, she would be through.

She glanced at the pharmacy next to the grocery store. One of these days she would have to find a specialist for Lizzie. The child seemed agitated lately. When she had a spell like this in Pennsylvania the doctor suggested Ritalin, but Megan didn't want to resort to such a strong drug. She waited to see if the hyperactivity would pass, and it did. Perhaps it would again.

Stashing the bags of groceries, she locked the car and headed up the street to the library. The collection of material on photography was meager and outdated, but miraculously, there had been a book that included some of Dorothea Lange's works. Megan had forgotten that in addition to the plight of migrant farm workers the woman had covered the rounding up of Japanese Americans into temporary assembly centers and the internment camps. The image of Japanese children pledging allegiance to the flag shortly before they were sent to the camps was uncomfortably moving.

She leafed through the volume one last time. The power was in the unrelenting truth of the faces. If only her own work with Corazón's people could be 10 percent as good. With mixed feelings Megan checked her watch. She was meeting Ben for lunch. After her mishap in the canyon, his anxiousness to help, and his apology, it was impossible to stay angry, impossible to think he deliberately sent the arrowheads off to keep them away from her.

On the other hand, she didn't need any more complications in her life.

Her grandmother, Elena, was a violinist who left New Mexico when she won a scholarship to Juilliard's school of music. One evening, homesick and walking back to the YWCA where she stayed, she found herself next to Carlos, a boy from home who was visiting a cousin in Brooklyn. As Megan's grandmother described it, he swept her off her feet. She gave up the idea of a music career. They would go home, have a family, and live happily ever after.

But with a fresh degree from the University of New Mexico and a taste of New York, Megan's grandfather saw himself as an intellectual. New Mexico was backward. He wanted to make his way in the East. Buy a bookstore. New York was too expensive, so they would try Pittsburgh.

Elena dutifully gave up both career and home. When her children were grown, she won a seat in the Pittsburgh Symphony. But Carlos complained that she was always practicing. So she quit. Her wistful regret was rarely mentioned, but it was always there in her eyes when she talked about music. After he died she looked at her hands and said quietly, "Why now, when it is too late?"

Sometimes Megan wished she had someone to share the decisions, the scares, and all the good things. But the price was way too high. Lizzie's father was an okay guy, nice enough to be a means to an end. And he didn't argue when she announced the relationship was over. Megan wondered what he would think if he knew he had fathered a child.

Ben might not be that easy. Remembering his lazy smile and the spark that ignited in his eyes when he was amused or pleased, she felt the color rise in her cheeks.

Chapter Thirty

Corazón gave Lupe Garcia's hair a final fluff and held the mirror for her to examine the back.

"*Linda*," Lupe said, the purple plastic bib crackling over her size forty-four bosom.

Corazón didn't answer. She was staring at the black-and-white tile floor.

"*Gracias*," Lupe said, a little louder, turning to look over her shoulder at the other woman.

"*Bueno*." Corazón untied the bib from the thick folds of flesh at the back of Lupe's neck.

When her customer had paid, Corazón didn't pause to sweep up the dark puffs of hair that littered the floor. She swung the strap of a bright-colored straw handbag over her shoulder and locked the door of the shop behind her.

Paper-white clouds that looked like they had swallowed something gray and bilious were building over the mountains to the east. A gust of wind sent a wadded up candy bar wrapper skipping ahead of Corazón's feet.

She always walked to and from work, with the step of someone on a mission. She grew up here. She loved stopping to chat with the Montaños at the bakery, Mr. López at the shoe repair shop, anyone, everyone.

This was her town, her people. The rural people in the mountains were hers, too. There, the people's heart, the center that held them together, was nearly used up. They could not be ignored any longer or they would die. Maybe Miguel was right. An omelet always meant broken eggs.

Today, Corazón didn't drop in at any of the shops. She went straight to the plaza. Most of the white iron benches arranged along the edges of the brown-splotched grass were empty. Here, with other toddlers, she learned to walk. Here she tasted her first ice cream cone, saw her first Christmas tree, sat nervously with her first boyfriend. She began to relax for the first time in three days. This, more than any other, was *her place*. If she sat here awhile she would know what to do. She chose a bench.

But there was no revelation. No easing of her mind. She watched the jays warring over some left-behind crumb and sighed. Should she just forget about it? Write it off? Abandon her dreams for her people?

". . . mad with me?" a voice was inquiring, a young voice with a catch in it. The face that accompanied it was red and glazed with tears.

"Maria," Corazón smiled. "I didn't see you. Of course I'm not mad at you. Sit." She drew the girl to the bench. Corazón's brother Emil was married to the child's aunt. "What is wrong?"

"Cico," Maria sobbed. Cico was Maria's brother. "He shouts and calls me names. He says he wants a lock on his room. It was just pictures. Stupid pictures of girls with no clothes. . . ."

Maria drew in a ragged breath. "We were telling secrets. And I thought if I showed one it would be better than just telling. Cico keeps them in his English book." She stopped sniffling and gave a half smile. "Nobody's secret was half as good as mine. Brenda's was just a peephole into her parents' room. And Lizzie's was just about a bunch of silly green stones."

*   *   *

147

Megan sat on the riverbank kicking her bare feet in the water while Ben perched on a rock next to her, the sun catching the broad smile under his ancient hat. The day was more like summer than what was technically still late winter.

A sudden gust of wind whipped the empty Kentucky Fried Chicken box from the ground and sailed it over the bank. Lunging after it, they both lost their balance and descended, with squeals from Megan and much laughter from Ben, into the Rio Grande.

A pale carp darted toward Megan's toes. She teetered, trying to keep her balance, the water an inch or so above her knees but barely halfway up Ben's shins.

"You're soaked!" he roared.

She shoved a big splash of water toward him. "So are you!" She waded toward the bank.

When he caught her shoulder, she turned, ready to douse him again, but his hands were framing her cheeks and his mouth was moving toward hers.

She drew back with something like panic in her eyes.

He shook his head and looked down. "Sorry." His hat fell into the water. He scooped it up. When he looked back at her, the web of creases around his eyes had deepened.

"It's not—" She paused. "It's just . . ."

He shrugged and smiled. "I understand." He turned toward the bank. "The water's chilly. Come on, I'll lift you out."

The smooth mud of the river bottom sucking at her feet, she moved deeper into the river.

"Look, I said I was sorry. Just let me give you a boost out."

Avoiding his eyes, she maneuvered toward him, half swimming, half walking.

He lifted her in the air, but instead of bending to sit on the bank, she put her arms around his neck and pulled his face toward hers.

His lips, motionless with surprise, began to soften. Slowly he lowered her against him, and her feet slid gently back into the water. For a long moment, neither moved. Then, like starving people who have stumbled upon a feast, they began to gulp each other in.

At length Megan leaned against the bank and began to unbutton his shirt.

The river lapped at their legs, making soft chuckling sounds. It no longer seemed cold.

Ben lifted her out of the water to the grass on the bank. She lay back in the warm sun until he scrambled up beside her. Then she sat on her knees and through half-closed eyes watched him watch her while she rid herself of the dripping blouse and bra.

The river went on chuckling.

It was still chuckling when they lay spent.

"That was quite completely shameless," she said, rolling over to nibble on his chin. "It's broad daylight."

Ben was looking at the sky. "Does Lizzie ever see her father?"

Megan drew back. "No."

"What was he like?"

She sat up cross-legged and reached for her blouse, only damp now after its time in the sun. "He's not important. I know this sounds odd, but he never was." She laughed nervously, struggling with her jeans. "We'll be lucky if we don't find someone selling tickets on the other side of those bushes."

Ben was trying to pull on his damp jeans.

Heavy clouds were building rapidly over the mountains, dulling the purple slopes. Megan waved a hand toward the scene, glad to find something to change the subject. "Look, where else can you find a sky like that? I love New Mexico. I don't ever want to leave here."

"I wouldn't mind seeing what the rest of the world is about," he said, fastening his belt.

Megan's glance darted to his face. "But your work . . ."

Ben tossed a pebble. It rolled a few feet and rocked to a stop. "That is what's known as a tender trap."

"What does that mean?"

"I guess it means the job is okay, but not much more." His voice faded as he caught her hard stare.

"That's why you're so interested in the arrowheads, isn't it. Not because of me, not even because of the emeralds themselves."

He was pulling on a boot that hadn't seen polish in a very long time. He reached for the other and pulled it on, too, before looking up. "No, it's mostly for you, but yes, also because it's pretty exciting to be part of it if they turn out to be the legendary arrowheads. And okay, I'm also hoping they might open the way to another job."

"Somewhere else."

"Yeah."

"I see." Megan gathered up the remains of the picnic and reclaimed the fried chicken box.

On the way back to Ben's lab, she tried hard to make conversation. Ben tried, too, but they only talked past one another.

She collected her car and was heading home when a strong blast of wind began bending the trees. Malicious black clouds were massing overhead.

By the time she pulled up in front of her garage a sort of free-floating anxiety was rising as quickly as the clouds and making her uneasy. The wind had stopped, but the silence seemed eerie.

Get over it. So you had sex. So he gets a job somewhere else. This is the end of the world?

She was barely out of the car when the rain came, not with a drop or two, but like the sudden gush of a hydrant. Something grazed Megan's cheek, then her arm. Hail. In seconds her shirt was soaked through for the second time that day. She jerked open the car door and got back in. Sheets of water sluiced over the windshield.

The rain stopped as abruptly as it started. And the wind began again. Bent nearly double, feet squishing in wet shoes, Megan ran for the house.

Grateful to be inside, she leaned against the door frame and was kicking off her shoes when a door slammed, not in the house, but somewhere nearby. One shoe off, she paused, listening. Lizzie should still be at school. The neighbors?

She drew back the dining room drapes, and one glance outside almost stopped her pulse.

The window in her garage, the entire pane except for three jagged triangles along the top, was gone. On the ground lay the shattered remains. No way hail could do that. That window, like the one in the dining room, was protected from the weather by the carport roof.

Megan slid the bolt on the kitchen door, crossed the carport, and avoiding the shards of glass pushed against the door. It swung open a few inches. Panic mounting, she threw it open hard, slamming it against the cement-block wall.

Lying in a tangle below the hook where she always kept it was the garden hose.

Chapter Thirty-one

Megan watched Corazón's hands as they steadied the steering wheel of the old pickup on the rutted gravel road. She hadn't yet shaken the uneasiness about the garage break-in. Whoever it was must know about the garden hose. And the arrowheads. But how?

No one knew except Ben, and he swore he didn't tell a soul. This time calling the police wasn't an option, because she had never told them about the emeralds. For the first time she was glad the arrowheads were in London.

The road was so narrow there was barely enough room for oncoming traffic to pass. Corazón's fingers were long and strong, slightly larger at the knuckle. The wild pink nail polish was chipped, and two nails were cracked. "You have beautiful hands," Megan said. "I'd like to photograph them sometime."

Corazón glanced at her fingers. "They need new polish. I have been too busy."

"They tell a better story like they are now."

Corazón was looking in the rearview mirror. Her eyes narrowed. "What the . . . ?"

Over her shoulder Megan saw a cloud of dust on the road behind them. As it drew closer she could make out the whitish nose of a vehicle. The headlights were on, although it was bright and cloudless and only a little past noon.

"*¡A la chingada!* What does he want now?" Corazón steered to the side of the road.

"Who is it?" Megan asked.

"My . . . friend." Corazón braked to a stop. "We had a fight. Now he wants me to forgive him. You know how it is." She got out of the pickup.

A dirty white panel truck had pulled off the road behind them, and its driver was getting out—a darkly handsome sort, with hair as perfect as a shampoo commercial. Even from a distance Megan could see the intensity about his eyes. He reminded her of someone, but she couldn't think who.

Corazón reached him before he took four steps. Angry words in Spanish jabbed back and forth like daggers, then abruptly halted. The man yanked open the door of the truck, got in, and turned it around with much lurching and grinding of gears. Red letters in a circle on the door spelled NMP&L.

Corazón's eyes were still fiery when she slid back under the steering wheel. Circles of red lit her cheeks. "*¡Cabrón!* Men are such pigheaded goats, they don't deserve to live!"

Megan agreed, but she was thinking that jealous men can be dangerous.

With amazing aplomb, Corazón drove on. By the time they reached their destination no trace of her fury was evident. She parked the pickup and led the way past two hens that were pecking at sparse patches of grass. The house beyond was barely more than a shack. Wooden crates for steps led to a door from which the screen had long since disappeared. Corazón stood squarely in front of the door. Sounds of someone scurrying about came from the room beyond.

Corazón called out something in Spanish, and the door opened. A stringy-haired, hollow-eyed young girl who looked to be thirteen or fourteen stepped across the crumbling sill. She was carrying an infant swaddled in blankets.

The child's eyelids were encrusted with something white and flaky; the rest of the face was a dry pasty gray. The little head was twisting back and forth, as if to avoid force-feeding. Around its neck on a silver chain, over a blanket that wrapped the infant tight like a papoose, hung a cross so detailed that Megan winced at the agony of the Christ.

Corazón said, "This is Carlita and Jesús," pronouncing the baby's name "hay-SOOS."

The girl looked anxiously from one woman to the other. She was so thin her collarbones stuck out in the V of her ragged blouse, and the flesh around her eyes was as dark and ominous as midnight shadows. A band of metal around her wrist looked more like a handcuff than jewelry.

Megan gave the infant a worried look. "What's wrong with the baby?"

"Nutrition here is not good." Corazón said it as if she were announcing the price of tomatoes, and she placed the girl and the infant against the wall.

Megan wondered if she deliberately chose the spot where the stucco had disintegrated, baring the adobe bricks. If so, she had a good eye. The slant of the sunlight made the shadows almost theatrical. The baby blinked against the brightness and began to wail.

Hurriedly, fearing the picture taking might be the source of his distress, Megan adjusted her camera, snapped the shutter, changed the settings, and shot twice more, trying to catch Jesús between the loud squalls that distorted his face. She worked quickly, saddened by the baby's apparent illness but encouraged by his powerful lungs.

The girl was nervous and self-conscious. "Talk to her," Megan said over her shoulder to Corazón. "Stand over there, so her eyes are on you, and talk to her. About anything."

Arms and legs restrained by the blanket, the baby was bending almost double with his effort to scream. A drop of sweat rolled down Megan's cheek. She flicked it away. "Maybe he's too warm," she muttered. Moving to the girl's side, she plucked at the blanket.

Corazón spoke loudly in rapid Spanish.

The girl grabbed at the blanket, trying to keep it wrapped tight, but one of the infant's arms came free, and he waved it wildly, leading his own chorus of howls.

"No," Megan said quickly. "Leave his arms free." She snatched the light meter from the camera bag and dangled it on its strap just above his chest.

The girl chattered in staccato Spanish to Corazón. The baby suddenly fell quiet, intently watching the swaying meter.

Megan hustled back to her shooting position and peered through the lens. The girl's air of distraction gave the scene energy. She was resetting the camera the second time when she realized something about the baby's appearance was not right.

*   *   *

Lizzie felt terrible. She dragged her feet along the dusty pavement, deliberately walking in the middle of the street. Maybe a car would come along and hit her. Good. Nothing was going right anyway. The Anglo kids were selfish and stuck-up and always asking stupid questions about the hearing aid. And the others—the HISS-pan-ics—acted like she was a spy or something and yacked away in their own language.

And now her mother was acting stupid. Spooky, even. Changing all the locks on the house again, and talking about how maybe they should get bars put on the windows. Bars! Well, Lizzie was in jail already, why not bars, too? Her mother didn't even want her walking home from school. Like she couldn't be trusted out of sight for two minutes.

She cried—real tears, even—and finally Mama changed her mind. Chewing on her lower lip, Lizzie watched a bird hopping from limb to limb in the tree in the Melendrezes' front yard. At least Bernie was fun, even if she was a *baby*sitter. Bernie seemed to understand things no one else did. Least of all Mama.

*   *   *

Megan lowered the camera and swept her eyes over the baby, who was frantically waving his hand despite the efforts of the girl. Jesús's arm was the color of dark honey. The pasty gray pallor was confined to his face.

Corazón and the girl were jabbering in Spanish. Amid a chorus of yells, the girl finally captured the infant's arm and wrapped it tightly inside the blanket.

Angrily, Megan bent to put her camera away.

"No," Corazón said sharply. "We need a few more. This will be good for your portfolio."

"I don't think so." Megan slapped the bag closed and stood up slowly, features stony as she faced the other woman. "The scene is a lie. I don't know why, but it's phony. And you set it up."

Silence stretched out like a rubber band seeking its own breaking point.

The color drained from Corazón's face, then came back like a blast furnace. "You call me a liar?" Eyes flashing, she took a menacing step forward. The girl and the baby melted away into the house.

"That baby may not have the best diet in the world," Megan said slowly, "but he's not suffering from malnutrition. I don't know about the girl. Maybe *she* doesn't get enough to eat, but that baby is as healthy as you are. What was the stuff on his face? Flour? Why do you want pictures of healthy babies fixed up to look sick?"

Corazón shifted her weight as a wrestler does to get into position. Megan stood her ground.

Insects whirred in the quiet. A long moment passed before Corazón's shoulders slumped, as if someone let air out of them. She sank to the ground, the brilliant colors of her skirt making a halo around her. Picking at a few bedraggled blades of grass, she said, "You are right. I will tell you the truth." She squinted into the sun. "It is not easy to get attention with ordinary pictures. And there are wrongs here. Many, many wrongs. Wrongs that are not so easy to take pictures of."

Megan's heart went out to this dynamic woman whose cause was clearly irreproachable. No one could make up at least some of the things Megan saw with her own eyes, the unquestionably forlorn and rundown shacks, the almost impassable roads, the dust and grime.

"My people deserve better." Corazón's voice separated each of the last four words with the fierceness of a sword.

"I know," Megan said. "But I will not take counterfeit pictures."

*　　*　　*

Lizzie kicked at a rock in the driveway, deliberately scuffing her high-top shoes and glaring at the small octagonal window in her front door. The sunlight felt like a warm cap on her head. A pickup truck with a new coat of red paint sat in the carport.

She hoped Bernie wasn't putting on an act, and now she would turn out to be an ordinary old babysitter. The kind who said, "Let's do something exciting," like play tic-tac-toe.

The door was slightly ajar, and Lizzie could hear a clicking sound. She poked the door with her foot, and it swung open. An odd smell hung in the air.

Bernie was sitting on the sofa, her red head bent over knitting needles. A huge blanket flowed across her lap and seemed to be creeping across the living room floor. From the saucer on the table at the end of the sofa, a thin stream of smoke curled upward from a blackened lump.

Looking over the round glasses that perched at the end of her nose,

Bernie fixed Lizzie with eyes like clear brown crystal. *"Buenas tardes,"* she said. "It is time you learn some Spanish. That means 'good afternoon.' Your mama will be home in two hours."

Lizzie headed for her room, wondering if she would have to spend all afternoon doing homework and saying "BWAY-nas TAR-days."

Bernie's attention returned to her knitting. "No, but I do think you should get your homework done now. That will make your mama happy. You can play later. And you only have to say *buenas tardes* once. Now would be nice."

Lizzie stopped in sullen midstride. She hadn't uttered a word out load.

Bernie's jaw was set. "You just charm the *tortuga* or is there other stuff, too?"

"What do you mean?" Lizzie asked in spite of herself.

The knitting needles clicked. "Other stuff. Like seeing strange things. Like knowing things you know you can't know."

Chapter Thirty-two

Megan went home from her confrontation with Corazón and into a funk. She shot no pictures. She ignored the file of photos on her computer and printed none she had taken on film. When Lizzie went to school Megan went back to bed and read mystery novels, although she couldn't remember the plot from one hour to the next.

When the phone rang she would roll over and stare harder at her book. Half an hour before Lizzie was due home she would get dressed and sink onto the old battered sofa to watch television until it was time to start dinner.

By the third morning she had slept so much she woke at 4:30 and lay in the dark thinking that this was not exactly a great way to live.

So Ben was planning to get another job, probably on the other side of the world. So he was interested in her because her arrowheads might help him make his getaway. So she was stupid. It wasn't the first time, and it wouldn't be the last. She wouldn't trade her career for his and that was that. Besides, who said it would come to that after one roll on a riverbank?

So someone broke into her garage, someone who apparently knew the emerald arrowheads had been hidden in the garden hose. Whoever it was couldn't steal the arrowheads because they weren't in the garden hose anymore. And that person couldn't be Ben because the emeralds weren't even in the country. Thanks to Ben.

So what if Corazón was lying to her, getting her to take pictures of people made up as if for a theater stage? Sure Megan should have realized it sooner, instead of embarrassing herself by showing the phony pictures to W. Brewster. So she had fantasies of becoming another Dorothea Lange. So what? She still had some good material. And maybe Corazón would let her do an honest job now.

No point lolling about in bed making a bigger fool of herself than she already had. Besides, it was boring.

*   *   *

When Corazón arrived at her salon, Megan was waiting for her. She minced no words. "I understand how you feel. I know what you were trying to do. Let me help you do it the way it should be done. They are my people, too."

Corazón studied Megan's face. "I wondered when you would remember that."

Two days later they set out on a new shoot. Corazón had not exactly admitted staging some of the other photos, but she hadn't denied it, either. She listened to Megan's argument that people determined to help themselves might generate even more support than hopeless people, and they both especially liked the idea of featuring women.

They arrived in a village fairly buzzing with activity. Megan wondered if that was what life in the mountain towns was really like. But this seemed to be a special occasion. So many people were in the road they had to slow the pickup to a crawl.

Two young women smiled broadly and held up a big cardboard carton as if it were a trophy. Jars with brass-colored caps jostled inside. Megan turned to Corazón, "Are they canning this time of year?"

"Any time there is extra food, they preserve it." Corazón pulled up under a tree near the church, which seemed to be made of gray mud. Bits of straw stuck out in some places, and young blades of grass were emerging from various crevices, but the walls looked sturdier than those of the huts scattered around its jagged circumference.

More women, these with sacks filled with loaves of bread, appeared. Megan opened her camera bag. "Looks like a fiesta."

Corazón was waving to someone. "Yes, of course," she said to Megan. "A fiesta."

Three large yellow drums of the sort that might contain gasoline stood in the shade against the gray wall. The color contrast was stunning. Megan started to raise her camera, but Corazón took her elbow and steered her around the corner of the church.

Scores of people were milling about. Smoke rose from various places behind the throng and the aroma of cooking made Megan hungry.

Corazón raised her hands above her head, clapped them loudly, then spoke quietly but authoritatively in Spanish. A hush fell over the crowd.

Fidgeting with her camera, Megan waited, wishing she could understand the words and marveling at Corazón's instant command of her audience. A few feet away was another yellow drum. She craned her neck to read the label: KEROSENE.

Corazón dismissed the gathering with a wave. The excited crowd cheered, and she motioned Megan to follow her.

Their first stop was at a round clay oven, where an old woman with no teeth, the map of a century on her face and eyes as bright as a bird's, was baking bread.

"She's beautiful," Megan breathed softly. "This is exactly what I meant." She took several shots. "What will she do with so much bread?"

Corazón shrugged. "Much bread is eaten at fiesta. This was the last of the flour from before the shortage. In the homes there are only a few tortillas, very little bread. For the next fiesta, maybe no bread, but for this fiesta, everyone will be happy and bellies will be full."

Megan made notes on a steno pad.

They visited half a dozen small enclaves of feminine industry, then passed a pit of glowing coals over which an entire small pig was roasting on a spit. Sitting nearby was a girl of eight or nine, knees pulled up under her chin. When she saw the two women she jumped up and pulled laboriously at the handle of the spit to give the pig a turn. Megan's camera caught the determined look on her face. "What's the reason for the fiesta?" she asked Corazón.

"First, to make people forget they are poor and often hungry, with almost no prospects. Second, to make them proud in spite of all that. Third, the celebration is for Cinco de Mayo, the fifth day of May. The anniversary of Mexican independence."

"Why are they roasting a pig now?" Megan asked. May fifth was more than two weeks away.

"This fiesta lasts until then, and they have to eat something," Corazón said, and abruptly turned away.

Megan wondered why Hispanics, who according to Ben had little to do with Mexico, would celebrate Mexican independence. But Corazón seemed edgy. Megan saw the woman's boyfriend in the crowd and guessed they were still having problems, so she didn't ask.

Some musicians were setting up in the plaza in front of the church as a small crowd watched. The music was not the brass of the mariachi bands. A violinist played a quick and happy tune that sounded a little like early American music. Another violinist played a tune that sounded very much like a polka. Megan loved best a high-pitched and plaintive melody played on a wooden whistle.

Corazón nodded at the whistle player. "That is Cleofes Vigil. He is everyone's favorite."

"Would they mind if I take pictures?"

Corazón spoke to the musicians. They each smiled and nodded at Megan, and she shot until she was out of film on one camera and nearly out of digital memory on the other.

As they retraced their steps around the church, the sinking sun made the contrasting colors of gray wall, black shadows, and yellow barrels even more stunning. "Wait," she called, and focused the camera. Only about three shots were left. "What will they use all that kerosene for?"

Corazón turned back. "Kerosene?" Her eyes swept to the drums. "Oh . . . there will be a ceremony on the last day of the fiesta. They will use it to light torches."

That would light a million torches. They must use it for cooking, too, Megan thought as she got into the pickup.

*   *   *

The fiesta photos were even better than she hoped: two ageless women making tortillas; another, this one toothless, stirring a stew in an iron pot; three worn but sturdy women shucking dried corn to grind into meal; the baker of the bread; the child using every ounce of her strength to turn the roasting pig; a couple of candle makers; the musicians, all were stunningly good. With careful selection and cropping, these pictures could be an exhibit all their own—a visual ode to the strength of women against tremendous odds.

Looking over the proofs Megan realized Dorothea Lange's mastery was not just her photography skills; it was also that she instinctively knew exactly what to shoot.

She waited impatiently for the prints to dry, then gathered them into a box with the digital prints and got in the car. She wanted to show them to Alma. And Corazón, and W. Brewster, as she now thought of him. But Alma first. Alma knew art better than anyone. Megan could trust her opinion.

Heading up the dirt road, she reflected that the seed for this project itself came from Alma. It was knowing Alma that helped her to face Corazón down in that mountain village. Alma's courage, her trueness to art and to life demanded it. And it was her admiration for Alma that led her to go to the salon and talk Corazón into doing the job right.

The cabin seemed oddly silent. Alma usually came out when she heard the car arrive. She must have gone for a walk. The battered old pickup truck sat where it usually did, seeming to snooze under its layer of dust.

Megan knocked and waited, then knocked again. She scanned the landscape. There was no movement anywhere other than the road runner, who strode into the yard to gawk at the newcomer. In the garden the tomato vines were wilted over their wire cones. She poked her head inside the shed. No sign of the animals. The feed pans were bare.

Icy little feet began to skitter up her spine as she went back to the cabin door and tried the knob. It turned. Pushing it open a little, she called. The cabin was dim and cool inside.

Nothing stirred.

If the pickup was in the driveway, Alma must be on foot. She *must* have gone for a walk.

Megan again scanned the mesa, but there was no sign of a tall woman with braids the color of the sky on a rainy day and the posture of a dowager queen.

Alma must have other friends. Maybe someone gave her a lift somewhere. Maybe it wasn't her habit to lock the door. Megan could almost hear Alma saying thieves would do more damage breaking in than walking in.

She would leave a note. Her handbag produced a pen but no paper. The back of a bank deposit slip from her checkbook would have to do. Holding it against the rough stucco wall, she wrote: "Have something to show you. Will stop back later this afternoon."

Where should she leave it? Outside it might blow away. On the floor just inside the door, it might be stepped on and overlooked. Inside. On the table. That would be best. Alma wouldn't mind.

Megan pushed the door open. Forgetting the low step up to the main room, she stumbled and dropped the note. As she bent to retrieve it, the air in her lungs turned to frost.

Alma's bed was unmade. That didn't seem to fit the woman's obvious discipline. But it wasn't the bed that closed Megan's throat as if a hangman had tightened a noose.

Next to where the worn brown chenille spread trailed on the floor was a lump of something. In the dim light from the cabin window, it looked like a severed thumb.

But no, there was a rudimentary nose, indentations for eyes. It wasn't a thumb, thank God, but a tiny doll.

Megan reached out for the little figure, then jerked her hand back. The doll's flesh felt startlingly real. Carefully, she picked it up and walked around the bed to examine it in the light.

But she never reached the window.

On the floor near the corner of the bed was what looked like the remains of a small bonfire.

Chapter Thirty-three

Megan threw Ben a worried look, then stared again through his pickup window at Alma's cabin. She had hoped Alma would be home by now, would invite them in for tea and explain away the odd scene Megan found that afternoon.

But everything looked the same. Except the evening light was now sending sharp-angled shadows to slice across the old adobe walls.

The roadrunner scurried toward the shed as soon as Ben parked his truck. Megan followed the bird to the little barn and came back shaking her head. "The animals are gone. Where could they be?"

"You said they roam pretty freely."

"But I got the impression they always came back at night. I poured out some feed and water before I left this afternoon, but it hasn't been touched."

"They won't starve," Ben said. "Goats, even sheep, can live off the land a long while this time of year. If worse comes to worst, someone will take them in. No self-respecting Hispanic will let a stray animal starve."

Megan pushed away the thought that they were talking as if worse had already come to worst.

Her call caught Ben just as he was leaving the lab. Now they both wore puzzled frowns as they went to the cabin door. "I think Alma would have told me if she was going to be away for some time. Where would she go without her truck?"

The knob turned as easily as before. Nothing inside stirred except a horsefly buzzing at the big window beside Alma's bed. The air held the odor of dust—and something else. Something peculiar. Megan hadn't noticed it earlier.

She glanced at Ben. He looked as wary as she felt, his lean frame poised for fight or flight. He snapped on the big red flashlight he had brought. His eyes below the shapeless hat, moved slowly over the cabin's contents one item at a time, as if he were cataloging them.

Megan scraped her foot through the burned bits of brush, the remains of the little bonfire that lay on the floor between the bed and the window. Her boot came away smudged with soot. She picked up a half-burned stub. Lacy, dried leaves and stems were tied together with string that was now charred. She held it to her nose. The pungent smell was not unpleasant, almost familiar, but she couldn't place it.

Her eyes met Ben's. "Something bad happened here," she said. "I can feel it."

He gave a cursory glance to the charred lump she was holding. Probing with the flashlight, he searched the bed. "You may be right."

"Alma would not make a fire in the middle of her floor, for God's sake."

"Probably not," Ben agreed. "Is she into New Age?"

"New Age? Alma? I don't think so. What does that have to do with anything?"

He pointed at the ashes on the floor. "*Curanderas* have used this sort of thing for years. Now it's become a fad, and Anglos do it for kicks."

"Make bonfires next to their beds?"

"These probably are spirit sticks."

"That sounds Wiccan. Alma might think Wicca is interesting, but I can't imagine her doing a ritual."

"Well, it looks to me like a smudging ritual was done to cleanse the place," he said. "Hispanic or Wiccan or whatever. If Alma didn't do it, who did?"

"Cleanse it of what?"

"That is the question," Ben said slowly.

"What's a *curandera*?"

"A sort of witch." Ben caught her look. "I keep forgetting you're more Anglo than I am. Not a bad witch. A good witch, a healer."

A last shaft of sunlight was giving something on the floor a pale glow—something that lay half under the brown chenille spread. Megan bent over to see what it was.

Leaning against the charred sticks but unbesmirched by the soot were two twigs in the shape of a cross, wrapped at their center with white string.

*   *   *

The deputy sheriff had small brown eyes and round rosy cheeks. He looked like a snowman made of newly tanned leather. His eyes were on Ben, although Megan was doing all the talking. Their chairs were jammed so tightly between the fronts of two desks they had to sit sideways. Both desks had been painted so many times the edges were rounded. The latest layer was black enamel.

The cop tapped his pen on the form he was filling out. The small lettered nameplate, all but swallowed by the mass of papers that covered the desk, said JUAN RIVERA. Annoyance wrote itself in the lines around his chin. He turned again to Ben. "That is all you know?"

"That's about it."

"No idea when she might have left or where she might go?" Rivera swung a reluctant glance to Megan. "No ideas? Even wild ones?"

"None." Megan brought her palm down on the desk in exasperation. "Where could she go without her truck?"

Rivera shot her a pained look, as though it was beyond him why women were allowed into sheriff's stations.

"If she went of her own volition, she would have to be on foot," Megan said sharply.

"She did not have any other friends?" Rivera's voice was so calm it was nearly monotone.

Megan's shoulders sagged. "Okay, maybe I don't know. But it's pretty unlikely she would just go off after building a small fire on her bedroom floor."

"And apparently smudging the place to rid it of evil spirits," Ben put in.

"Yes?" Rivera said in a bored tone, as if such reports were common.

Ben described the scene.

"More than one person has gone missing around here recently," Megan said to the top of Rivera's head as he wrote.

The deputy raised his eyes from his report. "Mmm?" He shook his head, clearly wondering how Ben put up with this woman.

Annoyed that even when she spoke the deputy looked at Ben, Megan almost shouted, "My newsboy disappeared. John Runyon. Has he been found? Is he back home?"

Rivera wet his lips, moved his eyes to hers, and gave her the answer she expected. "No, Ma'am. The whereabouts of the Runyon boy are not known."

"Maybe there's some connection between him and Alma. Has anyone thought of that?"

"Look, seventy thousand people in this country disappear every year," Rivera said. "Maybe it is just our turn here. Maybe the kid, he just wanted to get away from Mama and Papa. Maybe he just ran away."

Megan sat up straighter. "Maybe it's your turn here, but I really don't think it's my turn. I've never known anyone who went missing. Now, suddenly, two people I know have disappeared."

Rivera jabbed at the report. "Most people, they turn up. Believe me. This woman will probably show up. So mostly we don't do much until someone has been missing at least forty-eight hours."

"But Alma lived alone," Megan said. "We don't know how long she's been missing."

"Officially missing." Rivera pushed the report under the stack of papers on the side of his desk and gave her a nod of dismissal.

"I don't think she's just missing," Megan said to Ben as she dragged her feet down the brick steps of the sheriff's office. "I think somebody either kidnapped her or killed her. And so do you."

Chapter Thirty-four

Bernadette Ortiz was weighing Bermuda onions the size of grapefruit on the old-fashioned scale that hung from the ceiling in her shop. She was so pleased with herself she was even being polite to the woman who waited for her to tally the cost of the onions.

Under the counter on Bernie's side, in a cardboard box, a tortoise about the same size as the onions was peeking out from inside its shell.

The woman paid and Bernie dumped the money into the cash drawer. "You," she pointed her finger at the tortoise, "are just the thing." She had traded some cantaloupes to Julio Mondragon, who had found the baby tortoise in the pen with his sheep.

And very fine cantaloupes they were, too, all the way from the Imperial Valley in California. Bernie's cousin Ignacio moved there twenty years ago. He sometimes did "midnight harvests." This time he filled six gunnysacks with the best vine-ripened melons from some farmer's field and sent them to her, along with some fine corn and summer squash. His friend José, who drove a huge GE rig, delivered the sacks to her the day before yesterday. Bernie got a lot of the vegetables she sold this way.

The *tortuga* was for Lizzie.

Bernie was thinking a lot about Lizzie. She was over the alarm she felt when she discovered the child was *un vidente* with moments of *doble vista*, second sight. Maybe the Virgin had brought Lizzie to her. Maybe Lizzie was her own second chance. Maybe Bernie could protect her from the sight and limit it to animals. There was no harm at all in talking to animals.

She had already told the child that. She told her to ignore all the rest of the ridiculous stuff that might come into her head. With the baby tortoise, Lizzie would be so preoccupied she might not notice the other stuff at all.

*   *   *

Ben let the envelope lie on his cluttered desk at the archeology lab for two days. He had hoped it wouldn't arrive for at least another few weeks.

The return address was the University of Texas–Pan American. They had a team working in Cindad Perdida, the Lost City, in northern Colombia, and on the spur of the moment, when he learned that Megan's arrowheads might have originated in Colombia, Ben wrote asking if there was room on their staff for one more archeologist. He mentioned the arrowheads in the letter and mailed it with his résumé before that afternoon on the river with Megan.

Since then he had thought a lot about that afternoon. And now there was this problem with her friend Alma disappearing. He wasn't sure anymore what he wanted the letter from Texas PanAm to say.

So the envelope sat there like a black hole, pulling his eyes to it every five minutes. He glared at it as if it contained something toxic. He was not getting much work done. Finally, he picked it up and slid the end of his penknife under the flap.

The letter was from the head of the Department of Anthropology and began, "We are very pleased to be able to offer you an opportunity..."

A flustered look on her face, Bernie stood her ground, realizing too late that she should have considered that Megan might not approve of the baby tortoise.

Megan's right hand gripped the back of one of her dining room chairs as if she wanted to pick it up and throw it. "What on earth gave you the right to do such a thing?"

"Because I know what is happening with Lizzie." Surely the mother had noticed her child was not like others, was different in a way that had nothing to do with eyesight or hearing.

"You've only known her a few days. How can you know anything about her?" Megan wasn't sure why she was so angry. But the way Lizzie acted about that damn tortoise in the yard made her uneasy. How could this woman think she would allow one in the house?

Bernie drew herself up to her full five feet one inch and fixed Megan with eyes that were shooting so many sparks they looked like they might catch fire. "Because I'm old," she said, "older than you, older than your mama probably. Maybe even older than dirt. And for that reason, you will do me the favor of listening."

Megan twisted a nervous hand in her hair and said nothing.

"Maybe I see the little Lizzie better than you."

Megan's mouth flew open and Bernie quickly added, "This is because I am *not* her mama, I see the *niña*, not the *hija*, the little girl, not the daughter, yes. And I see other things because she is like me long ago."

Megan struggled to stay calm. "You never moved from your hometown," she said. "And you weren't deaf."

Bernie shook herself like a little red hen exasperated that some creature in her barnyard was so contrary. "Moving away? Deaf? *Insignificante.* Those things do not matter."

"Don't matter? Then what does?"

Bernie gave her a look usually reserved for customers who wanted cheap strawberries in December. "You are so stubborn, if you drown in the river you will float upstream. You do not see the tree in the forest even when it bites you in the face. The child has *la doble vista*. She must use it with care or it will run away with her."

Megan's mouth opened and closed and opened again. "She has what?"

"The sight. The second sight." Bernie pronounced the words as if she were teaching them to someone who spoke no English. She banged her fist on the table. "Have you not noticed that Lizzie sometimes thinks she knows things?"

Megan's eyes grew wider, her voice smaller: "Like when it's going to snow?"

Bernie nodded vigorously. "Like that, yes. Many times she will be right, but once in a while wrong. The more she is right, the more she will trust it."

"Even I paid more attention after seeing those snowflakes," Megan mused.

"This is important, what I say now. It is why I bring the baby *tortuga*. The child must learn *not* to trust it. If she gives her time, her thinking, to the animals—talking to animals is a good thing. Maybe she will become a *curandera* to the creatures, a healer of animals."

Megan was nodding very slowly. "A veterinarian."

Bernie wondered if she should point out the difference and decided it might be pushing things a little too far. "*Sí*," she said. "A veterinarian."

"You were like that?" Megan asked.

"Not with animals, no. I was proud. I was stupid. I thought I had special powers." Her friends, she told Megan, believed her. They wanted to go up in the mountains to cut Christmas trees, and maybe shoot a deer. The trip would take several days.

"They were taking two old wagons, pulled by horses. No one had an automobile." They came to Bernie to ask if the little expedition would be safe. She examined her mind and saw nothing worrisome.

Her friends were gone two days when the snow began. The wind blew and whistled like a monster. "Two minutes after you walked across the street, your footprints were gone. Thirty-three inches of snow. And that was here, in the valley." Bernie spread her arms to show how high. "It was weeks before anyone could get into the mountains. We found them, yes, the horses and the seven *amigos*, all dead."

"You must have been devastated," Megan said, a bit shaken by the thought herself.

"A grief I hope you never have. No one knew they had come to me, that I sent them up there to die."

"But how could you have known?"

"I knew many things. When old Pedro's mule got away, I knew it was in an arroyo a mile down the river, behind a smokehouse. When Lupe Gomez disappeared, I knew she ran off with a peddler and, sure enough, a year later she comes back with his baby."

"You were a witch?"

"No, no." Bernie stamped her foot. "Open the wax in your ears. I just knew things. Many times I was right. But sometimes I was not."

Megan stared at her for several seconds, then went to her bedroom and returned with something in her hand. "Have you ever seen anything like this?"

"*Ave María Purísima*," Bernie breathed.

Both women stared at the object on the palm of Megan's hand. It was the tiny doll she found by Alma's bed.

In the light of day the doll itself was just a molded lump of red-brown clay. It was the white wax that encased it that gave it an eerie look of flesh.

"Is it a hex?" Megan asked.

"Hex?"

"Would this have something to do with some sort of evil spell?"

"Evil? No. But a spell, yes. This was made to take away the badness of something." Bernie took the clay figure and turned it over and over in her palm. "Either it was never used, or it did not do what it was supposed to do."

"How do you know?"

"Because it would have taken the badness into itself. It would be black."

Chapter Thirty-five

The silence in the house reverberated with an intensity all its own. Megan locked the doors, turned out the light over the kitchen sink, and got into bed.

Lizzie had been ecstatic about the invitation to Mona Trujillo's slumber party. And Megan was pleased Lizzie was making new friends, but now a sharp-edged loneliness crept over her. Maybe too much had happened too quickly. For her as well as for Lizzie. Moving across country, getting her daughter settled, trying to launch a new career, her savings dropping to levels below her comfort zone. But she loved New Mexico in spite of the problems. There seemed to be more opportunities for her here than anywhere else. She tried to reassure herself that things would settle down.

But what about the arrowheads? That situation alone was enough to rob her of sleep.

Watching shadows of the tree outside her window play across the bedroom wall, Megan thought about how the arrowheads could give her what she wanted most. They could indefinitely stretch the amount of time she could afford to take to develop her photography into a paying career. On the other hand, there was the moral question. Or was she being too puritanical?

There seemed no way to escape the likelihood that the paperboy was the one who wrapped them in her *Journal*, which was why he went missing. And it was hard to think of a logical explanation for the ransacking of her house other than someone after the arrowheads. As to the garage and the garden hose, there could be no doubt at all about the reason.

The person or persons instigating all this believed she had the arrowheads, that she had hidden them. Would they be back? Very likely they would.

Were she and her daughter safe? Very likely they were not as safe as they were before the arrowheads. How much danger might be stalking them? Should they leave town? Move to California, as originally planned? Megan had no answers to those questions. Maybe the emerald problems were over when whoever was after them shook the garden hose and nothing fell out.

Good thing she gave the emeralds to Ben. She rolled over again. Just her luck to fall in love with a place and get interested in a guy, who then casually mentions that he wants to go live somewhere else. The blanket was twisted around her leg. She kicked it free.

And what about that cave in the mountains? There couldn't be any relationship between that and her own problems, but something weird was going on there. Where did all that trash come from? And the man shot at her. He missed, but she was sure he fired. Why? Because she invaded his privacy? Because she saw something he didn't want her to see? What was there to see besides a ton of trash?

And perhaps the eeriest question of all: Where was Alma? A sad ache flooded Megan. She hadn't known her long, but already they were like old friends, understanding things before they were even said. Surely Alma would tell her of any travel plans. Did she know Alma as well as she thought?

Unwilling to dwell on the possibility that something terrible had happened to her friend, Megan pulled at the covers. She was hungry. Milk and crackers, maybe. But the milk carton, she remembered, was almost empty. The digital clock on the night table said 10:41. If she hurried she could catch the 7-Eleven before it closed. Wearing jeans and a red shirt over her pajamas, she drove to the convenience store.

As she got back into the car with the carton of milk, a fresh wave of self-doubt rolled over her. She was out of her mind to move here. The move was too much for Lizzie to adjust to, and now they were embroiled in something she didn't begin to understand. Damn the arrowheads.

The store's neon sign blinked reds and greens across the hood of the car. If only she could talk to Alma. With the help of her down-to-earth wisdom, Megan might be able to sort things out.

Maybe the notion that Alma was a victim of foul play was melodramatic. Maybe an old friend had turned up and they decided to go to Denver or El Paso. Maybe Alma was already back home. And if not, it was time to call the cops again and insist on a real search for a missing person.

Megan started the car. At the corner, she didn't turn left toward home; she turned right, toward the road to Alma's.

*   *   *

She smelled it as soon as she got out of the car. A strong scent of burning wood tainted the breeze. The fireplace? Had Alma returned?

The moon was throwing flickering shadows against the cabin's adobe walls, but everything seemed about the same as when she and Ben were there. Megan leaned against the open car door.

Somewhere on the mesa a couple of coyotes gave a litany of chilling yips.

Retrieving the flashlight she kept in the glove compartment, she switched it on and aimed the beam at the cabin's chimney. No smoke. The smell must have drifted in on the wind. But when she swung the light to the cabin door, she knew better.

179

Wisps of smoke were leaking out around the edges.

She raced to the door and pushed it open. A roiling wall of black smoke in the main room rushed toward her like an evil spirit. Beneath that, red and yellow flames like glowing, clawing fingers were creeping along the floor in the vicinity of Alma's bed.

Gasping for better air, Megan turned to run for the car.

But maybe Alma was home, in bed asleep, or unconscious?

Megan drew in a deep breath and dashed into the cabin. Eyes blinded by smoke, she stumbled to the bed and searched it with her hands. It was empty. She remembered the water jugs stacked against the wall of the little kitchen. But her lungs were filling with pain. She tried to let her breath out slowly.

Air, she must have air. Too late for the water jugs. She had to get out. Now.

Making her way back to the door, her hand grazed something flat and square, knocking it to the floor. She kicked it aside. Outside, chest heaving, she took in fresh air. Inside the cabin the fire crackled and snapped as it savored its feast.

Slowly, it came to her what she had knocked to the floor: a painting. One of those paintings stacked along the wall near the door.

They are my only children.

Megan went back to the cabin, gulped as much air as her lungs would hold, and went in. The fire was in the main room. The smoke was far less dense on the sun porch, where the paintings were stacked five or six deep. She grabbed the two closest.

Something fell across her foot—a pale rectangle, an envelope. She snatched it up, jammed it between her teeth, grabbed two more paintings, and rushed outside. Drawing in clean air around the envelope, she leaned the paintings against a tree and went back.

Dizzy and choking on the smoke, she managed to rescue most of them.

She packed the car full and, with an anguished last look at the cabin, took the paintings home.

It wasn't until she got into her car the next day that she noticed the teeth-marked envelope on the passenger seat.

The flap was not sealed. Inside was a folded sheet of yellow-ruled paper. The words were written carefully in ink: "I, Alma Peters, being of sound mind. . ."

Chapter Thirty-six

The restaurant was old, with uneven floors, foot-deep window-sills, and heavy, dark wood furniture. Megan leaned back in her chair and stared at Ben through eyes that had begun to water. "Are you trying to kill me? I need some water," she said, in a voice so husky it was hardly audible.

"I take it this is your first green enchilada?"

"Are they always this hot?"

"Depends on where the chiles are grown, what altitude. The lower the altitude, the hotter the chile." Ben signaled a passing waiter and pointed a thumb at Megan. "Gringa," he said. "Bring her some milk."

The waiter nodded knowingly and hustled off.

Megan put down her water glass. "Milk?"

"Only thing I know of to put out the fire in the mouth. Water doesn't do it."

She took a sip of milk when it came. "People actually like that stuff? They eat it by choice?"

"Your family never ate chiles?"

"Not this kind. We ate the kind with beans. I've never even seen a flat enchilada." She caught his glance. "And don't you dare look amused. How do people get used to eating napalm?"

"It's like hating Texans—must be something in the water. In a couple years, you'll be craving it, too."

"I don't think so. It's hotter than hell. And it looks like . . . Well, you know what it looks like." She downed the entire glass of milk. "What do you mean, hating Texans?"

"One morning you'll just wake up loving chile," he deadpanned, "and hating those white license plates."

She laughed, and it made her face feel odd. She hadn't laughed much lately. Twisting the stem of the blue-rimmed water glass between her fingers, her expression went serious again. "Thanks for cheering me up. But I keep thinking I should do something about Alma's place." Water splashed from the glass. She mopped it up with her napkin. "What could have caused that fire?"

Ben leaned back. The straw chair seat creaked. "Any number of things. From lightning to a pilot light."

"The night was clear. No lightning. Besides, the fire obviously started inside. Could it have been a propane leak?"

"Good guess. The room was small. Once it filled with gas, just the refrigerator pilot might ignite it."

"Weird that she wrote out a will just before that." Megan folded her napkin into a small square. "She mentioned wanting me to have the paintings, but I didn't think she'd write it down. At least, not so quickly. You think maybe she knew something? Suspected something might happen?"

"No way to know unless she comes back."

Megan's eye's began to water again, this time for a different reason. "We still don't know what happened to her, or even if she's alive."

"She doesn't sound the type to have homeowner's insurance," Ben said. "If she comes back now, she won't have anywhere to live."

"She could live with me. I haven't known many people I thought I could live with, but Alma was one." A sudden tidal wave of sadness almost spilled the gathering tears. "*Is* one," she said.

Ben looked at her. Half of her face was in shadow, the rest was in the light from the candle on the table. He drew in a deep breath. "The London lab should be returning the emeralds soon."

"I guess I'd better rent a safe deposit—"

"That isn't what I meant to say," Ben cut in. "The thing is, I've been offered a job."

She took a sip of water, avoiding his eyes.

"In Colombia." In the back of the restaurant, someone dropped some glassware.

When she was sure she could trust her expression, Megan looked up. "When do you start?"

"I haven't accepted it yet." Ben looked at his hands. "I know the timing is bad, but . . ." He paused, then plunged onward, an unskilled swimmer seeking something solid. "I was wondering if . . ." He floundered.

She didn't help him out. Casting about for some distraction, her eyes fixed on a picture in a frame on the wall over his left shoulder, a still life with a blue glass pitcher.

Finally, he blurted, "I don't suppose you'd want to go with me."

Her head moved slowly from right to left before she dropped her gaze from the picture to her hands, which were twisting the napkin. "I can't. Lizzie has special needs. She's only now beginning to adjust to the move here. And I'm just getting started on a career."

*   *   *

W. Brewster Gillette's voice was low as he scrutinized first one painting, then another. "These are as fine as I have seen in a very long time. How many are there?"

"Forty-seven in all. Eight are a little smoke damaged. I'll have them cleaned as soon as I can afford it." Megan was almost giddy. First he was enthusiastic about her own latest series of photos, now he was regarding Alma's paintings with what could only be called awe.

"The museum here in Santa Fe can recommend someone for the restoration," he said. "As for these, I'll hang four at a time, and we'll increase prices as each group sells. And they will sell. You want to leave these?"

"I guess so, if you have room." Megan stopped, swamped by mixed feelings. "But . . . don't hang them quite yet." Alma was so set against exhibiting her work. And maybe there was still a shred of hope she was alive, would come back and want her paintings.

"If the rest are like these, and we handle them right, we can build the artist quite a reputation, to say nothing of the money."

If Alma returned, she could use the money for a new home.

"Not quite yet," Megan said again.

*   *   *

Lizzie was very pleased. She stopped on the sidewalk and opened her report card again.

An A in Spanish, and the rest almost all Bs. She couldn't restrain a giggle. Well, two Cs, but they hardly counted. One was in PE, who cares about that? The other was in music. Okay, so she didn't have a very good voice. She didn't care much about that, either.

She tossed her head. Her mom had taught her to braid her hair, and it was kind of cool to feel the braids swing back and forth. Lizzie wanted to let her hair grow long and have it loose, but her mom said it either had to be cut or braided or put in a ponytail. That was after the bubblegum got stuck in it. Mom was kind of easy to upset lately. But braids were kind of fun.

With a happy little hop, she put the report card back in her math book, where it wouldn't get wrinkled. Mama was going to be so pleased.

*   *   *

On her way home from the art gallery, Megan stopped at the super-market. She selected a plump roasting chicken that was on sale, a head of lettuce, and some tomatoes. The only lettuce that didn't look like it was past its sell-by date was the Bibb. Even those leaves looked a little limp, but she had a taste for salad. The chicken would be good for two dinners and maybe a lunch. And she could make soup from the bones.

She paid the cashier and crossed the parking lot, wondering again whether to let the gallery hang Alma's paintings.

"Hey," someone called. "Hello."

Intent on her thoughts about Alma, Megan didn't notice. She opened her denim handbag and dug out the car key.

"Megan!"

She glanced up, squinting against the sun, which was almost directly behind the head of an approaching woman.

"Hello." Corazón's cloud of dark hair floated around her shoulders as she reached Megan's side. "I just wanted to tell you how much everyone likes the last set of pictures," she said, a little out of breath and overexcited even for her. "They are *magníficos*." She kissed her fingers and held them up like a salute. "Can we talk a minute?"

Megan glanced at her watch. Lizzie was due home soon, but she obviously couldn't say no. "I guess so. If it won't take too long."

*   *   *

As soon as Lizzie got home she went to the kitchen to get a cookie for herself and a snack for Theodora. She was supposed to go over to the Gonzalezes', but Mom would be home any minute, and Lizzie wanted to tell Theodora about the report card.

She dug up the dandelions herself and thrust them roots and all into the vegetable drawer at the bottom of the refrigerator. Mom complained that there were more leaves than Theodora could eat in a lifetime, but Lizzie wanted to be sure there were enough. After all, they were free to anyone just for the digging. She selected a few small, young leaves, washed them carefully in the sink, and went to the garage.

Inside, it was shadowy and musty, but she could hear the slow pad, pad of little feet. Mom said Theodora had to stay in the garage when they weren't home, but she helped Lizzie make a safe place for the little tortoise in a big cardboard box. They put it by the window and kept it supplied with grass clippings and water.

A small, blunt head appeared in the rectangle of sunlight from the open door. "Hi," Lizzie said. "Are you hungry?"

She wondered if dandelions and lettuce and grass were enough. She told her mom that Theodora said she would like some grape leaves, and maybe some aloe vera once in a while, but Mama had given Lizzie that look again.

The tortoise blinked and took a slow step forward. The little girl squatted down and held out a dandelion leaf, but Theodora stopped.

Lizzie didn't notice the long shadow that fell across the grayish shell. "Come on," she coaxed. "You know it's safe here. I came to show you my report card!"

When Theodora still ignored her outstretched hand, the little girl reached out to pick her up. She had barely touched the tortoise when its head and legs vanished into its shell.

"Poor baby, what are you afraid—?" A gloved hand stopped her mouth before she could scream.

Chapter Thirty-seven

Megan sat on the sofa in her living room blankly staring into space, knowing exactly how it would feel if someone tore the lid off hell and forced her facedown to take a good look.

If she had just come home sooner. If she hadn't been so damned eager to hear Corazón's compliments. If she hadn't stopped at the grocery store.

The cops had come and gone. Megan told them everything she knew, which was practically nothing.

She called Mrs. Gonzalez as soon as she got in the door and saw that Lizzie wasn't home. Half an hour past the time her daughter usually arrived home, mouth dry, breath coming a little shallow, she walked Lizzie's usual route all the way to the school.

The teachers and clerks still in the school building suggested the child probably stopped to play with someone and forgot the time. But Lizzie never did that. She always came straight home. Always. That was the rule.

Retracing her steps back toward home, Megan looked into empty lots, empty yards, hoping against hope her daughter had broken that rule, and she would find her with a friend or digging dandelions for that damn tortoise.

Mrs. Thomas down the street stopped sweeping her front stoop to say she thought she saw Lizzie skipping down the road toward home more than an hour ago. Mr. Melendrez next door hadn't seen Lizzie. The only movement he saw on the street all day was a truck that drove past and parked under the globe willow half a block up the street. He figured it was probably the cable company or the gas company.

Gripping the phone so tightly her knuckles whitened, mouth so dry she could hardly form words, Megan called the sheriff's station. The arrival of a squad car brought all the neighbors, gaping, into their front yards.

When the two deputies finished asking their questions and searching the house and yard, Officer Córdova, the man with the beagle-sad eyes who told her about the paperboy's kidnapping a few weeks before, asked if she wanted a doctor, a sedative.

"No." Megan struggled against full-blown hysteria. "I want my daughter."

When they left, she sat on the sofa, staring but seeing nothing. Eventually, a strange calmness came over her. The pain numbed and shock set in. She telephoned Bernie and recited in a flat voice what had happened. Then she called Ben and repeated the same statement.

She no longer remembered what Bernie or Ben said or how long ago she talked to them.

She went into Lizzie's room, pulled the comforter from the bed, and hugged it to her. It smelled a little of Lizzie's favorite cookies. "Nooooo," she keened, sitting down on the bed and rocking back and forth. It wasn't true. It couldn't be. How could this be happening?

Dragging the comforter back to the sofa, she sat down and put her face into it. A few cookie crumbs stuck to her cheek, and she realized that tears were dripping slowly off her chin. She fought down the urge to scream. If she started, she was afraid she wouldn't be able to stop.

She didn't get up when Ben arrived. He knocked and let himself in the unlocked front door to find her sitting on the sofa, eyes unfocused and fixed on an invisible spot in space. If only she hadn't stopped to talk to Corazón. If only . . .

"That's nonsense," Ben said. "So you were five, ten minutes late. Whatever happened probably didn't happen here. More likely it happened on her way home."

His eyes searched hers. He put his hand on her shoulder and shook her gently. "Megan," he said. "Stop it. You aren't going to do Lizzie any good this way."

"First the paperboy, then the burglaries, then Alma, now Lizzie." Megan's voice rose to a scream and broke. "What is going *on*?"

Ben sat down and put his arms around her. Slowly the anger and hysteria gave way to sobs.

"This can't be happening." She kept saying it over and over.

"I know," he said. "But it is."

"It's the arrowheads," she said. "The goddamn arrowheads."

*   *   *

Bernie stood, feet planted in the middle of the living room, elbows like the ends of wings, hands planted on broad hips, red hair scrambled as though she had run an eggbeater through it, giving her a wizened punk look.

After listening to Megan who, face blotchy and swollen, was still rooted to the sofa, Bernie issued an order: "Stop blaming yourself!"

Bernie was angry with her own self, and that was bad enough. Why hadn't she seen this? She had begun to forgive God a little, but now she was angry with Him again. How dare He give her dreams about other children in trouble and nothing about Lizzie?

"You think this is your fault?" Bernie said again. "For five minutes you think that?" Her voice rose to a roar. "That is nonsense! That is *bullshit*!"

A short, squat whirlwind moving from room to room, she opened every window and turned on every light in the house before disappearing into the kitchen. Megan dropped her face into her hands.

"Now I say something, and you listen," Bernie declared loudly. "This is hard. This is *muy terrible* for you. But your daughter lives." Blazing brown eyes held Megan's like a vice. "I am never certain of anything, but I am certain of that. The little Lizzie lives."

The woman spun on her heel, disappeared again into the kitchen and returned holding gingerly between thumb and forefinger something that looked like a very fat cigar. A small stream of smoke curled up toward her face.

Bewildered, Megan watched as she resolutely crossed the room, first on one diagonal, then another, the cigar making a smoky X from corner to corner.

Ben began to pace. Bernie told him to sit down. He sat.

"Bad energy," Bernie muttered as she stalked back and forth across the room. "I can feel it. I do not think the person who took Lizzie was in this house, but I can feel the bad energy. This will send it away." She moved toward the bedrooms, trailing smoke from the stub in her hand.

"What is she doing?" Megan asked Ben, her voice a little steadier.

"Smudging. They make the sticks from plants: sage, cedar, sweetgrass, copal, lavender."

"Why?"

"Just what she said. It's supposed to remove negative energy where something bad has happened. I think it was the remains of some kind of smudge sticks that we found in Alma's cabin."

"A spell?" Megan asked. "Bernie is casting a spell?"

"Sort of."

"Aha!" Bernie's sharp exclamation came from the direction of the back door.

Megan and Ben found her outside, at the side door to the garage, staring at the charred stub in her hand. "It went out," she said in a low voice. "Here the bad energy is very strong. Get for me another match."

Megan found a box of wooden matches in a kitchen drawer. Bernie slid open the box, shook one out, and struck it. When the flame flared, she held it to the fat cigar-shaped wad of dried stems and leaves until it began to smoke again. Then she opened the door to the garage and Megan flipped on the light.

"Oh God, I forgot about Theodora. I'll have to give her some dandelions and fresh water or Lizzie will never forgive me." Bending over the little tortoise's box, she swept her hand through the grass clippings, first slowly, then again, quickly. Face troubled, she glanced at the others.

"It's gone."

Then she noticed something white under a corner of the box. When she picked it up, she moaned and put her hand on Ben's arm to keep herself steady.

He took the white card from her limp fingers and turned to Bernie. "Lizzie's report card."

Chapter Thirty-eight

Lizzie was sure her eyes were open, but she couldn't see. Was she blind? Or blindfolded? She touched her eyes. Her glasses were there. She squeezed her eyes tight shut and opened them again, slowly. Still nothing.

The ground under her was cold and clammy. Something next to her squirmed. She jumped. Was she dead and in hell? Mama said there was no hell. But what if Mama was wrong?

Whatever it was wriggled again.

Lizzie sat up. The air smelled of dirt. The squirming thing was inside her jacket. She unzipped the front and felt inside. Something like the sole of an old shoe brushed her hand.

"Thank you, thank you, thank you," she breathed aloud, and brought Theodora into her lap.

Lizzie remembered now. She was standing in the garage, trying to feed Theodora. She had just grasped the tortoise when a hand slammed across her face.

She tried to scream. When she couldn't, she tried to bite the hand that was blocking her mouth. The arm imprisoned her chin, making it impossible to turn her head to see who it was.

She had slipped Theodora inside her jacket to keep the baby tortoise away from that horrible hand. Something was jammed over her head and pulled down over her eyes, pinching her glasses into her nose, making her give a little yelp. It smelled of someone else's sweat. To her left, someone grunted, and she knew there was more than one of them.

A cloth had been stuffed into her mouth. She tasted dust, started to gag, and tried to spit it out. Big hands pulled her arms forward, and her wrists were tied with another rag. Her heart began to flutter like a bird beating its wings against a cage.

Someone lifted her, carried her to a car, where someone else—a woman, she thought—held her—gently, not roughly—on the floor in the backseat. A woman started to say something. A man shouted something she didn't understand. After that everyone was silent and the car drove off. Several minutes later the car stopped, and someone else got in.

After a long time the car came to a stop again. A man picked her up, slung her over his shoulder as if she were a Raggedy Ann doll, and carried her a long way over uneven ground, grunting a little with the effort.

Eventually Lizzie knew she was no longer outdoors. She didn't hear any doors opening or closing, but she could tell from the smell. The odor wasn't like an ordinary house, though, more like the basement of her grandmother's house in Pennsylvania.

The man had put her down on a hard, flat chair. Someone with hard, cool hands untied the rag around her wrists and bound them, this time behind her, with a narrow rope that felt like the clothesline her mother sometimes used. It cut into her wrists, even though she didn't struggle.

A woman yelled something Lizzie didn't understand. The man must have moved away, because gentler hands untied the rope and tied her hands together again, but this time with something soft, like a scarf.

"Okay," a man's voice said roughly. "Now where the hell . . . ?"

"No!" A woman's voice cut in sharply. "Go. Get out! Leave us!"

Lizzie, the hat or cap or whatever it was still pulled down over her eyes, had felt chilled to the bone. A chunk of ice rolled over in the pit of her tummy. She could see a little light through whatever was covering her eyes, but that was all. Drawing a ragged breath, she wondered what they wanted. What were they going to do to her? They treated her roughly, but so far they had not really hurt her. So far.

The voice next to her ear had been very soft: "Please. No one will be hurt if you tell me. Do you understand?"

"Tell you what?" Lizzie's words were weak and thin and flat, like day-old tea.

The woman's voice went on—low, coaxing, urging, wheedling, but always gentle.

Once Lizzie thought she heard an edge of fear in the voice.

In the end, she told it most of what it wanted to know.

*   *   *

Clothing rustled as the woman moved away. Where did she go?

"Hello?" Lizzie called softly. No one answered.

The cap was making her forehead itch, but she couldn't do anything about it. She could see only light and shadows through fabric that felt like a wool sweater. Choking back the tears that were right behind her eyes and in her throat, she told herself sternly that crying won't help.

Someone—the woman again?—placed a cold metal spoon in Lizzie's mouth. Without meaning to, she swallowed. It tasted like applesauce, but a bitter taste lingered on her tongue.

She wasn't hungry, but she was getting sleepy. She roused a little when a man came, took the awful cap from her head, and untied her hands. Lizzie thought he didn't mean to be rough, but he couldn't seem to help it. She kept her eyes closed. The whole place was so dark she still couldn't see anyway.

Did she sleep again? She wasn't sure. Why was she so tired? The next time she opened her eyes there was a light—a pale, yellowish light that faded before it reached her.

Now, sitting up, she stared through crooked, smudged eyeglasses. The light came from a lamp that looked like a candle under glass, except there was no candle. Next to the lamp, on the uneven floor, sat a plate of food. She patted the front of her jacket and jumped to her feet in panic. Theodora was gone.

She was reaching for the lantern when a short round shadow emerged from behind it. Lizzie scooped up the inverted bowl–like shell and hugged it to her chest. Instead of snapping head and legs into the shell, the little tortoise rubbed her head slowly against Lizzie's cheek.

Theodora was safe. Nothing else mattered.

The little girl tapped the top of the shell with her fingertips, then stopped, then tapped again. She could not hear the sound her fingers should have been making. In fact, she hadn't heard anything since she woke up.

She said, "Hi, Theodora," and her voice sounded far away, high and tinny. She moved her hand to her left ear, but she already knew the hearing aid was not there. She must have lost it when the man yanked the awful cap from her head. On hands and knees, still holding the tortoise close, she patted every inch of the floor of the windowless room that now made up her world.

The hearing aid was gone.

Rubbing her hand against her forehead, she tried to stop the sobs. She wouldn't even hear anyone when they came back to get her.

If they came back.

Lizzie bit her lip and sat down, wondering for the first time who brought the applesauce and the lantern. Why was she here?

Staring about her, she saw that the walls and floor were hard, like rock. Barely visible in the lantern light was an opening, a rough doorway, covered top to bottom with chicken wire. Three quarters of the way up the opening, a board formed the top of a makeshift gate. Just below the board was a padlock. The small space at the bottom wasn't big enough for even a thin little girl to slip under. Beyond the wire was darkness.

The dank chill of the floor slithered up her back. She let go of Theodora and took off her jacket, folded it, and sat down on it, crossing her legs under her. Without the jacket, her arms were cold.

Where was she? Where was her mom?

Something nudged at her toe. She jumped, but it was only Theodora. She put the little tortoise in her lap and rubbed her fingers along its legs. The animal stretched its neck and leaned its head against Lizzie's chest.

Holding her palms to her cheeks, she sniffed until her head cleared. No more tears. She cleaned her glasses with the tail of her shirt. Now she felt a little better, but her stomach was rumbling with hunger.

On the plate by the lamp were two cold burritos and a mound of applesauce. The spoon was old and didn't look very clean. None of it looked very appetizing. Suspiciously, Lizzie tore a burrito open, hoping she wouldn't find the center full of chocolate-covered chicken, but there were only a few chunks of greasy sausage inside.

Water, she saw, was in a tall plastic cup. Some of the applesauce had sloshed onto the burritos. *The applesauce is bad. No*, she reminded herself, *it's probably okay*. Bernie said not to pay any attention to that kind of thinking.

Kneeling, she drank the water down in one gulp. She didn't realize she was so thirsty. The burritos were dry on the outside, but the taste wasn't bad. She tore off a bit of tortilla and put it on the floor in front of Theodora. The tortoise cocked its head to stare at it, and backed away.

Lizzie downed both burritos, then, still hungry, tossed down the spoon and licked the apple sauce from the plate. Now she was almost okay. If they left food for her, maybe they didn't plan to kill her.

She got up and went to take another look at the gate. Without warning, a bluish light erupted behind it, and the gate itself began to sway. The blue faded to gray, then to white, then exploded in orange.

And something black and shapeless was moving toward her.

Chapter Thirty-nine

Ben's movements were smooth and efficient, as if he had cooked on this stove a hundred times. Megan sat on a chair in the corner of her own kitchen watching him. She wasn't hungry. She wasn't anything. She couldn't even smell the chicken and onions sizzling in the pan.

He turned a piece of chicken with a fork and looked over his shoulder at her. "I forgot to tell you. I guess I was just so shocked at what happened. Anyway, I got the arrowheads back. What do you want me to do with them?"

Her shrug was almost imperceptible. "Throw them away. Keep them. I don't care. I want my . . ." She paused, as if she couldn't say the word. "My daughter." The words came out in a thin, shapeless wail.

He put down the fork, lifted her from the stool, and held her. "I know," he said, clasping her upper arms and giving her a little shake. "We'll find her. We will." He turned back to the frying pan before she could see the look of frustrated fury on his face.

Megan stared at his back. "Maybe we could use the arrowheads for ransom."

Fork halfway to the frying pan, Ben turned. "We don't know if there will be a demand for ransom. But if there is, yes, there should be some way to turn the arrowheads into cash. Not as much as they're worth, but probably more than any kidnapper would think you could raise."

"Unless the kidnapper knows about the arrowheads. He probably does, you know."

Ben glanced at her. "Whatever the reason Lizzie was taken, it's now beside the point. What does matter," he went on calmly, "is what we do about it."

Struggling for control, she said quietly, "Like what?"

"Like what if we put up notices with Lizzie's picture and ask people to call if they've seen her? What if we offer a huge reward for her return?"

"That would virtually invite the kidnapper to ask for ransom."

Ben nodded. "Maybe. That might be the whole point. To get them to make contact. I don't know what the cops would think of that."

"I don't give a damn what the cops think. She's my daughter. I want her back!"

When they sat down to eat, Megan cut the food, put it in her mouth, chewed, and swallowed, but it might as well have been sawdust.

Afterward, Ben washed up the dishes while she printed out copies of a picture she had taken of Lizzie. Below the picture she wrote, "Have you seen this girl? Very large reward for information leading to her location," along with her own and Ben's phone numbers.

Ben finished the dishes, put on his jacket, and drew a plastic envelope that held the emerald arrowheads from its pocket.

Megan stared. "You have them here? They're our only bargaining chips."

"Sorry. I'm not thinking clearly. I shouldn't be walking around with them."

She went to the refrigerator. "Whenever I've got extra money I stash it in the vegetable drawer. Lizzie calls it our cool cash stash. . . . Good heavens!"

"What is it?"

She stepped back to let him see. The drawer was jam-packed with leaves. "Dandelions. For that damn tortoise. If I put the arrowheads in there I'll never find them again."

Ben reached for the trash basket. "Dump the dandelions. Just keep enough for cover."

"No," she said sharply. "Lizzie put them there. That is where they'll stay until she's home."

As she started to close the refrigerator door, the head of Bibb lettuce she bought that afternoon fell from a shelf. She picked it up and inspected it. "Well, why not." She held out her hand for the arrowheads and tucked them here and there among the leaves and put it back in the refrigerator.

A mournful look passed over her face. "How am I going to tell Lizzie that Theodora is gone?"

*   *   *

Using a flashlight, sometimes on foot, sometimes in Ben's pickup, they put the notices on the bulletin boards of the town's two supermarkets, on the front doors of four convenience stores, and on prominent telephone poles from Main Street to the edges of town. Now that she was doing something useful, an achy scratchiness in her eyes replaced the tears. It was nearly midnight when they finished.

The carriage light flashed on when Ben pulled into the driveway. He cut the engine. "You want me to stay?"

"No." Megan stared with unfocused eyes at the dashboard. "I have to get used to it." Her body feeling like it belonged to someone else, she got out of the pickup.

Ben said, "If you can't sleep, call. Promise?"

"Okay." She closed the truck door, crossed the grass, and mounted the front steps.

He rolled down the window and called after her, "In any case, phone when you get up tomorrow. It's Easter week. I'm not very busy."

She nodded.

He waited until she opened the door before driving off.

At first, she didn't realize what was wrong.

Inside the house a vague feeling that something was not right set off an alarm. Maybe it was just all the stress. And knowing Lizzie wasn't there. Struggling to control a rising panic, Megan turned on the light.

The scent of onions still hung in the air, and for the first time all day she was hungry. She was in the kitchen before her mind registered that the house had been completely dark. She always left the small fluorescent light above the kitchen sink burning in the evening. Maybe it burned out. But the bulb flashed on when she pressed the switch.

All thoughts of food vanished. The door of the refrigerator was open and the floor was littered with dandelion leaves; the vegetable drawer itself was upside down on the heap.

Even in her slow-witted state, she knew that someone was after the arrowheads. And in the back of her mind, something more important dawned as well.

Body leaden, she crossed the kitchen and bent down to look for the lettuce. The plastic produce bag was still on the shelf. Megan took out the head of lettuce and slipped her hand into the leaves.

The arrowheads were still there.

*　　*　　*

The following day was dismal, much worse than the day before, when the sheriff's deputies, Bernie, Ben, and the posting of notices filled the time.

Now there was nothing, except fear.

When Megan, unable to sleep, finally stopped twisting and turning and got out of bed, she didn't bother to get dressed. Instead she wandered through the house in white pajamas, closing, reopening, then reclosing drapes and curtains. She unlocked the doors and windows. When Ben called, worried because he hadn't heard from her, she said she didn't want company.

She didn't tell him about the refrigerator.

Whoever dumped that vegetable drawer knew where her daughter was. Megan wanted them to come back.

For hours she drank cup after stale cup of coffee, staring numbly across the room, mind racing, seeing nothing,

Whoever took her daughter had come for the arrowheads. That much was clear. Only Lizzie knew her mother kept small valuables like money and credit cards in the refrigerator drawer. No windows were broken, no sign of a door being forced. But the back door was left unlocked. They entered the house with Lizzie's key.

Megan clung to the belief that this meant Lizzie was alive.

But what did they do to her to make her tell about the vegetable bin?

Would they harm her because the arrowheads weren't there? Would they think she lied? Would they punish her, even torture her?

Mechanically, Megan sifted through every stray idea in her head, trying to find something, anything, that might help her find her daughter.

The paperboy disappeared. Megan's home and others on the same street were burglarized. Wrapped in her newspaper she had found five emerald arrowheads. She hid them in the garage in a garden hose. The garage was ransacked. The thieves didn't find the arrowheads, but only because Ben had them.

Suddenly curious, she checked the garage. The hose, which she had rewound neatly on its caddy, was now strung out like a giant snake amid a hodgepodge of miscellaneous items on the concrete floor. Nearly the full length of it had been slashed down the side.

But Lizzie didn't know about the hose.

There were too many things Megan didn't understand. She went back to the house without bothering to clean up what was left of the garden hose.

What about the man at the cave in the mountains? Was he shooting at her? Or was all that just coincidence? Why were all those people at the cave the day she and Lizzie were picnicking?

She didn't know for sure if the man she saw in the cavern was the same as the one who fired the shots. Maybe it was just a hunter shooting at a deer. And maybe people held their community meetings in a cave because it was cool and conveniently located.

There were more important factors. Worse things. Alma disappeared, and then her cabin burned down. Lizzie was abducted. And whoever took her came back for the emeralds.

The wind rose, whipping around the house as if searching for an entrance. Megan had brought her daughter to this godforsaken place. She allowed those arrowheads to cast their tantalizing spell, had kept them instead of turning them over to the authorities.

No matter how she turned and twisted the events, there was no escaping her own verdict. Whatever happened to Lizzie was her fault.

When the late afternoon light began to fade, Megan went into the bedroom and got dressed.

The lights were on in the house across the street. She called and asked Mr. Gonzalez if he and his wife would keep an eye on her house, just in case a miracle happened and Lizzie came home.

She wasn't sure what she was going to do, but she had to do something.

Chapter Forty

In the gathering dusk, the charred remains of Alma's cabin looked like the ruins of some ancient culture.

Megan got out of her car, leaned against a fender, and took in the painful scene. The chimney still stood, a lonely silhouette against the dimming sky, its upper parts eaten away by the fire.

A feeling of helplessness was sapping her energy. Now that she was here, she wasn't sure why she had come. Nothing had changed. Apparently there were no other visitors. The sight that would greet Alma if she did somehow return was a grim one. And Alma wouldn't even know how to contact her or what happened to the paintings. The cabin had no phone, but maybe she should leave a note—just in case.

The sun was sinking fast. By the time she found some paper and a piece of twine in the trunk of the Honda, it was almost dark. She got out her flashlight and tied the paper to what was left of the chimney, wondering sadly what became of the roadrunner, the goats and sheep.

The shed she and Alma had coated with mud wasn't damaged, but its warped and ill-fitting door gaped open by at least a foot. The hinges rasped and groaned when she swung the door back. A scuffle of movement came from the dark interior. The narrow beam of her flashlight caught the puzzled gaze of a sheep standing next to an overturned wheelbarrow. A brown goat clambered to its feet and lowered its head questioningly.

Megan's fingers flew to her mouth, but she made no sound. The shed's single room looked like some titan had picked it up and shaken it. Shovels, rakes, trowels lay every which way amid rolls of wire. A hen pecked nervously at a sack of feed that was spewing its contents through a jagged slash in its side.

She saw the shed's interior the day they spread Alma's muddy concoction on its outside walls and again on the day she first realized Alma was missing. Both times it was amazingly tidy. Could the animals have strewn things about? She found two more bags of feed. Big slashes in their sides looked like they were made with an ax. At least the critters, as Alma called them, were back, and they wouldn't be hungry for a while.

The door moaned as she backed out into the night. The moon was washing the landscape with a bluish glow. From beyond the shed came a mournful cooing. Megan moved the flashlight in that direction. Something rose against the darkening sky—a large bird. It landed on a rock, lifted its head, and cooed again.

"Rodolfo?" Megan moved slowly toward him. The roadrunner sat perfectly still, watching her approach. As she neared him he leaped to a post where a pile of stones spilled over a large oval mound. The bird flapped his wings but stood his ground. She realized he was perched on a slightly tilted, uneven cross.

The stones sank a little beneath Megan's weight as she tried to get a better look at the cross. It was made of rough pieces of wood cinched together with wire. Pushing two of the rocks aside, she found clods of recently turned earth. It resembled the grave in the little churchyard where she had taken pictures of a funeral. Was this one of Alma's beloved critters?

At the base of the cross was a sprig of flowers. She touched the petals. Plastic. She smiled sadly at the practicality of those who live in the desert. Then she saw what was holding the flowers and her breath stopped.

Moonlight was outlining the brim of a hat. Alma's hat.

Alma might have buried one of the goats here. She might have put a sprig of plastic flowers on its grave. But she would not have parted with that hat.

*   *   *

Later, she had no idea why she didn't turn back. She was too numb, too tired to think straight.

Strange as it seemed, the likelihood was inescapable. Someone had killed Alma and, for some peculiar reason, buried her there with a crude cross to mark her grave and plastic flowers in her straw hat to decorate it.

Megan crouched, staring at the scene until the muscles in her legs began to ache. She was easing her cramped body upright when something flashed far off to her right, across the mesa. The tangle of trees and brush stretched all the way to the slightly paler horizon. Another light flared and disappeared like a distant firefly.

She stared at the place where the light had been until her eyes were dry and she had to blink. Letting her breath out in a slow sigh, she made her way back to the car. She must have imagined the light.

She went back to her car. The thought of those empty rooms in her home made it almost impossible to start the engine. She squeezed her eyes closed trying to stop her thoughts. Just as her eyes blinked open, another light flared. Several seconds elapsed as it moved slowly east. Then it vanished.

She got out of the car.

*   *   *

She wasn't sure how much time had passed by the time she could hear the voices muttering in Spanish, the sound of feet crushing the brush.

There were at least twenty people. From time to time, someone turned on a flashight. They slowed to cross the sandy bottom of an arroyo—one of the many ditches cut by rainwater cascading from the mountains. Illegals who had sneaked across the border? They probably were heading north hoping to find a place where they might safely look for work. *How sad*, Megan thought, *that they must brave arrest in order to find jobs.*

The migrants avoided the highway, skirted the town, and now, to her puzzlement, they seemed to be heading into the mountains. Surely there were no jobs in the mountains. Perhaps they would just spend the night with some sympathetic Hispanic family and move on.

The night was like the flat side of a cool knife against her cheek. Her mind still shying from the thought of going home to sit and think, she, too, went on.

Following what she thought must be a cattle path, the trekkers wound their way through the foothills. Megan stayed at least a quarter mile behind, her climb becoming a little more difficult as she edged through piñon, juniper, and bushy chamisa covered with last year's now dry flowers. On the ridge above her, the people looked like shadows moving single file.

Suspending all thought, she plodded on under a net of cold white stars that in the black desert sky seemed to breathe like a single huge organism.

In the bright moonlight a splotch of blood from a hand scratched by prickly pear looked like an ink blot on her shirt. Despite the boots Ben had recommended, her feet hurt. Her back began to ache, and she longed to lie down. Her only coherent thought was that at the very least she would wear herself out and be able to sleep.

An arroyo snaked its way around from the north, separating Megan from the people, whose path apparently ran along the high rim. She scrambled down the side and walked along the bottom. Here, where racing water had scoured away some of the brush, and the sun had dried the earth to a crust, the way was easier. Running a little to wake herself up, she found she could keep up with the men who were still about a quarter mile ahead.

What would it be like to sneak into a foreign country, knowing that every step you took could bring you closer to jail, or even to death at the hands of a trigger-happy rancher?

She plodded along the bottom of the canyon for some distance before glancing up again. This time, no shadows moved along the ridge. Straining her senses, Megan searched for some sign of them. Only the sound of a car on some distant road broke the quiet. She had lost them.

Wearily, she sat and hugged her knees to her chest. What was she thinking of to have followed them this far? She would rest a little and then go back to her car.

Chapter Forty-one

Wool rasped against Lizzie's cheek. It smelled like old clothes. She would tell Mom it needed washing. Her eyeglasses went lopsided on her face as she rolled over, and the bitter hand of reality closed around her chest. She was someplace awful. But where?

She plucked at the raspy woolen thing. While she slept someone had brought a blanket and covered her. The lantern in the corner had gone out, but a dim yellow glow from somewhere beyond the gate to her cell-like space saved her from the earlier total darkness.

Pulling the blanket up around her, she saw that the edges were torn. Lizzie closed her eyes. Maybe this was just a bad dream. Maybe when she opened her eyes again she would be home in her own bed, and there would be the smell of bacon frying. And she would get up and complain about having to do homework.

Her eyes went wide and a scream rose to her throat. She bit it off, staring instead toward the yellow glow beyond the gate, remembering.

Something horrible had come at her from that tunnel. Something black and wavy, like what happens to your reflection when you toss a stone into a puddle. But she couldn't remember what happened after that, whether it touched her or just went away.

A slight aroma of food was coming from somewhere. She raised her head and looked toward the lantern. Another plate had been left. Burritos again. And more applesauce. Theodora was standing next to it, watching her.

Afraid to take her eyes off the passageway, she thought about the food. *Something was wrong with it.* The thought was like a voice inside her head. Bernie said to ignore such thoughts, but Bernie was wrong. Lizzie was sure the applesauce had made her sick.

But she was awful hungry.

She gobbled down the burritos. Leaving the applesauce, she got up and examined the gate, moving her fingers idly along the wires that formed squares about four inches wide. Boards—no, two were only sticks, really—ran along the top, bottom, and sides of the gate.

She tried to pull apart two of the wires by moving them back and forth. The fencing was old, and there were traces of rust, but neither wire broke. She sat down and tried two more, then two more. Finally, at the very bottom, one of the wires split away from its partner. She worked earnestly at the next pair.

Her fingers began to hurt where the wires cut into them. At last, another snapped. She moved her hands up to the next pair and let out a little squeak of surprise. One was already broken, the end poking out toward her. If she could break maybe three or four more, she could bend the fencing back and try to fit through.

Lizzie leaned forward, wrestling with the wires in excitement. As the last one broke, her hands froze in midair. What if someone came down the tunnel just as she was slithering between the wires? She had no idea what time it was or whether someone was just around the bend in the tunnel.

Without her hearing aid, she couldn't even hear anything. She was trying to puzzle out what to do when Theodora crept across her thigh. She started, then gave a weak smile. "Yes," she whispered to the tortoise, "we have to try to look around, see if there's a way out." Otherwise . . . But she didn't want to think about otherwise.

She gently patted the little tortoise's shell. The animal lifted its head and watched her. It was too risky to take Theodora. She promised to come back, and under the tortoise's lidless gaze, she wriggled through the wire.

Slowly at first, then faster, she threaded her way down the tunnel toward the light.

At the place where the passage narrowed and jutted to the right, Lizzie flattened herself to the wall and peered cautiously around the corner. The tunnel was empty, but a ragged archway loomed ahead. The light was coming from beyond that.

She slid along the rough tunnel wall. The glow came from what looked like a huge, round room. Making herself as small as possible, she slipped through the archway.

A sea of empty folding chairs and camp stools flowed toward a box-like stage made of what looked like old boards. On the stage, a man and a woman were gesturing wildly at each other.

Lizzie hugged the ground and inched along the base of the wall toward a big sheet of plywood that leaned against it a few yards away. The triangle of space between the board and the wall was barely big enough to hide her. Praying the plywood wouldn't fall and give her away, she slipped inside. The shelter stood firm. She had to lie prone, and it took awhile to get even halfway comfortable.

A desire to suck her thumb almost overcame her, but she didn't do it. This was no time to be a baby.

She edged her head out from behind the sheltering board just far enough to see the stage. She must have made some noise, because the man and woman had stopped shaking their fists at each other and were staring in her direction. Quickly drawing her head back, she almost giggled, thinking it was just like what Theodora would do. She strained to hear something, but the blurry sounds didn't tell her much.

Lizzie held every muscle still, waiting for someone to yank the board away and seize her.

But no one did.

She peered out again. The eyes of the pair were trained again on each other, as they moved stiffly in a sort of semicircle, making sharp, angry motions. Lizzie could hear a faint, staccato babbling she knew must be their voices.

The man and woman were about the same height. The woman's hair was long. As she shook her head defiantly, it seemed to stand out about her face like a lion's mane. Skirt swinging about her long legs, she lunged toward the man's chest and grabbed his shirt.

He took a step backward and swung. The flat of his hand caught the woman on the side of the head, and she fell. Even Lizzie could hear the high-pitched shriek that followed.

The child ducked her head back into the plywood shelter. Should she try to run? Maybe the man and woman were so busy fighting they wouldn't notice her.

No. That was too risky. She would wait until they were gone.

Her body ached everywhere. There was no room to straighten her legs. Her knee rubbed against the board. Forcing herself to count the squiggly lines on the plywood, she settled down to wait.

*   *   *

At first Lizzie felt the sound more than heard it: a deep, rhythmic pounding that seemed to smash like a fist at the center of her body just beneath her rib cage.

She closed her eyes, trying to understand where she was. A man and a woman were fighting. After that, she must have gone to sleep.

The rhythmic pounding grew, then abruptly stopped.

She leaned her head against the board and peered out.

Four large lanterns stood along the wall. One was quite close, and she could smell something like gasoline. She glanced to the right and jerked her head back inside her shelter.

The huge room was filled with people who were facing away from her, heads bobbing slightly, attention riveted on the woman who stood on the platform.

Lizzie realized her own head was moving with the rhythm. A drum?

Another noise rose, a sort of dim roar—without her hearing aid, it was hard to tell what it was. Voices? Yes, probably voices. Were they singing? No, it was more like calling, all together, like one huge voice.

Craning her neck, Lizzie could see riotous black hair and a short but flowing dress of blue. On the feet that moved resolutely along the platform were sandals made of rope. The woman lifted one arm and the heads of the crowd followed her hand. Lantern light painted the edge of her outstretched arm with gold. When she dropped the arm to her side, the crowd made a humming sound. Lizzie could barely hear it, but she could feel the vibration.

She couldn't understand the woman's words, but she could hear enough of the voice to be pretty sure she had heard it before. This was the woman who was fighting with the man. The hair was not quite as wild, and the dress was different, but it was the same woman.

Lizzie was now fairly sure of two things. First, this was the woman who asked her questions after the man had grabbed Lizzie from the garage and brought her to this place. Second, a deep, basic goodness was emanating from that platform. Lizzie was sure of it, but she wasn't sure *how* she knew it.

A long, graceful arm stretched again above the crowd to point at something, and Lizzie stretched her neck to see what it was.

With no warning, the board that protected her suddenly tilted away from the wall.

A hand clamped itself across her nose and mouth, cutting off her breathing.

The hand swung her around and she saw a man, his dark eyes not so much angry as determined—and sad—a little like her mother looked when she announced some punishment for Lizzie's own good.

The fingers pinched her nose and her mouth gaped open for air.

A cup was held to her mouth and something cold and mushy was poured into her throat.

Lizzie gagged and coughed.

Applesauce. And it was bitter. She tried to spit it out, and it ran down her chin. The hand pushed her head back. She choked. And swallowed.

The man's face was very near hers. It looked anguished, like the pictures of saints in the Gonzalezes' house.

Then the face stretched, grew larger, and became a dog with huge teeth and a very red tongue.

Chapter Forty-two

Megan watched the black sky become purple, then blue shot through with streaks of white. A wave of panic washed over her, unbearable at first, as she remembered that Lizzie was missing, kidnapped, or worse. Slowly the horror all tapered off into numbness.

Body so cold and stiff it could barely obey the directive to move, she rolled to her side, groaning softly. She must have been out of her mind. How many miles had she walked? Even with an hour or two's nap, she knew she couldn't walk much farther without falling over in her tracks. She would have to call Ben, tell him about the grave that was surely Alma's, and he would come to get her.

Chilled to the bone and limping, she managed to put one foot after the other in the arroyo she had trekked through the night before. How far would she have to go to find a phone?

Half a mile on one side of the arroyo began shrinking, and she found a place to climb out. An hour later she stepped out of the brush onto a narrow dirt road. Wondering which way to turn, she was trying to make up her mind when she heard the music. Encouraged, she turned toward it. Where there was music, there must be a phone.

The sound was thin, reedy, and distant. She kept going as the dirt road narrowed, then became a well-trod path through the trees. Clearer now, the music became a slow, plaintive rhythm. Ahead, the path led to some sort of clearing. When she reached it, she saw the space was not clear at all but filled with people—old women in black, men in mirror-shiny shoes and pants with knife-sharp creases, children in stiff, dark clothing, all with their backs to her.

Some instinct prickling along the back of her neck told her a stranger might not be welcome here. She ducked back into the brush.

Cottonwood trees lined one side of the roughly circular open space. The crowd's attention was focused on three huge boulders on the other side. The music stopped. A tension spread through the crowd, revealing itself in stiffened shoulders and heads tilted toward the ground.

Shuffling and throat clearing died away to absolute silence. Something began to rise above the heads of the throng—a heavy, weathered, timber cross.

On the cross was a man in a brown loincloth, smears of red at his hands and feet.

What little color there was in Megan's face drained away as she gaped. Slowly, her muscles began to respond to her brain's demands, and she backed away, barely breathing for fear of drawing attention. She tripped on the knobby root of a cottonwood, but the people were so intent on the spectacle, no head turned in her direction. Scrambling to put the cottonwood's thick trunk between herself and the crowd, Megan turned and ran, not knowing where she was heading, wanting only to get away.

Lungs and legs aching, she slowed but staggered on.

Nothing she saw registered on her dazed mind until she realized she was approaching crumbling walls like those of an old fort and a shallow ditch carrying a tiny stream along the wall and under a small wooden bridge between two huge cottonwoods.

The worn wooden gate was swung back against the wall. In the court-yard, the church seemed to kneel, tombstones drawn about it like a ragged peasant skirt. Modest bell towers rose on either side of the doors. A ladder of weathered gray slats of wood, tied together with rope, leaned against one of the towers, for access or escape.

The sun was not much above the horizon. If the church was open, there would be a phone. She remembered wanting to see it from the inside, but this was hardly the way she had in mind. For one fleeting second she wished she had her camera.

Crossing the tiny bridge, she followed the flagstones past a grave mounded with plastic flowers to the heavy wooden doors. They gave inward, and she stepped inside. The floor and ceiling of the church, as well as its benches and simple square pillars, were wood dark with age and a black-brown stain. The walls were brilliant white.

A single clear window above the door directed a pale shaft of light past the altar to a carved wood panel where some of the paint had flaked from once brightly colored images. A dark wooden door in the wall to the left of the altar indicated there must be another room. A candle burned in a glass in front of a doll-like Madonna.

Drawn by the eyes of the statue, Megan moved down the aisle. She couldn't remember the last time she was inside a Catholic church, but she looked up into the candlelit face.

Please, help me.

She was still gazing at the painted eyes when the door next to the altar opened.

The priest wore the traditional black shirt and white collar, but his pants were made by Levi Strauss. His face was young. The cheeks and round chin in need of a shave made him look like he had been up all night. He halted, and for a moment they stared at each other.

Relief made Megan almost giddy. "Father! Thank God. I need to borrow your phone."

He led her through a long room filled with icons. Crutches, braces, and other devices were fixed to the walls—apparently relics of invalids now cured. At the base of the wall, beneath a small square of clear glass, a recessed light focused on sand dug from under the floor. They filed past framed letters from people who apparently were healed by the saint, past old photographs and hand-lettered pleas for donations, and down a dim hall to a small study as barren of decoration as the preceding room was cluttered.

The priest guided her to a chair and sat down behind the simple desk of dark-stained pine. "You are troubled. What is it? What can I do to help?" His voice was strong but gentle, like a parent coaxing a child to spit out whatever had poisoned her.

Megan opened her mouth to ask again if she could use the phone, but other words began to tumble over her tongue. She told him about Lizzie, and tears flooded down her cheeks.

He sat quietly, saying nothing.

Tasting salty tears but not bothering to wipe them away, she told him about finding the arrowheads, about the grave near Alma's cabin, and, finally, brows knit together in a straight, horrified line, about the awful crucifixion scene she had stumbled upon nearby.

When she finally ran dry of words, the priest handed her some tissues from his desk drawer. Looking directly into her eyes with a comforting, sympathetic smile, he said, "I am so sorry about your daughter. I'm sure she will return to you very soon. And it is unfortunate, especially in these terrible circumstances, you became so frightened about . . ." He gestured toward the ceiling. "We have only a simple Easter ritual here. What you saw was not a real crucifixion. How could you think such a thing?"

Megan stopped wiping her face. "But I saw the blood. Dripping from his hands and feet."

"Not real blood," the priest said gently. "Paint. It is only a Passion play. The man was tied, not nailed, to the cross. Believe me, it is not a torture. It's a great privilege. After an hour he will be cut free to lead a procession here for Mass." He stared for a moment at some spot over her head, then added, "I was just going to prepare some tea before I saw you. Will you join me?"

Megan nodded, the phone call she had come here to make forgotten for the moment as she tried to stuff back into her subconscious all the awful things she had blurted.

The priest was gone for what seemed a long while, and she began to fidget, thinking she should not be wasting time with tea; she should have asked for a phone. There was no telephone on the desk, and she wondered if the church had one at all.

When he returned with a dented copper teapot and two cups, she tried to smile. "I guess I was overwrought and jumped to a silly conclusion about the crucifixion."

"It is understandable." He poured a clear greenish tea and handed the cup to her. "Especially with your mind so troubled about your little girl. Strangers are not familiar with our ways."

She set the cup on the desk. "Before I have tea, I must use your phone."

"It is better you drink the tea first," he said gently, "and calm yourself."

Of course he was right. A little more time might take the edge from her voice. She didn't want to worry Ben any more than necessary. She took a sip from the cup. The liquid was hot, its original taste masked by a good deal of sugar.

"I've been so upset since my daughter . . ." Megan's voice broke, and she took another swallow of tea. It burned all the way down, leaving a trail of bitterness.

She sat on the edge of her chair holding her cup. "My daughter has been taken somewhere," she said, her voice oddly calm. Then she realized she had already told him that. The priest's eyes were soothing, compassionate.

Then his cheek began to swell until the bulge became another, very different face.

A chill spread from the top of Megan's head and congealed deep in her gut. She opened her mouth to scream, but no sound came out.

Chapter Forty-three

The outside world was as dark as it was behind Megan's eyelids. She could see nothing. Nothing at all. She blinked her eyes to make sure they were open.

She lay on her side, cheek on her arm, the ground beneath her cold and hard as stone. The air felt thick and smelled of dust. As she tried to twist herself onto her back, a groan escaped her lips, and the sound of her own voice startled her. Every bone in her body ached. Had she been beaten? She couldn't remember.

She recalled trying to find a phone, and coming by chance on a crowd of people who were crucifying a man. They put him on a cross, and he was bleeding. But the priest said it was just a harmless Easter ritual.

The priest.

He gave her tea. Was there more than tea leaves and hot water in that cup? *Did he poison me? That's not possible. Priests don't poison people.*

But nothing else was possible, either. Where was she? Why was she here? How did she get here?

Megan ran her hands over the gritty, uneven ground around her. She leaned on her hands and tried to stand. A spot of pain detonated eight inches or so below her shoulder. She fell back, breathing as heavily as if she had just run a race.

Then she remembered Lizzie. . . . The realization that she didn't know where her daughter was thrust its way into Megan's mind, pushing everything else out.

In the blackness, something touched her shoulder.

Startled, she bit back the hysteria that rose in her throat.

"Are you okay?"

She froze, heart thumping. The voice sounded young and worried, and it cracked halfway through the last word. An adolescent boy?

"Who are you?" she croaked, hardly recognizing her own voice. Her mouth felt like it was full of Styrofoam and so dry it almost hurt to speak.

"John," came the voice. "John Runyon."

She tried to sound normal, but the words came out thin and shrill. "Where are we?"

"I don't know. I've been here a long time. Bobby's only been here a couple days."

"Bobby?"

"I call him that. I don't know his real name. He's pretty little."

"Why is he here?"

"I don't know. Maybe he belongs to someone here. But no one comes to see him. I don't know if he has a mother. I can't understand much of what they say, but it sounded like he kept wandering off, so they decided I should babysit him. I tried asking him stuff, but he doesn't talk. He's old enough, maybe four or five, I guess, but he never says a word."

"Where is he?"

"Over there in the corner, asleep. Sometimes they light a lantern and you can see."

"Who are they?"

"I don't know," John said. "Different people bring food. Mostly men, one time a woman. Usually they bring it while we're asleep, or they shine a light in your eyes so you can't see their faces. But you can tell by the hands. And they take away the bucket." He made a small disgusted sound. "At least they're decent about that."

"The bucket?"

"Their version of a port-o-potty. It's got bleach or something in it and a board to cover it, so it doesn't stink too bad."

Megan squeezed her eyes tight shut, as if seeking light somewhere inside her head. "Do they beat you? Hurt you in any way?"

"No," he said. "They're not mean."

She hugged herself and rubbed her arms, feeling better. Her companions might be children, but at least she was not alone. "Why are we here? I'm sorry," she interrupted herself. "I'm Megan Montoya."

"I was afraid of that." The boy's voice was almost inaudible.

She peered toward him, though she couldn't see anything in the impenetrable blackness. "What do you mean?"

"Well," the boy paused, and Megan could hear him swallowing. "I don't know about Bobby, but I guess I know why you and I are here."

"Why?"

"Because of the arrowheads."

The realization came like a brisk wind whisking the fog from her brain. "You're the paperboy? This is where you've been since . . . ?"

"Since I got captured. Yeah. . . . I knew they were following me. I was afraid they were going to grab me and beat me up and take the arrowheads. And once they had them, I figured there wouldn't be any reason to keep me around. So I rolled them into your newspaper." John stopped, then added, "I'm sorry. I swear I didn't tell anyone about you. I told them I put the arrowheads back where I dug them up. I even told them how to get to that big old tree. A couple days later, they said there was nothing under that tree. I said someone else must've found them. I didn't know they would figure it out. I didn't think they would hurt you."

"The arrowheads are yours?"

"I guess so," he said. "I found them."

"Where?"

"There was this goat out on the west mesa. I was riding my bike one Saturday, and I saw this goat, so I chased it. I don't know why. Not to hurt it. Just for the heck of it, I guess. The goat disappeared, and I was kind of lost, like, I wasn't really sure which way was the road. I stopped under a tree to take a good look at everything, find some landmark. After I sat there awhile, I saw this place between the roots of the tree that was sort of dug out. The dirt was lower than between the other roots. So I found a stick and I dug. And there they were, all wrapped up in yellow oilcloth."

In the darkness Megan could hear John dejectedly blowing air between his lips. The sound was sad and weary. "But how did anyone find out? Did the package you found belong to the people who brought us here?"

"I don't know. I don't think so. I showed the arrowheads to a guy at school. José Quiñones. He borrowed them to show his brother, who's studying mineralogy down in Socorro at the Mining Institute. I don't see how José could be mixed up in this, though. He gave them back right away and said he thought they might be worth a lot of money."

"How did you know they were arrowheads?"

"That's easy. You can find tons of them around here, once you learn how to spot them. I've got a couple dozen really nice ones."

"Did you know that the ones you put in my paper are made of emerald?"

"Emerald?" John's startled voice cracked on the word. "Geez! I thought José meant they might be worth a couple hundred bucks, max. Like for a history museum or something."

"Where did you say that tree was?"

"On the west mesa."

"I mean, how far from town?"

"I don't know. Five, six miles. Not more than ten. I don't ride farther than that."

"But you could direct these people who kidnapped you to the tree?"

"Oh, sure. There's a cabin near it."

Megan could hear the boy shifting his position.

"What did they do to you?" he asked, and his voice cracked again.

"I don't know who did what," she said. "Burglary. My little girl disappeared. Then a priest. I was talking to a priest. It sounds crazy, but I think he poisoned me."

A soft snore came from behind them. "That's Bobby," John said. "He doesn't talk, but he sure does snore."

Suddenly, a dim light spread over them, spattering mottled shadows on the walls.

Now Megan could see John a half-dozen feet away, his body all sharp angles. Legs that seemed much too long were drawn up, the knees under his chin. She had forgotten he was black. Behind him a shapeless wad lay in a corner like a pile of discarded clothes.

From somewhere came a dim rasp of footsteps.

John gave a whispered shout, "They're coming!" He dove to the floor. "Lie down. Pretend you're asleep."

Megan did as he said, then lifted her head and looked toward him. "Why?"

"It's just easier."

The light was coming from what seemed to be a hallway. She could see a crude, uneven gate made of chicken wire blocking the opening to the tunnel-like corridor. Ponderous footsteps plodded toward them.

Megan twisted her fingers in her hair until it hurt. It was almost impossible to turn her face away from the hall. Every instinct demanded she see her captor. A tiny shudder ran along her spine, but she turned her head.

The footsteps stopped, and someone fumbled with a lock. The gate grated against the floor, and there was the sound of something soft and bulky being laid on the ground. Then the lock clicked, and the footsteps moved away more quickly than they had come. With them went the light, which faded until the room was in absolute blackness again.

When all sound had trailed away, Megan lifted her head. "What did they leave?" She cleared her throat. "John?"

"I don't know." His voice sounded like the breaking of a hollow stick.

"Are you frightened?" she asked.

There was a long pause, then a whispered "Yeah."

"So am I. But I guess we should see what it is."

She crawled toward where she thought the bundle had been placed. Her hand bumped against cold, hard rock. She ran her fingers over it. "I can't find it. I'm at the wall."

"When it's dark like this, it's hard to know where you are."

John's voice helped to orient her. She crept a little to the left, toward where she thought the gate should be. The floor was rough and seemed to slant downward. "Nothing yet. You still with me? Say something. It helps."

"Okay." His voice shook a little.

Megan's palm came down on something soft. Pure reflex snatched her hand back. "I found it." She pulled herself into a crouch, one foot flat on the ground so she could get up quickly, although there was nowhere to run. Hesitantly, her hand reached out again. This time it encountered something flat, something that felt like rubber, like the tread of a tire. But it was small and rounded at the ends.

"A shoe? No! Dear God! It's a person!" The ankle above the shoe was very narrow. "A child."

Her probing fingers elicited no response. For a horrified moment she thought the child might be dead, but the thin leg was warm. Gently she moved her fingers along the body. A sigh escaped from lips Megan couldn't see.

"Are you okay?" John whispered behind her.

She nodded, then realized he couldn't see her. "Yes."

The child's shoulder was thin and bony. Across it lay a thick rope. No, not a rope, a braid. Megan's heart fluttered toward her throat. Her blood deserted her brain, leaving her light-headed as an impossible thought careened through her mind.

"Oh my God," she said softly, touching the cheek she knew so well. She ran her thumb across the narrow chin and cupped the face.

"Lizzie?"

Chapter Forty-four

M ama?" Lizzie's voice was thick and sluggish.

Megan pulled her daughter to her and rocked her back and forth for a long time. Wherever they were, for whatever reason, she felt like a whole person again.

"How did you get here, Mama? Did the men bring you?"

"Sssh, sweetheart." Megan went on rocking.

Lizzie was quiet a moment, then she struggled to sit up. "This is a bad place. They give you applesauce that makes you sick."

So they poisoned Lizzie, too. "We will find a way out."

"But where are we?" Lizzie asked loudly. Megan felt gently around her daughter's ear. The hearing aid was not in place. She put her finger gently across her daughter's lips.

*   *   *

A dim bloom of yellow light crept over the walls, then flickered out, dousing them again in darkness, then returned, as if someone had passed in front of a distant spotlight.

Lying curled around her daughter, Megan snapped awake, tightened her arms around Lizzie, and glanced over at John. He shook his head, as if to say he didn't know any more than she did.

A small head popped up over John's shoulder. The eyes were huge and dark and as round as bottle caps. A thumb was anchored in the mouth, and the lips were making soft sucking sounds. A small hand snaked to an ear and scratched.

"Hello, Bobby," Megan said softly, but the child just nodded and sucked on his fist. He looked familiar. Was this the child from the church parking lot? What was he doing here? A wave of dismay engulfed her. What was she to do with these children?

John said, "They brought more food. It's over by the wall."

Lizzie sat up. Then her face puckered, and her shoulders shook with deep, wrenching sobs.

Megan hushed her, exaggerating the words so Lizzie could read her lips. "What is it?"

"Theodora. Where is she?" The words began as a wail, but Lizzie slapped her hand to her mouth.

Megan said, "She's gone, Lizzie. I looked for her, but she wasn't in the garage. I'm sorry."

"No. She was here with me." Between gulping sobs Lizzie told of leaving the little tortoise in her cell, creeping along the tunnel to the big room where the man and woman were arguing, later seeing the huge number of people, then being caught by the man who forced applesauce into her mouth and pinched her nose shut to make her swallow it.

Megan rocked her daughter until the sobs quieted.

In an old pie tin next to half a roll of paper towels and a plastic milk jug of water were four peanut butter sandwiches. They ate in silence.

Megan said, "At least we're all together. Now all we have to do is figure out how to get out of here."

She had already spotted the space at the top of the chicken wire above the gate. The gap looked wide enough for someone to slip through.

John tried, but with no toehold, he couldn't reach the top. Megan managed it standing on John's shoulders.

Once outside the gate, she mustered a reassuring smile, gave a mock salute, and inched her way up the corridor.

A noise startled her as she began crawling down the second of two corridors beyond the cell where she left the children. The yellow light was getting steadily brighter. She didn't want to think about what she would do if it went out.

A faint breeze ruffled her hair. Looking down the seemingly endless, shadowy tunnel, she wondered if she was near an entrance. A few minutes later she reached a big oval room. Here was the source of the light: two bright lanterns sitting against a wall.

Megan gazed around the big room. Things had been moved, but she had been here before—the day she was shot at. Some part of her had expected this, but it was a shock all the same.

She crept along the wall to where another corridor led away from the light. Was this the passageway that out of curiosity she entered not too long ago? It must be. If so, the entrance wasn't far. But now she couldn't chance walking in plain view.

But she had to be absolutely certain this was the way to the entrance. She couldn't risk bringing the kids this way only to be trapped like mice in a sewer. The light faded as she left the lanterns behind. The air was stale and silent. Perhaps it was very early, and whoever brought her to the cell was asleep in a distant part of the cavern. Or maybe the captors didn't stay here but would arrive any moment.

Inching forward along the base of the wall, she hoped anyone glancing down the corridor would take her for a mere ground-level bulge in the wall. Ahead on the left she thought she saw an opening. The trash room? If so, she wouldn't have to go farther. She wriggled on her belly across the tunnel to the opening.

Yes, this was it. The garbage sacks now reached nearly to the ceiling.

Their telltale yellow handles glimmered in the gloom. The place stank of rot. Megan's stomach churned. Did they never haul it away? She tried to breathe through her mouth but the odor seemed to seep in through her pores. Propping her back against the wall, she willed herself to block out the smell.

She was stretching her arm out in front of her to relieve a cramp in a tense muscle, when her hand began to glow bright purple.

And her fingers became snakes with neon tongues.

A scream began, but she trapped it in her throat and shoved it down. The snakes vanished.

Unnerved, no longer trusting her own senses, she sank down, her back against the wall of trash. What the hell . . . ?

The answer came from another part of her brain.

Did the priest give her something like LSD? Was this a flashback? She passed hot fingers across her clammy forehead, waited for her stomach to stop seesawing, then began inching back toward the doorway.

A faint, fluttery hum behind her made her turn her head. Something like a huge insect flitted at her hair, and she couldn't completely strangle the scream that rose in her throat. Another hallucination? Please let it be that. *Don't let it be real.*

Seeming to lose interest in her, bigger than any insect could be, it loosed its grip on her hair and flew away. She was daring to breathe again, forgetting not to breathe through her nose, taking in the stench, when the thing swooped into a turn and fluttered back toward her. Again, it clutched at her hair.

Megan threw her head violently to the side. A bat. Just a bat. No more than a flying mouse. *Harmless*, she told herself. But when it turned and dove at her again, she wasn't so sure.

Then, as quickly as it appeared, it was gone. She lay, almost without breathing, for a full minute. The bat, if it was a bat, didn't return.

She got to her knees, thinking the wall should be very close on her left. But it wasn't. Her fingers brushed something. A mountain of some-things. Metal rods? A small hole in the center of each. Two of them rose into the air.

Two triangular heads glowed red, their tongues yellow. Megan squeezed her eyes shut. *These . . . are . . . not . . . snakes*, she told herself, her brain meting out the words one at a time. *They are pipes*.

She forced her hand to touch one. It clanked against the other. She jerked her hand back and froze, as the snakes' yellow tongues flicked the air. Willing herself to reach out again, she slid a quivering hand along the metal until it dipped. Her thumb brushed something curved, and she knew she was wrong. These were not pipes.

They were guns. And there were many.

Anxiety squeezed her breath into little pants. Slightly dizzy now, she crept backward again, toward where the doorway should be. Her foot scraped something, and the sound seemed to echo as whatever it was tee-tered. She swung her hand back and her fingers found a gallon-size con-tainer. A paint can? She pried at the lid with her thumb and reached inside. The contents were grainy, like salt. Megan brought a pinch to her nose but couldn't smell a thing beyond the reek of the garbage.

The light came from nowhere, piercing her eyes and seeming to bore all the way to her brain.

She froze, mind empty of everything but the light, torso half ele-vated, like a jackrabbit transfixed by headlights.

The beam bobbed. A hand grabbed her hair and dragged her into the corridor. She kicked at the hand's owner, but her efforts accomplished little.

"She risks everything with her stupidity," a voice, flat and oddly sad, grunted. "It was not a kindness to put them all together. It was weak. I should not have permitted it."

A rag was stuffed into Megan's mouth, and strong fingers pinched her nostrils closed until she stopped kicking.

Chapter Forty-five

Someone was moaning. Eventually Megan realized the sound was her own.

A damp rag lay across her eyes and forehead. The back of her skull pulsed fiercely, as if pummeled by fists. She could almost hear the blows. Behind her eyes a dot of orange exploded into jagged scarlet.

"Mama?" Lizzie's voice rose with panic. "Mama, are you okay?"

Megan ran her tongue over her lips. Several seconds passed before she managed to form the word, "Yes."

"Mrs. Montoya?" This from John. "I think you need a doctor."

She took a long time to answer. "Let's hope not."

A tiny, ineffectual bit of light had found its way to their cell. Feebly, she moved her gaze across the wall toward the gate. It was no longer a gate. It was now a door of hastily hammered together boards. Three or four holes gaped where the boards were rotted or didn't meet. Such places were now patched with chicken wire.

Any chance for escape was gone.

A veil like a soft, sticky spiderweb spread itself across Megan's mind, and she let go of consciousness.

When she woke again, something was touching her shoulder. "Lizzie?" she asked, her voice blurry.

A hand moved to her arm and shook it gently. The voice was low. "Megan? Wake up."

She knew that voice, didn't she? A female voice. Had this woman taken the children? Had the creature now come to get her? For a moment she wondered if this was another episode from whatever the priest put in the tea. "What?" Megan's voice cracked in her dry throat. "Who are you?"

The voice was now close to her ear. "Listen carefully. You must do exactly what I tell you."

Megan struggled to sit up. Someone's hands supported her back so she could pull herself upright. Eyes between puffy eyelids made out the outline of the woman kneeling beside her. Was she part of the insane scheme of kidnappings or was she another hapless captive?

"You do not know me?"

Megan glanced toward the sleeping children. "Should I?"

The woman sat down on the floor, took Megan's face gently in her hands, and turned it to her. A wisp of the pale light flowing weakly beneath the planks of the door showed her features.

"Corazón? What are you doing here?"

The woman's clothing rustled as if in a faint breeze, paused, then rustled again. "I believed in something. I trusted someone. Now . . . I am here."

"I don't . . . understand." Megan's mind was beginning to work, but her tongue was thick.

"He talks of liberating my people from poverty. He has enormous intellect. Nothing is beyond him. He says we should control our own fate, we should defy injustice, not endure it. His words are so . . . they make you feel drunk, *comprende*?"

"I don't know."

"It has never been this way for you?" Corazón asked. "When you are more than yourself, better than yourself. When you are huge with happiness and goodness."

"I don't think so."

Corazón was gazing at the wall as if she saw something there. "You are a Montoya. You told me once your people are from here. Then your people are my people. Did they never tell you what it was like? Were they born rich?"

Megan shook her head. "I don't know, but I don't think so. I told you, they never talked about it much."

"How could they not talk about it?" Corazón shot back at her. "It is who you are."

"I don't know," Megan said slowly. "Maybe they didn't want to be part of it. Maybe they had a chance to get away, to not see it every day of their lives. Maybe that's why they went to Pittsburgh. I guess I didn't want to know any more than they wanted to tell me." She finished defensively, "Why should I?"

Corazón put her hand to her temple as if her head hurt. "For me, it is the center of my being."

"But what has any of it got to do with me?" Megan waved her hand at the sleeping children. "Why are we prisoners here?"

Again, Corazón went silent for several seconds. "He is a good person. You must understand that. Like a saint. He would give his life . . ."

"Who is this saint?"

"Miguel."

"This saint goes about abducting people?"

Corazón ignored that. "He said the people will believe me, do as I say. He said we must make a separate nation. In the beginning, I think this is book talk. I think he means we must draw strength from ourselves. The pictures you took for me—Miguel said that for everyone to know how poor some of our people live, they must look terrible. Okay, I fix it so they look terrible. But I think now you are right. It is better to be more true, more real."

Megan frowned into the long heavy silence that followed. At length she said, "It was the arrowheads, wasn't it? You people tried to steal them. You found out I was a photographer when you broke into my house. You saw the lenses, the enlarger, the equipment."

Corazón shook herself, as if the words had doused her with water.

In the pale light Megan saw the woman's silhouette nod. "But how did you find out about the arrowheads? Why did you think I had them?"

"We knew about them for some time. My cousin Tonio told us about them. His brother borrowed them from some kid at the school. Tonio thought they might be very valuable. Miguel said such a thing is a gift from God. These are not ordinary arrowheads. They are very special. They are *las esmeraldas.*"

"What made you think they were emerald?"

"Tonio said so. He is a student at the institute in Socorro."

"Why didn't you just keep them then?"

"Tonio is a very honest man. By the time he talks about it he has already given them back." Corazón turned her head toward the door for a moment before continuing. "This makes Miguel very excited. He says these arrowheads, made long ago by people like ours, give us the way to free our people. And we must have money to feed our army—"

"Army?"

"That is not your concern," Corazón said fiercely, then she went on more casually. "Mexicans from Arizona and California bring food in trucks. I think maybe they steal these things, the oranges, the chiles, the chickens, maybe even the trucks. But Miguel says these people have suffered many bad things at the hands of the gringo. More important is, they want to be paid for their work and the supplies or they will become very angry."

"So Miguel planned to pay for these things with the emeralds?"

"He says our cause is good, and when we need, God blesses us. He says God meant the emeralds for us and we must take them—that we only steal back what is ours, what God has given us."

For a long time there was no sound in the room but the sleeping children's measured breathing. "Even when we bring the boy here," Corazón said, "I think it is something we have to do only for a little while."

"And what did you think when you killed Alma?"

There was a ragged intake of air in the dark and then a very long silence before Corazón said mechanically, "One must break eggs if one is to have an omelet. That is what Miguel says."

Megan had expected Corazón to deny Alma's murder, wanted to hear denial. Now she could only blink away the stinging in her eyes and fight down the hopeless dread that rose and swayed like a cobra inside her. "You thought Alma had the arrowheads. So you killed her."

"The arrowheads will help our people. There is much cost. Not only the food." Corazón's words were strong, but her voice sounded discouraged. "Luis hired a coyote. A person who helps poor people to come from Mexico."

"Luis?"

"A friend of Miguel. This coyote brings men from there for months now. The price is very high, because each man must also have two guns. This coyote is not a saint. He is demanding his money."

"Why do they need guns?"

"For the plan."

"How do you pay for this now?"

"Miguel is a very good forger. He makes much money forging passports and birth certificates and other documents. But it is not enough. Now he pays with promises. Miguel is an honorable man. He will keep his promises."

Corazón made a sad smile. Then her eyes flashed in the dim light. "He is right. We have tried the *políticos*. We have tried even guns, in little, foolish ways. And we were laughed at. But he hears how Anglos blow up their own people in Oklahoma, Arabs blow up people in New York and Washington. This happens all over the world.

"He says this is how the poor make the rich pay attention. They blow up big buildings and as many people as they can. They do not stop, they do not give up. They blow up even themselves to make the rich and powerful afraid. Miguel says we will make a small war, and then we will be noticed. We will be arrested, yes, but the TV cameras will come. And the police will be very careful not to hurt us. And the eyes of the world will see us. When the eyes of the world look into the eye of . . ."

Megan waited, but Corazón didn't go on. "The eyes of what?"

"Of the Mountain God." Corazón hesitated. "It is something Miguel says. He believes the arrowheads were *sent* to him to pay for *el plan*."

The black cloud of hair bounced as she tossed her head. "I want teachers. And jobs. Miguel's plans are much, much bigger."

Chapter Forty-six

Megan's drug-befuddled brain struggled to take in what Corazón was saying. "A war? You can't be serious."

"I assure you Miguel is very serious. *We* are very serious."

Megan thought about that. "The people in that village in the mountains. The fiesta. What were they really doing?"

Corazón's shoulders slumped forward with a look of anguish and desperation. "They were preparing for a fiesta. But also for something else."

Suddenly, Megan understood. "He can't mean to arm them. That's insane. What would he do? March on the capitol in Santa Fe? With guns? That's not just insane, Corazón, it's stupid. Some of them will be injured, even killed. And all of them will be thrown in jail."

"He will begin with the electricity. There is a place—he knows it, I do not—where the power can be cut off. Everything will be dark. The airports, the televisions, the gas pumps, the telephones. Even the cell phones will run down and stop. When this happens by accident in other places it is many days before everything works right again. And there is looting. Angry people do bad things just because they can," Corazón said. "What he will do after that, he does not tell me the detail. He speaks of someone who knows how to enter a big computer system."

"A hacker? There's a hacker with you?"

"That is the word, yes. Luis found a person to change the main computer so it will take a long time to repair the electricity. He says it is ready now to obey as soon as the electricity lines blow up." Corazón shrugged. "It is much easier than you think. This person learned in a class in California."

"There are classes in how to hack a computer?"

"Oh, yes. Many places. Miguel says this person learned at a university."

Megan tried to swallow her disbelief. "If it's that easy, why not just use the computers to bring down the power supply?"

"Because violence will bring the television cameras. The computer will be used to make it last longer, so other things can be done. Miguel speaks of blocking roads, airports, and about something he calls dirty bombs." Corazón stopped, then added, "The coyotes have taken many men to the pueblo lands, the reservation lands."

"The Indians are in on this?"

"They own millions of acres."

Megan rubbed her forehead. "Do they think this is a good idea, cutting the electric power, the guns, the rioting, the looting?"

"The *indios* have been angry with the Anglos for a very long time."

Megan considered that. "I was drugged in a church by a man who appeared to be a priest."

"Yes, there are priests with us. They care about their people; they see the hopelessness. They think they see a way to do something, to bang the drum, you understand? To point the finger. It is the first hope in a very long time. And each step is very small. The priest who brings you here, he is a little like Miguel. He says sometimes a price must be paid. But the reward is much bigger than the price."

"Why are you telling me this?"

"Because you must understand this is very, very important." Something like fear edged Corazón's voice. "You must understand what will happen to the children if you do not give him the arrowheads."

Megan didn't want to ask but couldn't stop herself. "And that is . . . ?"

Half her face in darkness, Corazón's eyes drilled into Megan's. "When you give us the arrowheads, we will give you the children. But then you must leave here. Go as far away as you can. That is the best I can do. I tell you all this so you will believe me. You will give me the arrowheads, then you will leave immediately. You will not even go home. You must swear it."

Megan just stared at her, trying to take in all that Corazón implied.

"Miguel says we wasted too many days. Already someone has discovered one of the ways to come into the mine. We think they do not know anything about us yet, but they may be watching. We will have to block that entrance. I tell you this as your friend. You must leave New Mexico immediately."

"If anyone starts shooting, they'll call out the National Guard. Your people may be shot."

"I pray to the Virgin it will not be many." Corazón's voice sank to a whisper. "No great cause is without cost."

"You think this is okay? You agree with all this?"

"I . . ." Corazón turned her head, and for the first time Megan saw the puffy swelling and the cuts on her cheek and forehead.

"He has beaten you."

"We have the *pelea*, yes. An argument. It was nothing. He was drinking."

"He must be stopped. You must know that." Megan tried to size up the other woman's role in Miguel's scheme. A coplanner? A victim? Or something in between?

"Can you find out when and where he plans to bring down the electric power?"

The other woman seemed to have turned to stone.

"Corazón?"

Still she did not stir for a full minute. Then she stood and moved toward the patchwork door. When she reached it, she turned. "I cannot do that. You must listen to me. You must give him the emeralds, or he will kill you. And he will kill the *niños*. You have no choice."

"You may not believe me," Megan said, "but it isn't giving up the arrowheads that bothers me. It's this plan of yours. You must know it's crazy. Worse than crazy. It will hurt the people you want to help."

"If you love your daughter, you have no choice. You must give us the emeralds."

Megan gave a sad sigh, aware she had no options at all. "Okay," she said finally. "The arrowheads are in—"

"No." Corazón cut her off. "He has searched too often and found nothing. You will go. Now. I will take you to the entrance. You will get the arrowheads and bring them here."

"And leave my daughter?"

"For now, yes. It is the only way he will allow you to leave."

"No. I can't do that."

"For your child's life, you must do this. She will be safe here. I promise you. On the grave of my mother, I swear it."

Remembering the marks on Corazón's face, Megan said, "I'm not sure you are able to keep that promise."

"You have no choice but to believe me. When you bring the arrowheads, you can take the children. Then you must leave. Go far away."

She opened the door. "Come."

Megan glanced at the sleeping bodies. "Please. Let me tell them where I'm going and why. They'll be frightened if they wake up and I'm not here."

Corazón looked down the corridor, then at the children. Bobby rolled over in his sleep.

"All right. It is very early. The men still sleep. I have to help the women with the *desayuno*, the breakfast. I will come for you in one hour. One hour," she said again, and shut the door behind her.

Megan wondered if she could do what she had to do.

It was several minutes before she realized the door had closed but the lock had not clicked.

Chapter Forty-seven

Behind her, the children's soft snores rose and fell.

Megan tiptoed to the door and pushed gently against it. Creaking a little, it swung outward. Corazón had left the door to the cell unlocked. Deliberately. The men were still asleep, the women were preparing breakfast.

She struggled to think clearly. She would gladly give the arrowheads to Corazón. They had all but ruined her own life; she wished she had never seen them. But she could not leave Lizzie behind. She would take the children with her. Now.

Shaking each gently, she whispered to them to get up.

In the faint light that seeped beneath the door, Lizzie and John seemed like wraiths from a dim, mirthless world. Bobby, sucking his thumb, merely squatted, frowning, near Megan's feet.

Megan pushed the hair Corazón had cut so beautifully—limp now, dirty and disheveled—from her face. If she failed, they all might be trapped. What would Miguel do if he found out?

Head close to the three worried faces, exaggerating each word so Lizzie could get the gist of it by lip-reading, Megan whispered her plan.

Tiny beads of sweat slid down John's forehead as he nodded.

Bobby shrank back into a corner and sat.

"Come on," John said to him, holding out his hand. "Let's go."

Bobby blinked at him over the fist that still anchored his thumb in his mouth.

Megan was wondering if the child belonged to someone there, if he understood English, but he hesitantly rose to his feet. She looked from Bobby's face to John's to Lizzie's. Then she stared at the door wondering if she could do it.

"Yes, you can," Lizzie said.

Megan looked into her daughter's face. She hadn't spoken out loud, and even if she had, without the hearing aid Lizzie couldn't hear her.

The little girl's eyes held her mother's. "It's not silly, Mama. I just know it."

"What else do you just know?"

Lizzie glanced away, then looked back at Megan. "Three very bad things are gonna happen," she said slowly. "One will be real soon. But . . ." Lizzie stood, mouth slightly open, eyes on something Megan couldn't see.

"But what?"

"We will be okay." Lizzie nodded twice, slowly, but a look of pain crossed her face. "You and John and me, we'll be okay."

They all moved to the door. At Megan's shove, it swung open a few feet, then stopped. She pushed a little harder, wedged her head through the opening, then uttered a muted cry of alarm. Something was on the floor of the tunnel behind the door, something the size of a big teacup. It was moving.

A tarantula? Dear God, that's all we need.

The head of the thing arched high and inquisitive, as the creature padded slowly to the door.

Peering around Megan, Lizzie yelped, "Theodora!" then slapped her hand over her mouth. "Back up, Theodora," she whispered. "Back up so we can open the door." And the tortoise did so.

This time Megan found it much more difficult to hug the wall and inch along that horrid corridor. Something like hot Jell-O seemed to fill the top of her skull and the space behind her eyes till they throbbed. Her ribs shrieked in protest with each step.

The aroma of coffee and bacon wafted down the tunnel, and she realized she was very hungry. The kids must be hungry, too. She could hear the stealthy sounds of their feet moving over the ground behind her. How far had they come? It seemed like miles.

Lizzie had Theodora inside her jacket. Megan wasn't sure that was going to be practical, but she didn't have the heart to tell her daughter to leave the tortoise behind.

When they reached the big room and the corridor leading from it, she dropped to her hands and knees and motioned for the children to do the same. Now, if someone caught sight of them, it would probably be from behind. Best to be as small as possible.

The entrance to the trash room was a blacker shade of darkness in the wall just ahead on the left. Megan eased herself to a sitting position and turned to face the three sets of solemn eyes watching her. She held up a finger. *Wait*, she mouthed, and turned to crawl forward again.

Snaking her body across the corridor to the entrance to the trash room, she flattened herself, first to the floor, then to the wall. Motionless, she held a finger over her lips, eyes warning the children to be still, and listened.

Nothing. The trash room was dark and soundless. Trying to recall her first foray into the mine, she estimated the exit would be maybe a hundred yards farther.

Signaling the kids to stay where they were, Megan crawled several more yards. Now there was a whiff of fresh air, giving the smell of coffee and bacon the scent of a campsite breakfast.

Ahead, a faint glow appeared. The entrance. She looked back. She had come farther than she realized. Lizzie and the boys were several dozen yards behind her.

She was swinging her arm in an arc to signal them to join her when a sound erupted with a violence that pitched her against the wall at the tunnel entrance.

Coughing, covering her face against spewing clouds of dust, she struggled to turn back. Behind her, ruptured rocks crunched against each other. A powerful wind seemed intent on wrenching her hair and clothing from her. Bits of flying stone strafed her cheek. She squeezed her eyes shut.

When she opened them the corridor was gone. Where it had been was a solid wall of loose rock.

Megan threw herself at the rubble, clawing at it until her hands bled. But the stones she scraped away were quickly replaced by a cascade of more bits of rock.

The children were trapped.

If they were alive.

Chapter Forty-eight

Like a wind-up toy at the end of its run, Megan lurched away from the rocks, willing her legs to move. Her knees shook. She wobbled and fell. Tottering to her feet, she forced herself on.

Without attempting to search for a path in the weak light of dawn, snatching at branches of shrubs and outcroppings of rock to keep from sliding backward, she dragged herself up the craggy canyon wall.

What seemed like eons later, she ran along the road at the top, knowing only that she had to find a phone. As far as she could see, nothing but desert mountain brush lined the empty pavement. Swaying, barely able to stay on her feet, she staggered on.

Rounding a bend, she was narrowly missed by a van so old and dusty it was impossible to identify the make. It creaked to a halt. Children leaned from every window. The driver, so broad and weathered that he looked like a potato, asked if she was okay.

"Please," Megan asked, her voice like a squeaky hinge. "Please. I need help."

The man said something in rapid Spanish.

She shook her head and tried again, almost sobbing. "*Teléfono*—I need a telephone."

"Ah. *Sí.*" He hopped out of the van and slid open the side door. The vehicle's interior was so crammed with children, Megan had to sit in the open door, feet dangling above the pavement.

Barely hearing the din of young voices, choking on the van's exhaust, she clung to the door to keep from being jounced onto the road as the van did a bump and grind into a town.

The gas station looked closed, but she called to the driver and pointed at a phone booth. He hit the brakes, nearly throwing her out the door to the pavement.

She repeated one of the few Spanish words she knew. "*Gracias.*" Thank you.

He took four quarters from a box on the dashboard and pressed them into her hand. Astonished at his thoughtfulness, she watched him drive off, then limped toward the telephone.

As she pressed the first digit of 911, two images, like a split-action television screen, leaped into her head: A squad of cops clearing the rubble at one end of the cave; the children being silenced on the other side.

She pressed the disconnect lever, slipped the returned quarters into the slot again, and dialed Ben's cell phone.

Sitting on the ground slumped against the phone booth staring at nothing, she was neither awake nor asleep when Ben arrived.

"What the hell are you doing here?" he shouted, braking his pickup to a halt. "Where have you been?"

"Take me back," she wailed. "I have to get Lizzie."

"Back where?"

But she only repeated the same words over again. "Please. I have to find Lizzie."

He shook her gently. "Megan, stop it. I don't understand. Help me to understand."

At last the words began to come, tripping over each other in haste, but coherent, as her eyes stared at a horror he could not see but could hear in her voice. She told him about the children, the explosion that blocked their exit from the cave. The threat to kill Lizzie and the others. "Please," she said, in a tone beginning to shrill again with hysteria, "take me back to the cave."

"No."

She wrenched away from him. "Then I'll go alone!"

He caught and held her until her fists stopped pummeling his chest. "Megan, they might kill the kids the moment they sense someone is trying to get into that cave. And they have all the aces. If there's another entrance, we don't know where it is. Even if we could dig through the rock, they would have hours to—"

"We have to *do something*." She broke in and began to sob, but it was like the dry heaves. No tears came.

He lifted her chin until his eyes held hers. "I was wrong. They don't have all the aces. We have one."

She gazed back at him dumbly.

"The arrowheads. They won't harm the kids. They will trade them for the emeralds."

Chapter Forty-nine

When Ben's pickup swung at fast speed into Megan's driveway, a familiar figure was sitting on the stoop.

Bernie dropped her knitting needles to her lap. "I thought you might be coming home this morning."

They went into the house, and while Ben scowled and hovered, Bernie, making clucking noises like a disgruntled hen, bustled back and forth preparing sandwiches. When they finished eating, Ben guided Megan toward her bed, with Bernie, muttering, close behind.

Megan lay down and curled into the fetal position. "Lizzie is dead. I just know it."

"Stop," Bernie said. "You have worn yourself out with the weeping. You are not good for yourself or anyone else like this." She plumped the pillows, disappeared, and returned with a cup of something she insisted Megan drink.

"No," Megan said weakly. "I don't want anything."

"Yes." Ben's eyes were full of pain, but his voice was firm. "Take it. Swallow it. Do it now."

She stared at him over the cup for a few seconds, then took a sip. The liquid was strong and sour. She made a face. Bernie's eyes, boring into her from the foot of her bed, reminded Megan of her mother. She was a child again, feverish and frightened and believing her mother could make her well. She drained the cup.

"You do not know that Lizzie is dead," Bernie said slowly and clearly. "Trapped, yes. Alive, dead, we do not know."

Megan looked first at Ben, then at Bernie, then at something inside her own head. "You don't understand. Killing children would be nothing to this Miguel. He would chalk it up as just another small price. Another broken egg needed for his omelet."

Bernie pulled up a chair and sat.

"If he hasn't killed them already, he will." Megan's voice was that of a last-place long-distance runner.

Bernie leaned back. "A child will die, but it will not be Lizzie. She is a fine girl, your Lizzie. You must listen to her. She will ask you to do something you think is silly or unnecessary, but you must do it. Near a house that has burned down, you will find this man."

Megan's voice snapped across the line between despair and anger. "I don't want any phony hocus-pocus hope."

Ben said, "I think we should call the cops."

Megan sat up. "Not until Lizzie is safe! Think what a god-awful mess cops could make of it. You said yourself that if Miguel heard anyone trying to get into the cave, he would kill the children."

When they didn't argue with her, she lay back against the pillow again. "You were right. If he isn't threatened, Miguel won't do anything to the kids right away, because he needs them to barter for the arrowheads." She felt quieter now, more sure of herself. The gauzy curtain cloaking her mind was lifting. Perhaps it was Bernie's medicinal concoction. "Corazón said that once he has the emeralds he will sabotage the electric power. The entire state will go dark."

"The whole state?" Ben said. "That seems unlikely."

Megan disagreed. "Remember how it was when the power went down all around New York? It may be like a house of cards."

"Even if he could, why would he do it?"

"Corazón thought he only meant to attract the national media. Now she says he talks of roads and airports, of people taking back what is theirs. He even mentions dirty bombs. I do know there are guns in that place. Many guns. And apparently the Indian reservations are involved."

"He must be mad," Ben muttered. "It sounds like Tijerina all over again."

Megan frowned. "It's what?"

"Reies Lopez Tijerina was jailed in 1970," Ben said. "His plot was not so massive, not such a broad sweep, but it was the same sort of thing. This Miguel may be capitalizing on the fact that geographically this is a big state, with little more than a couple million people. The roads are sparse, only three real interstates, and there aren't many airports of any size." Somewhere in the bowels of the house a water pipe rattled and groaned.

Megan searched Ben's face. "So he could do it? Miguel could cut off the state? Take it over?"

"He could sure get a lot of people killed trying. And you're right, a long, widespread blackout probably is possible, and it would make one hell of a mess." Ben scratched his head where the band of his hat left its mark. "But that blackout around New York, wasn't that some failure in the system itself?"

"Corazón says Miguel knows exactly where to go. And I've heard that all the power lines enter the state at one place."

Bernie had been listening intently to their discussion. Now she looked at Megan. "What you say may be true. It is near the ruins of a house."

"But how could this guy know where it is?" Ben asked.

In Megan's head, the image of a man, complete with detail, floated out of the fog. He was standing in her living room tapping a clipboard against his leg. An empty clipboard. And it was a dirty white panel truck that followed Corazón's pickup into the mountains. She had seen the decal on the side of that truck when it turned around: NMP&L. New Mexico Power and Light.

"He was right here in my living room. He works for the electric company. But that wasn't why he was here. He already knew I had the arrowheads. He came to look the place over. And now he has Lizzie. God *damn* him."

"Once we have the kids," Ben said, "we go to the cops."

"How do you know some of the cops aren't part of it?" Megan asked. "It was a priest that poisoned me. If a priest is with them, why not a few cops? Maybe more than a few."

Bernie cut in, "Tell me about this poison?"

Megan described the taste of the tea and the hallucinations.

Bernie's red head rocked back and forth, then gave a sharp nod. "*Toloache*," she said. "They use jimson. This *hombre* exploits the old traditions."

Ben sat down. The line above his eyebrows looked like it was made with a knife.

Megan looked from one to the other. "Jimson?"

"A drug. A hallucinogen," Ben said.

"For the warriors, for battle," Bernie added.

"They say it gives people a sort of lethal optimism," Ben explained. "And visions of glory."

"It sure didn't give me any visions of glory," Megan said. "It made me sick."

"They didn't want you to do battle," Ben said. "They wanted you to be sick. No doubt that calls for a different dose."

Bernie put in, "*Muy peligroso*, this man. Very dangerous. And very smart."

Ben agreed. "My guess is he's manipulating ancient ideals in people who want to believe."

Megan said, "He has Lizzie." Her words seemed to hover in the air like poisonous insects.

When the phone next to the bed rang, it startled all three of them. Megan's eyes found Ben's.

The phone rang again.

Chapter Fifty

The road from the main highway was long and very straight. Chuckholes showed clearly in the headlights, but Megan neither slowed the car nor swerved to miss them. Each jolt seemed to hammer the reality harder into her mind.

The owner of the voice on the phone didn't trouble to disguise himself. It was the same male voice that belonged to the hands that had grabbed her by the hair in the tunnel near the trash room. It had to be Miguel.

"Listen most carefully." The voice was sure of itself. He had something to trade, and he knew he had a taker. "If you wish to see your daughter again, you will do these things."

When Megan and Ben left, Bernie was in the kitchen, sleeves rolled up, pots on the stove, apparently prepared to cook for an army. "You will not feel like cooking when you come home," she told Megan. "So I will fix and freeze."

In his pickup, Ben took Megan out to Alma's cabin to retrieve her car. Then he followed the Civic to the turnoff from the highway. There, Megan insisted he wait. Ben's protests fell on deaf ears. Miguel had told her to come alone.

So now she was speeding toward Santa Rita Pueblo. Ben had explained that neither the federal government nor the state had jurisdiction there. That was Indian land. And she was a long way from help.

Her handbag bounced about on the passenger seat. She reached into it to feel the shape of the arrowheads in their plastic bag. Also in the handbag was Lizzie's spare hearing aid.

Megan's relief that the emeralds might buy Lizzie from her captors was dimmed by a sadness. When Miguel had the arrowheads, how much death and destruction would they buy?

He must be insane. Brilliant, perhaps, as Corazón said, but insane. A deadly combination. He would go after what he wanted, with or without the emeralds. The only thing Megan had a prayer of accomplishing was Lizzie's release. Along with John and Bobby.

The voice on the phone had said all three children were safe. Megan knew there was only one reason to believe him: She had the emeralds. She didn't want to consider that he probably would say anything to get her to cooperate until he got his hands on them.

Over and over she heard Lizzie's voice saying, just before the explosion, *We will be okay.* Megan hoped Bernie was right, that her daughter did have some peculiar window on the future.

The car's tires thrummed over a cattle guard. At the edge of the headlights' glow, she could see picnic tables. Slowing the Honda, she found the road that matched Miguel's instructions. It should lead to some partially reconstructed cliff dwellings. Ben said the Indians were developing the site as a tourist attraction.

The road was gravel and wound in a huge S for a mile or so before widening into a very large, very empty parking lot, exactly as Miguel described. A lone vehicle sat dead center in the farthest row of parking spaces: a white panel truck.

Megan parked, got out of the car, stuffed the arrowheads into one jean's pocket and the hearing aid into another.

Whitish cliffs loomed above. Hazy moonlight lay like a fog across a long wall where the prehistoric dwellings sat like condo apartments on ledges that began halfway up the cliff.

Gravel crunched beneath her boots as she threaded her way along a path that led between the dark hulks of two modern buildings, a café and a gift shop. The moon emerged from behind a small cloud, sending a bluish light shimmering across the face of the cliff—a cliff that now seemed almost chalk white, except where it was riddled with dark splotches that marked prehistoric doorways.

A few yards ahead, propped against the cliff, she saw a ladder apparently fashioned by stripping two young trees of their bark and nailing pieces of a third between them as rungs. Two more ladders were visible on ledges farther up. The first seemed newly made and solid.

Once she began to ascend, she would be a clear target. And when she scaled a mere half dozen feet of the fifty or so above, she would not be able to escape gunfire, or even thrown rocks. The higher she climbed, the greater the odds against surviving a fall or a jump.

Megan thought a light flared off to her left, but it was gone so quickly, she couldn't be sure.

She lifted her foot to the bottom rung of the ladder.

Miguel had devised a clever advantage for himself. She was to climb to the fourth level. He would watch the parking lot, would know if she had disobeyed his orders to come alone. And she would be at his mercy. He could simply kill her and take the arrowheads from her body. She had to believe he would prefer to hand over the children, to get them off his hands and off his conscience. If he had a conscience.

And if the children were still alive.

Megan climbed as quickly as she could, clenching her teeth against the needlelike pain that stabbed at her side. The day she injured the complaining rib seemed a year ago.

Near the top of the second ladder, a rung seemed to give beneath her foot. The ladder swayed with a creaking, scraping sound. The hot hand of panic squeezed off her breathing. In the moonlight, the ladder's shadow marked the wall with bold black lines. The space below seemed huge and empty and ominous.

Something above her moved, and a small hailstorm of dust and pebbles clattered down the wall of the cliff. Before this she had been only mildly uneasy about heights. Now an overpowering terror bubbled up, flooding her mind, paralyzing her. A dreamlike sensation of falling into nothing engulfed her. Her leg, as she lifted her foot to the next rung, began to shake uncontrollably.

Knuckles of both hands were blue-white in the moonlight. She put the trembling foot back down and leaned her face against the smooth wood of the ladder.

"Is she all right?" A woman's voice.

Megan's head snapped back, eyes searching the cliff. If Corazón was here, Lizzie was alive. Megan didn't know why she believed that, but she did. She raised her foot again and pulled herself up. A bit of debris bounced across her cheek, whipped along by a small breeze. She began to climb more quickly.

Reaching the next ledge, she saw a low doorway to the right. This was the fourth level. Clinging for dear life to the rocky surface, she hauled herself over the last rung onto the ledge. Too frightened to stand, she crept toward the doorway.

The room was tiny. Small rough bricks rose on three sides; the cliff formed the fourth. Poles lay across the tops of walls, and the moonlight played across the chalklike floor, making uneven bars of shadow.

She inched her way to a corner and sat facing the doorway in the eerie stillness, wondering if she only imagined hearing Corazón's voice. Mind empty of everything but Lizzie and her own raw determination to survive, she waited.

Minute after minute passed, her mind bending under the strain. By the time she finally heard the footsteps, she welcomed anything they might bring.

She barely saw the form darkening the doorway before a beam of unbearably bright light seared her eyes. "Where are the arrowheads?" a voice demanded.

"Lizzie," she faltered, and drew a rasping breath, "I must know the children are safe first."

A mirthless laugh, as sad and chilling as the wail of a coyote, came from the dark blot behind the light. "You have nothing left for the bargaining."

Chapter Fifty-one

Her request is fair." Corazón interrupted from somewhere behind the man. "I will get the children." Quick steps moved away.

Mouth dry as cobwebs, Megan swallowed, covered her eyes to wipe out the awful light, and waited for the steps to return.

When they did, the beam trained on her swung away. A child so small it had to be Bobby was handed to Miguel. "You do not even know if she has a gun," he hissed to Corazón.

"Mama?" Lizzie's voice was high but controlled. "She says to tell you we're okay."

A tall form stooped, slipped through the low doorway, and made its way toward Megan. Corazón searched her quickly, then turned her head toward the light and said quietly, "There is no gun, Miguel." She turned back and whispered to Megan, "The children are safe. Believe me. He is many things, but he is not a cruel man."

"He tried to blow us up," Megan grunted under her breath.

"He did not know you were there." Corazón whispered warily. "He made the explosion only to close the entrance, because some people discovered it."

"I don't believe you."

"I did not know he would blow it up so soon, but this does not matter anymore. Give me the emeralds."

Megan wanted to be rid of the arrowheads. Stiffly, she straightened one leg so she could remove the packet from her pocket.

Corazón started to move away, then turned back. Her whisper was barely audible: "He will turn off the electricity just before dawn tomorrow." Her voice regained a normal level. "You must leave. If you value your life and the lives of the *niños*, go as far from this place as you can. Immediately. Tonight."

She darted a look over her shoulder. "Tonight he is *loco*," she breathed. "He believes that to bring the eyes of the world to my people, he must sacrifice himself. He says, 'Always it is the leader they nail to the cross.' Tonight, he drinks jimson tea."

A foot stamped somewhere nearby as Megan touched Corazón's arm, "Where—"

Instantly, a finger silenced Megan's lips. Turning her head again toward the low entry, Corazón said loudly and calmly, "She has no weapons. I have *las esmeraldas*."

"Are you sure?"

"See for yourself." She tossed them through the small opening to the ledge.

"The electricity. Where?" Megan murmured.

Corazón didn't answer. She bent down to pass through the doorway.

Miguel's voice shot out of the darkness, and the light bored again into Megan's eyes. "Where is the other one?"

Megan gazed dumbly at the light. Her mouth opened, but no sound came out. Finally, "I don't understand."

"The other one, where is it?"

"There are no more."

"There were six."

"No," Megan gasped. "I swear it. Only five. I never had six."

The beam of light swept across the wall. When her eyes recovered from the dazzle, she could see beyond the doorway Miguel's outstretched arm. In his fist was Bobby's thin little arm. The child's feet dangled near Miguel's knees.

At first she didn't realize he had thrust the child into midair beyond the ledge.

The little boy tried to cling to the arm above him, but it swung him even farther into the void beyond the cliff.

"No!" Megan screamed, scrambling to the doorway. "I never had six. Please believe me. I would not—"

Out of the darkness, Corazón lunged toward Miguel. Her voice struck out like a sword: "No! Miguel, do not do this thing."

"It is not you who must climb onto the cross and let them drive the nails. I will have all the *esmeraldas*," he thundered. "If I cannot give our people freedom, I give them *dinero*." He shook the bag of arrowheads. "These belong to our people. And this woman has stolen one."

"It is only the *niña* who said six," Corazón shouted. "Maybe she did not count right."

Miguel swayed, lost his footing on the uneven, sloping ledge, staggered backward, and teetered on the precipice.

Corazón plunged forward to grab Bobby.

Trying to regain his own balance, Miguel swung the little boy away.

As her hand grabbed at the child's arm, Corazón's feet slid along the rock, then left it almost gracefully. For a hideous moment she seemed to hover there, her body forming an impossible angle with the cliff and the child.

Miguel's face was like a frozen scream as Corazón's weight carried her and the child away from the cliff, into the void.

Her shriek rose like a siren, driving everything from Megan's head but unmitigated horror.

It seemed to go on a very long time.

Then, it stopped.

Bobby hadn't made a sound.

Chapter Fifty-two

An emptiness swallowed all sound after the horrible thud at the bottom of the cliff. No insect chirped, no coyote called, no rabbit scuttled.

Megan didn't know how long she sat silently staring.

At length, Lizzie's small voice broke the stillness. "Mama?"

"I'm here." Megan could barely make out her daughter sitting a dozen yards to the right, her back to a mud-brick wall, next to John, who stood flattened against it. There was no sign of Miguel.

Megan got up and, fighting down a desire to do anything but this, approached the ladder.

"He went down it, I saw him." John's voice broke on the last syllable. His eyes were hollow places in his moonlit face.

"Poor Bobby," Lizzie choked. "I didn't want to know."

Megan held her daughter until the sobs ebbed. Something squirmed against her chest. Lizzie looked up at her, face smeared with tears. "It's just Theodora."

John stood like a bas-relief carving against the cliff, his face so stricken that Megan put her arm around him. He burrowed his head in her shoulder, his whole body shaking. Then he turned his face and awkwardly moved away. "He was so little."

Lizzie was looking at the sky, her face as ashen as the moon.

"Don't stand so close to the edge," Megan called.

Lizzie didn't respond.

Remembering the hearing aid, Megan fished it from her pocket. She was placing it in her daughter's ear when the empty ladder rocked against the cliff, swayed sideways, and ever so slowly, scuffing the rock face, it toppled.

John moved to the rim of the ledge and looked down into the void until two quick thumps and a sharp crack announced that the ladder had struck the ground below. He shifted his gaze to Megan. A haunted look had set in around his eyes; his face looked creased and too old for his years. "He must have pushed it over."

Pressing fingers to eyelids, wishing there was another adult, wishing she was one of the children, she asked, "Why would he do that? He has the emeralds."

John shrugged. "To keep us from following."

For tense minutes they waited for the second ladder to topple, and then the third.

John's eyes were intent on the parking lot. "There goes the truck," he said finally, pointing. "He even turned on the headlights."

"At least he's gone." Megan watched the truck circle the parking lot, like some strange creeping insect. "There must be another way down. The people who built these rooms must have had other ways besides ladders."

Lizzie was looking intently at the place where the van had disappeared. She turned her face to her mother. "They used little rock stairways."

Megan said carefully, for once hoping her daughter really did have a sixth sense, "Do you know where any of those little stairways might be?"

Lizzie squeezed her eyes shut and thought for a moment. Then she looked down at her boot, where a shoelace was coming loose. "No," she said in a disappointed voice. "Sorry, Mama, I don't know."

"Maybe if we walk along the ledge we can find a place that leads down," John offered, exhaustion thickening his voice.

Single file, they walked the full length of the ledge. No obvious exit appeared. Megan leaned wearily against a crumbling wall. "Maybe we should wait until the sun comes up so we can see."

"That will be hours," John said. "And it's kind of cold already."

"Are you okay?" Megan asked.

"I guess I just want to go home. I want to see my mom and dad and sleep in my own bed. Seems like I've been in that awful cave forever." A tear escaped and traced its way down a jaw that was trying very hard to be strong.

"Okay, we'll go," Megan said. "There has to be some way. Let's look again."

They reversed direction and examined the cliff's edge again. "There." Megan pointed at what looked like a rough, sloping, stone path.

Three pairs of feet moved cautiously onto the path, but a few yards along it changed direction and ended at a rocky barrier.

"We could climb over it," Lizzie said. "There's a stairway on the other side."

Megan looked at her daughter, then at the barrier. There was no way Lizzie could see over it.

Standing on tiptoe, John hoisted himself high enough to peer over the rock. "It does look like there's a path. It goes a ways, then drops off. It could be steps."

"But what if it isn't?" Megan said. "What if it dead ends?"

John looked again over the rock "We'd have to climb back up from a really bad angle."

Worry etched itself across Lizzie's features. What if she was wrong? Would they all fall to the bottom and die? "Maybe we shouldn't," she faltered.

With the cold night air seeping through her clothes all the way to her bones, Megan said, "We don't seem to have a lot of choices. And John's right. It's cold."

"I'll go first," John said, hiking up his pants legs.

"You can't," Megan said. "You'll have to help Lizzie get up there. I'll go first so I can catch her on the other side. You come last, John."

"Okay." He stooped and held out his hands, making a stirrup for her foot.

When all three were on the downside of the rock, John leaned back to examine the face of it. "Man, I hope we won't have to try to get back up."

"No kidding," Megan agreed.

At the end of the path, she eyed the descending row of shallow niches in the rock. The slope was steep, the niches shallow. *A stairway to hell,* she thought.

"They were little people," Lizzie said. "They had little feet."

John said, "I think we can do it if you want to try, Mrs. Montoya."

"We can barely even see the niches. God help us if the moon goes under." She paused for a moment, then, "Well, let's go."

With John in the lead, they descended a few dozen feet. At the slightly wider space where the steps switched back, he waited for the others to catch up.

Megan tried to sound confident. "So far, so good."

Here the way was steeper yet. John's shoe slipped. He tried to hang onto the rock but skidded farther.

Above him, Megan cried out as she reached the same place and began to slide. The pain in her rib caught fire. "Lizzie," she gasped, trying to catch her breath. "Wait. Don't come any farther."

John turned sideways, his hands and face scraping along the rock. At last his foot struck a flatter surface. He explored it with his toe, then eased his body onto it. "It's okay," he called. "I made it. The rest looks much easier."

By the time he was able to grasp her legs to steady her, Megan's forehead was beaded with cold sweat and her cheek was bleeding. "I'm all right," she grunted, as much to reassure herself as John.

She looked over her shoulder to where Lizzie was clinging to the rock above them. A gust of wind caught Megan's back, and she struggled to keep her balance. "Lizzie," she called. "It's not as bad as it seems. Just let yourself slide. It hurts a little, but it's the only way."

"I can't."

"Yes you can. John did it. I did it. You can do it."

"No."

"Lizzie, please. There's no other way."

"No."

"Why?"

"Because I'll crush Theodora."

Megan crumpled into a sitting position and ran a hand through disheveled hair.

John shouted, "Take the turtle out of your jacket and let her come down by herself." He waited. "Lizzie?"

"I don't know if she can do that," came Lizzie's troubled voice.

"If she falls, I'll catch her," called John.

"What if you can't? If her shell breaks off, will she die?"

"I don't know. But that won't happen. I'll catch her. I promise." John injected a certainty into his voice he couldn't possibly feel. It would be hard to even see the little tortoise.

Megan stood and shouted up the rocky incline: "And if you slip, I'm right here. I'll catch you."

Above there was silence. They could see Lizzie's hand, and in it the little tortoise outlined by the moonlight. "She can't come down by herself. It's too steep," the little girl said plaintively. "I put her on my shoulder. At least she'll have a chance if I don't fall."

And Lizzie began her slide.

Megan, eyes pinned to her daughter's small form as it bumped, teetered, and bumped again, felt every scrape as if it was her own.

Suddenly Lizzie's body spun sideways and stopped. "I hit someth—" She began to slide again. The jolt jarred the tortoise from its perch, and the round, compact body arced into the air.

Dodging to the right, John held out his hands for what seemed an achingly long time.

The tortoise landed in them like a softball.

And Lizzie's legs slipped into her mother's trembling hands.

Compared to the nightmares they had already survived, the rest was easy.

In unspoken agreement, they didn't stop at the base of the cliff but picked up their pace and were making their way through the shadows between the cafeteria and the gift shop when headlights swung through the parking lot toward them. All three flung themselves into the shadows against the right-hand wall. Had Miguel returned?

"Megan," a voice called from behind the lights. "Are you there? I saw someone drive out. I couldn't wait any longer."

"Ben!" she yelled hoarsely. "Thank God!"

They broke away from the wall and crossed the pavement.

Ben swept all three into his arms. "What happened?"

"First, give me your cell phone. Miguel is headed for a place where he can blow up the state's power lines."

"Corazón told you where?" Ben asked.

"No." Megan paused for a long moment, trying not to relive the horror of it all. "Corazón is . . . is dead, Ben. She fell. I almost think she meant to. She was trying to save Bobby—the little boy who didn't talk. He fell, too. It was . . . awful," she finished, her voice barely above a whisper. "We have to go. Now." Grabbing Lizzie's hand, she moved toward the Honda. "Leave the pickup here."

Ben took his rifle from his truck and stashed it behind the backseat of the Civic. "We don't know where he was headed," he said, sliding under the Honda's wheel.

Megan helped John and Lizzie pile into the backseat. "I know someone who does know where it is."

Chapter Fifty-three

The cell phone didn't get a good signal until they reached the main road.

It rang nine times before a voice, blurry with sleep, answered. "Yes?"

Megan held her breath. "Mr. Gillette?"

"Yes?" The sleepy voice was tinged with annoyance.

"This is Megan Montoya."

"Who?"

"The photographer."

"It's 1:04," he grunted. "In the morning."

"I'm so sorry to wake you. . . . Are you there?"

"Yes."

"The day we first met in your office, the lights went out, and you told me that all the state's power lines came together at one point. You said you knew where because your father worked on the original project."

"Yes?" The one word conveyed astonishment. Now he was awake. "Have you taken leave of your senses, Ms. Montoya?"

"I have reason to believe someone will try to sabotage the state's power lines or power supply or whatever you call it. I know that sounds crazy, but it's true."

"Perhaps we can talk about it tomorrow."

"He's going to do it tonight. There's no time to explain more."

This was greeted with a long silence, as if W. Brewster Gillette was sniffing her breath from the other end of the line.

Megan was afraid she had lost the connection. "Hello?"

Finally, warily, "What do you want from me?"

"Those power lines, do you know where they all come together?"

Slowly, reluctantly, he either decided to believe her or pretended he did in the hope it might make her go away. "Not exactly, no. I don't know the name of the road, but I can give you fairly good directions."

"Where's Four Corners?" Megan asked Ben as she closed the cell phone. They were still on the road heading toward the main highway.

Ben frowned tiredly. "Where Arizona, New Mexico, Colorado, and Utah come together."

"How far is that?"

"A couple hours or so."

"The main power tower is near there. Close to three ponds or small lakes. You think we can stop him?" She looked into the backseat at Lizzie's and John's drawn faces.

Ben stared at the dark, empty road for what seemed an endless moment, then he blew a long breath through pursed lips. "Megan, I really don't know."

"Don't you think we have to try?"

"You're exhausted. I don't see how you can even think."

"It's pretty damn certain that Miguel is, too."

"A trigger-happy, exhausted, fanatic, madman. That makes me feel so much better."

They were nearing the main highway. He pulled to the shoulder and cut the motor. In the backseat Lizzie and John sat in numb fatigue, barely blinking.

"Should we take the kids home first?" Ben asked.

"No!" Lizzie was suddenly wide awake. "I don't want to go home."

"Miguel can't be much more than an hour ahead," Megan said, brushing her disheveled hair away from her face.

Ben nodded and started the car. They had not yet reached the edge of town when Lizzie began to whimper.

"Sssh. We'll be okay." Megan reached over the seat back to comfort her daughter.

"He was so little. He never hurt anyone. It was so wrong."

"I know, sweetheart. We have to find a way to live with that." Lizzie's earlier words filtered into Megan's mind. *You and John and I will be okay.* Not Bobby. She hadn't included Bobby.

"Did you know? About Bobby?" Megan turned until she could see her daughter in the backseat. The child was sitting upright, nodding slowly.

By the time the town lights faded behind the Honda, both Lizzie and John had fallen into an exhausted sleep.

The empty road ran straight as a ruler through a region of the state Megan had never seen. "Are there no towns?" she asked.

Ben's eyes darted from the road to her face and back. "A lot of this is reservation land."

Body riddled with aches, bruised fingers feeling like bunches of bananas, Megan squirmed in her seat, trying to find a comfortable position. "Corazón said Miguel stashed a lot of men and guns on Indian land. I keep thinking maybe you were right. Maybe we should call the cops. Maybe if they searched the reservations..."

Ben let out a long breath. "No, you were probably right. The cops wouldn't do much searching any time soon. I don't even know for sure how the law runs on that. If we go to the sheriff, they would first assume we're wacko, or doing drugs, or both. Then they'd probably call in the feds. States and counties don't have much jurisdiction on Indian lands. The feds would spend days if not weeks wringing their hands about the PR problems involved in doing a massive search of Indian lands. The last thing they want is to look like jackbooted, antiethnic thugs. In the end, maybe all they would do is demand the Indians search their own lands."

"That's not exactly helpful." She thought for a bit. "If *they*—Miguel and that makeshift army, or whatever it is—actually, at least for a while, took over some part of the state . . . What would they do to us?"

"I doubt it would be very pleasant."

"You can't imagine how crazed he was at the cliff dwellings."

They both fell silent, considering thoughts neither wanted to contemplate.

Like how easy it was to arrive at concepts like *them* and *us*.

Chapter Fifty-four

For more than an hour Ben hardly lifted his foot from the accelerator. Fatigue drew tight lines from his temples to his chin.

The sky was very black. Stars sparkled coldly above a road lined with lumps too small to be hills, too large to be rocks, barren and ghostly as the moon.

"Our version of the badlands," he said.

Megan looked up from the map that lay across her lap. "You said 'our.' You're more attached to New Mexico than you think."

"Sure I'm attached, like we're attached to our parents. That's why kids want to leave home. And why it's so hard. I'm getting old, and I've never known anything else."

"Will that university still want you now that the emeralds are gone?"

"I found out they actually existed, that they weren't just a myth. That's probably worth something."

"Can you prove it?" she asked.

"The lab in London can. They made digitals and slides and wrote it all up."

"I guess whatever happens here, the way the arrowheads were lost again will generate plenty of publicity for you, too."

"That may spice it up some." He put his hand on Megan's arm and searched for her hand. "Go with me, Megan. If it doesn't work out, you can always come back."

She took his hand in both of hers, and they rode for a time in silence. "For a long while now I've believed that a good, enduring relationship is about as likely as finding a diamond in a box of Cracker Jacks."

"Ah, well," he said, and moved his hand back to the wheel.

"And, of course, there's Lizzie. . . ."

"She's one of the toughest, most adaptable kids I've ever met. Already she's picked up a little Spanish."

Megan swallowed. "I can't just follow you around to Colombia, Egypt, wherever. I need to do something, be something myself."

"You're a photographer. Photographers can work anywhere, can't they? Maybe they could even use you on the site in Colombia. I'll ask."

"Have you noticed that Colombia isn't the safest of countries these days? Is it a good place to raise a little girl? I don't think so. And I should shoot artifacts? 'Turn it a little more to the left so we can see the blue marks'? That isn't photography."

Ben didn't say anything for a long time. When he did, his words were held together with resignation. "That's your answer, then?"

She listened to the thrum of the car's engine and the clicking of her own thoughts. "I don't know. So many things have happened at once."

Ben watched the road as if he might miss something important on it.

"I'm sorry," Megan said. "It's just that I can't make life decisions while we're driving ninety miles an hour in the middle of the night trying to stop a maniac from blowing up the power lines that feed the whole state."

Ben rubbed his chin where the day's growth of beard had roughened it. "I understand."

She wondered if he did. "What will happen if the state does go dark?"

"Chaos. Hospitals have emergency generators, but I don't know about air traffic control towers. Water pumps, gas pumps, refrigeration—it's hard to think of anything that doesn't need electricity. Computers, streetlights, heating, cooling. To say nothing of gangs of looters. For a while it might be really bad. And it could be days, even weeks before order is restored."

Megan sighed. "I guess that's what this guy wants. Then he could launch his little army . . . and what? Does he really think he could take over the state? And supposing he could, what would he do then?"

"He'd sure get plenty of media attention."

"And that's what he's after."

The tires hummed along the starlight silvery ribbon of pavement that seemed to stretch forever. They turned north on Route 491, and the barren, hippopotamus-hump landscape revealed in the headlights gave way to flat, open spaces, then to brush, then to trees.

Megan said, "I keep thinking it might be better to just turn it over to the cops. Even if they can't do much. At least it wouldn't be our problem. Maybe I should see if I can get an answer on 911."

"You were the one who pointed out that a lot of cops are Hispanic." Ben glanced at her. "So are you."

Megan looked at his grim profile in the pale light from the dashboard. "I was wondering when you were going to say that."

"I didn't mean—"

"Don't be ridiculous. It isn't them and us," she said. "Or them and you. It's one solitary madman."

"What I meant was, if the power supply goes, if anyone gets hurt, every Hispanic in the country will be blamed." Ben lifted his hands from the steering wheel for a moment, trying to make his point. "Even the Puerto Ricans in New York who never set foot in Mexico or the Southwest. Hate is cheap and easy to sell these days. I know that, and so do you."

This time the silence pulsed with unuttered thoughts.

An hour later, Ben motioned at the road. "The river is up ahead. It slices right through the Four Corners area."

Megan looked up from the map she was studying by flashlight. "It always looks easier on paper. If only we knew the name of the road."

"A lot of them aren't even marked. But maybe we can find the ponds your friend described."

"If we can find the power lines, we can just follow them."

The tires and minutes sped on. In the backseat, the children had not stirred.

"Oh my God," Megan said suddenly. "What if it isn't just Miguel? What if there are a lot of them and they're armed?"

"I guess we punt. We head for Farmington and take our chances with the cops. We've only got one gun. You know how to shoot?"

"Barely," she said. "I'm glad you do."

"I can target shoot okay," Ben said. "I spend a lot of time in isolated places. I keep the gun clean and oiled, but I was only thinking about coyotes, bears, and bobcats. I never thought I'd have to take on a human."

The headlights caught a small sign. "Shiprock is coming up," Ben announced.

Megan turned on the flashlight and bent over the map again. "Looks like there are two roads, one on each side of the river. It has to be one of them. And maybe you could call these three wide spots on the river lakes. But if the power lines aren't right there to follow, how do we know which road?"

"We don't."

Megan began to fret. "Even if there are power lines at the intersection, how do we know they're the right ones? If we don't get it right the first time, it may be too late."

"So we try for a lucky guess," he said. "Fifty-fifty chance."

She tried to blink away a sudden sense of hopelessness. "I suppose I'm the one who has to make the choice."

"You're the one with the map."

At the first road, Ben pulled to the shoulder so they could take a closer look at the area.

"No power lines," Megan said.

"Doesn't necessarily mean anything. The lines could easily join the road or cross it half a mile down. Too dark to see from here. We just have to make a guess. And maybe pray. If you believe in such a thing."

"I wouldn't know whether to pray we find him or pray that we don't," Megan said. "I hate to use up the time, but I want to see the other road."

He nodded and drove on.

The second road looked very like the first. Megan contemplated it, fatigue burning her eyes. She leaned her head against the seat back, stared at the car's ceiling, and let out a long breath. "I don't know."

Ben examined the intersection. "Too bad they don't put up signs: 'Most vulnerable place on the state power grid, two miles east.'"

"They don't put up any signs at all." Her gaze circled the intersection again. "Wait a minute." She was staring at a sign barely visible behind the branches of a tree. "The road *is* marked. Oh my God, Ben, this is it!"

The sign read BURNT CABIN ROAD.

He swung the car to the left without asking how she knew this was the right road. It was rough but passable. After a few miles, it bent south, and the river appeared on their left.

"You may be right," Ben said. "But there's no sign of a pond."

Ahead on the right something loomed, stark and huge, like some gigantic erector-set creation on a swath of open land that cut through the trees.

"Transmission tower," she said quietly. "This is it."

He pulled off the road and stopped the car under a tall pine. "We have power lines and the river. From here I think we'd better walk."

She glanced at him. "We'll be sitting ducks if anyone is watching."

Lizzie's face appeared between the front seats. "No."

Megan turned to her. "We have to leave you and John here for a while, maybe as long as an hour. We'll lock the car."

"No," Lizzie said again, this time sharply. "We can't park here. Back up." Her eyes held her mother's. In the icy starlight, the freckles stood out across her cheeks like splatters of mud. "Please," the little girl insisted, "not by a pine tree. Any other tree is okay, but we can't park by a pine."

Megan turned to Ben. "I guess it can't hurt. Let's back up."

"Just a little farther to walk." He turned the key in the ignition and shoved the gearshift into reverse. In the dark they couldn't tell one tree from another, so he backed up the car a quarter mile to an open meadow.

They left the children there.

Chapter Fifty-five

I n the narrow clearing beneath the power lines they walked single file, first Ben, stiffly holding the rifle, barrel pointed to the ground, then Megan. In some places tires had crushed the coarse stubby grass, but the tracks didn't seem fresh.

Behind them, a pale, purplish bruise was beginning in the sky beyond the trees. The woods were thin here. In another life Megan would have enjoyed the bracing odor of pine. She quickened her step to catch up with Ben, who was moving quickly, almost soundlessly. She tried to do the same, but no matter how carefully she picked up her feet they made little crunching sounds in the low brush.

Their plan was simple: Find the transmission tower nearest the pond—the one W. Brewster Gillette's sleep-dulled voice had described—then find a place to hide and wait. Miguel shouldn't be expecting trouble. He might be alone, might not even be armed. With Ben's rifle, he could be subdued. And it would be over.

Above, the power lines swept like a bridge, high and barely definable against the still-dark sky. Ben picked up his pace, almost disappearing into the night. Megan had to run to keep him in sight. She passed another transmission tower, but there was still no sign of a pond. A sudden breeze whipped her hair around her face. She stumbled over a root, righted herself, and plodded on. Did Ben realize he'd left her behind? She didn't dare call out.

A sharp grunt came from the right. Ben was standing very still beneath a tree. She couldn't see much more of him than his old hat.

"What are you doing?" she called softly, making her way toward him.

"Stop, or I will make *menudo* of his brains."

The air in her lungs froze. Now she could see the forearm locked around Ben's neck, the fallen rifle at his feet. He began to topple to the ground like a heavy rag doll in slow motion, his weight, for a moment, taking Miguel with him.

Megan charged left, into the trees. She dropped to the ground behind a rock, praying he would not kill Ben.

Miguel was saying something she couldn't quite make out. She inched her head forward to peer around the rock. He was bending over Ben. The rifle still lay on the ground.

"You can do nothing," Miguel said quietly as he stood up. "For many miles there is no one." He tapped Ben with the toe of his boot, then turned and hissed in Megan's direction, "You are a traitor to your people."

Peering from behind the rock, watching him tie Ben's hands behind his back, whatever had been holding Megan together broke. Remembering Corazón and Bobby, her spirit crumbled.

Miguel jerked Ben to his feet, swept up the rifle in one hand and with the other grabbed what looked like a gunnysack. "Come out now, or I will kill him." His whisper was like a spider crawling through the still night air. "To kill him is nothing to me. And you. You are only a woman. What can you do?"

He was right. What could she do? Helpless and horrified, Megan held her breath, waiting for the shot, knowing that when it came, he would simply stride to the rock and kill her, too. What, then, would become of Lizzie and John?

The silence drew out and collapsed under its own weight.

But the shot didn't come.

"Stay then. It is no matter," Miguel hissed. "The people will take back what is theirs. You cannot stop them."

Megan strained to hear him. If Miguel was afraid someone might hear his words, he must also know that a shot would be very, very loud. How far was the closest house? The pond must be nearby. There might be campers, early fishermen.

She poked her head out just far enough to see him prodding his captive with the rifle. He seemed to be having trouble handling the sack and keeping the rifle trained on Ben.

Jerking Ben around, Miguel fastened the hands still tied behind his back to the neck of the sack. "Even an Anglo can be a pack animal."

Ben took a few wobbly steps, dragging the sack, then steadied himself and walked slowly, the rifle barrel a scant few feet from the back of his head. Unlike before, this time his footfalls were almost impossibly loud.

When the two men were nearly out of sight, Megan began to follow. All but paralyzed with fear, she stole from tree to tree.

They walked that way for some time, the men moving openly along the narrow clearing beneath the power lines, Megan darting stealthily from the trunk of one pine to the next.

Overhead, the sky began to pale. Thorns in the brush snatched at her jeans. When she twisted her ankle and fell to one knee, she waited until she could barely hear the faint sound of dry pine needles being crushed underfoot ahead, then rose and hurried on.

The earliest rays of sunlight ignited something ahead to the right. Mirrorlike water glowed among the trees like a phantom pool of silver. The power lines swept up to the edge of the pond, where bold columns of steel, straighter than God could draw, rose to hold them.

Her safety growing more precarious as the sky brightened, Megan sank down behind some scrubby brush. Struggling with an almost overpowering urge to flee, to race back to the car and get the hell out of there, she forced herself instead to creep cautiously a few yards more, then a few more. At last she could see Ben sitting on the ground, hands still behind him, legs at an odd angle, at the mercy of a man who had little to lose.

Next to Ben were what looked like two big, white flour sacks. Miguel must have brought these sacks earlier. She knew nothing about explosives, but there was little doubt about what the sacks contained.

Suddenly she realized why Ben's legs were at that angle. A hideous thought raked her consciousness: Ben would be left there—ankles tied, unable to run—to be blown up, while she and Miguel raced to save themselves.

Where was Miguel now? Had he circled around to stalk her from behind? She shot a quick look over her shoulder. Then, craning her neck to get a better look at the area where Ben sat, she caught sight of Miguel marching toward the sacks. She flung herself to the ground.

Turning his back, Miguel bent almost casually over one of the sacks, fiddled with something inside it, then tied a rope around the neck of that bag and reached for the other. He seemed to have lost interest in Ben and her, one a bound prisoner, the other an unarmed woman.

When he seemed intent on the contents of the second bag, Megan bolted from cover.

Miguel didn't begin to turn until she was almost upon him. Swerving, barreling her shoulder into his chest, she knocked him off balance.

Ben ducked and rolled his body to cover the rifle as Megan jerked her knee upward with all the strength she could muster, high and hard into Miguel's groin.

But not hard enough.

Staggering back, Miguel dropped to a crouch and punched a fist toward her face, grazing her cheek a split second before she dodged. She shot out a foot and dug her toe deep into his crotch.

With the sound of a punctured tire, he bent almost double.

She raced for the rifle as Ben scrambled to roll away and uncover it.

By the time she grabbed the gun, Miguel had risen to one knee. She

pointed the barrel at him and released the safety with the cold knowledge that she would have to fire, would have to injure him or he could
easily overpower her and take the weapon.

With the primal roar of a cornered animal, Miguel rose to both feet.
Seeming bigger than life, like some creature in a horror film, he started
toward her, chin lowered like a bull's.

Chapter Fifty-six

Megan raised the rifle. "Stop, or you're a dead man."

Miguel took two more stiff-legged steps.

She aimed for his gut. The stock bucked against her shoulder.

Still, he came.

She brought the rifle up and fired again, wincing as the pain flared in her ribs.

Miguel took another step, then another. A small smear of blood several inches above his belt marked the fact that her bullet had not missed.

Cocking the rifle, she again rammed it against her shoulder.

Slowly, Miguel began to fold up like a marionette with a broken string. He sagged to his knees, both hands clutching his gut.

"I don't think he'll be going anywhere now," Ben called as he spun to face her, hands straining helplessly against the rope that bound his wrists.

She put the rifle down and slipped her fingers into the rope. "Have you got a pocketknife?"

"Right front." He nodded at his jean's pocket.

She found the knife and sawed at the rope. At last it frayed and gave way. The rope binding Ben's ankles took longer but finally surrendered to the dulled blade.

Miguel had not moved. He seemed to be staring at them. A terrible low bubbling sound came from his mouth. A rivulet of blood trickled down his chin.

Unable to look at him any longer, Megan turned to Ben.

"Leave him. He won't get far. We have to find some cops."

Miguel rose to his hands and knees and began to crawl toward them. "*Las esmeraldas,*" he grunted, voice full of gravel. "Take them." One hand fumbled at a pocket. The packet of arrowheads showed in the early light as he held it out.

Megan stared in horrid fascination.

Miguel coughed. "For my people. Take them."

Ben's voice ripped the air. "Don't go near him!"

She backed away, eyes still riveted on Miguel as he crawled toward the sacks.

He was trying to pull himself to his feet. It seemed to take a very long time, but he succeeded.

Against the paling sky, he stood with one foot against each bag and stretched out his arms.

Megan stumbled backward over a rock and almost fell. Ben grabbed at her elbow, and she was turning toward him, beginning to move back along the shaved path beneath the power lines, when the white light erupted.

Miguel became two blinding bolts of lightning, crossed pillars of brilliant exploding gases.

As it might have been when the world began.

The light burst through her eyes to her brain. Then she saw nothing.

Chapter Fifty-seven

Mouth open, eyes fixed, Megan stood, unable to move. She smelled smoke, heard the crackle of flames. "Ben! I can't see." A strong hand gripped her arm, pulled her forward. She tried to run. Twice she fell to her knees. Twice Ben yanked her to her feet and pulled her on. "You're doing fine! You're moving faster than I could carry you."

They lurched on through air malignant with sour smoke that seared and clogged their lungs.

A tree branch lashed Megan's face. "Please," she gasped for breath. "I can't go on."

"No!" Ben's shout hit her like a gunshot, almost knocking her over.

The forest was alive with heat. The fire seemed to be closing in on her from every direction. She couldn't tell which direction was safest. "Which way?" She shouted to Ben. "I can't see."

He didn't answer.

She ran, screaming his name, swinging her arms, searching for him. "Ben. Don't leave me! Where are you?" Breath coming in rasping, painful heaves, she slumped to her knees.

A hand grabbed her shoulder, spun her around, tied something wet over her face. "I went to the river. That's my T-shirt." Ben's mouth was at her ear. "Crawl. The fire is above. Keep your face as close to the ground as you can."

"I can't," she sobbed. "Dear God, Ben, I can't."

A horrible scene stole into her head: The fire would slow a little, when it ran out of trees, but then the flames would rage again, across the brush. They would reach the car. And Lizzie.

Alma's face floated before her. *I have wanted to be weak.* No. Alma said those words, but she was never weak. Never.

Megan forced herself forward. Her jeans tore, her knees bled, her frantic hands, flesh ripped by rocks, began to bleed. Then they went numb, and hurt less. "Keep moving," she mumbled doggedly. "Just keep moving."

She knew when she reached the road only because the brush stopped mauling her face. Now it was gravel scraping at her fingers.

"Get up. Run!" Ben's words came in short bursts from behind. "You're in the clearing. The car is straight ahead."

Megan rose and ran into the darkness.

She ran until she could not take another step. Her legs went out from under her.

She heard Lizzie screaming, John calling.

She heard the car door open, felt Ben lifting her into it.

She huddled in the corner of the passenger seat.

Darkness had come to her eyes. Now darkness blotted out her thoughts.

Chapter Fifty-eight

A big straw hat shaded Megan's eyes from the sun on the mesa. Ben sat cross-legged on the ground watching as she propped the butt of his rifle against her shoulder and fired at a can he had placed on a rock.

The bullet tore a hole through the can.

"Seven out of ten," Megan said. "I'm getting better."

Ben adjusted his sunglasses. "Damn good, if you ask me. I hope I never get you really mad."

"I don't ever again want to wonder if I can fire a gun and actually hit what I'm aiming at."

She set the safety and laid the rifle on the edge of the old Army blanket Ben had spread over the needles shed by a twisted old juniper. She took two turkey sandwiches from a battered red-and-white cooler, seated herself, and handed one to Ben. "I still play out that horrible scene in my head almost every day." This was the first time she was able to talk much about it.

"Not an easy scene to forget." Ben opened the cooler and poured himself a glass of iced tea. In the sun, the tea was the color of good scotch.

"The cops said there was no trace of Miguel out there by the tower. I find that hard to believe."

"An incendiary bomb is pretty intense."

Megan gazed at the mountains for a moment. "But it didn't take out the power long enough for the hacker to take over the computer system."

"Fires can be weird. I've heard of houses where a fire destroys furniture in one room but leaves a candle in another area almost intact." He scratched his head under his shapeless hat.

Catching herself beginning to like the hat, Megan plucked at a tuft of grass at the edge of the blanket. "I still find it hard to believe."

"How did Miguel hook up with a computer hacker?" Ben asked.

"A friend of a friend, I guess. There's a university in California that teaches people how to hack into computer systems."

Ben drew back his chin in disbelief. "Is that some kind of joke?"

"That's what Corazón told me. No reason for her to lie." She picked up a napkin and wiped her hands. "If there's no sign of Miguel, I'm beginning to worry they may think he never existed and you and I set off the bomb. Maybe we shouldn't have mentioned the arrowheads."

Ben's glance lingered on the backpack next to the cooler. "I suggested they contact the lab in London for confirmation, but they didn't seem interested in anything that would complicate what they saw as a simple case of someone who kidnaps kids for ransom."

"And since Miguel is gone, there's no case."

"Apparently not," he agreed.

"I told them everything I could remember about the cave," Megan said, "the weapons, the so-called plan. But they just sort of brushed it off. Like maybe I was hallucinating because of my eyes and the fire and all. They kept assuring me they understood I was overwrought." Her eyes went to Ben's. "Miguel would be horribly disappointed. No drumbeat. No attention to his cause."

"I'm sure he would."

She stared into the distance. "Somehow that seems kind of sad."

Ben looked over his sunglasses at her. "Now *I* think you're overwrought."

Megan pointed with her chin toward a rock-covered mound forty feet away among the piñons. "I need to get new flowers for Alma. Those are getting faded." Slanted above the mound was a cross made of two small tree branches. Sunlight glinted from the glass jar that held the plastic flowers. "I miss her," she said around the lump in her throat, and touched the crumpled brim of her hat. "I'm glad I rescued the hat."

Ben said, "I still wonder if we should call the sheriff's office about the grave."

"What would be the point? Alma's gone, Miguel is gone, Corazón is gone, even Alma's cabin is gone. And the last thing I want is for them to dig her up. What would they learn from that? Even if they did learn something, what could they do about it?"

She plucked at the plastic that held her sandwich. "I'd heard of incendiary bombs, but I didn't really know what they were."

"One of the easiest bombs to make." Ben unwrapped his sandwich and bit into it.

"I guess so, if you can get the makings at a welding supply shop. He meant to *melt* the transmission tower?"

"Probably would have done it, too, if the bombs were strapped to the legs of the tower. Forty-four hundred degrees Fahrenheit would melt damn near anything."

"Instead, the sacks were at his own feet." A small shudder rippled across Megan's shoulders. She stared again at the distant mountains that were just a shade darker than the sky. On the worst nights, she still woke, sweating, with the image of Miguel, his arms outstretched, engulfed in flames, scorching the darkness behind her eyes.

Ben watched her, two lines deepening above his nose.

"For a while," she said, "I really thought I would never see again."

"So did I," he said, not quite concealing the small catch in his voice. When they escaped the fire, he'd taken her to the emergency room in Farmington. A few days later, her sight had returned.

"Funny how quickly everyone lost interest," Megan said. "A huge barrage of questions, then nothing."

Only a few fortune hunters, attracted by the rumors, showed any interest in recovering the "alleged arrowheads," as the press put it. Those few had given up. The press itself, hyped and goggle-eyed at first, had touted big headlines. But their interest was cut short when a film star who owned a ranch near Taos tried to have a private wedding. The people who called themselves reporters breathlessly followed that buzz.

As far as Megan knew, no one had looked for the old mine or found the cache of weapons, if it was still there. She had no desire to see for herself. The main entrance was blown up, and she didn't know where the other one might be. The people who did know were almost certainly gone, dispersed to other places, other lives.

Ben had reported hearing about the disappearance of a priest from a mountain village church. Whether he was ill, recalled by the church, or had left the priesthood, no one seemed to know.

For a week or so after their ordeal, Lizzie was uncharacteristically quiet. One night Megan heard her sobbing in her sleep. She'd gone to Lizzie's room, lain down on the bed, and wrapped herself around her daughter. Some nights, she herself woke, hearing Corazón say, "It is only the *niña* who said six." Without her hearing aid, Lizzie could not have heard. And Megan would never tell her. How could a child bear what that mistake led to?

Then one morning Lizzie had bounded out of bed and begun teaching Theodora to fetch a small rubber ball. The little tortoise now came toddling toward anyone who called her name.

When Lizzie insisted that Theodora would like a few special food items, Megan broke down and bought some grape leaves from a gourmet shop in Santa Fe and an aloe vera plant at a garden center.

It was even beginning to look like Megan might actually make a real career for herself in photography. The gallery had sold five of her pictures, including two of Alma. And John's father had introduced her to his brother, who was a graphic designer in Santa Fe. The next thing she knew, she'd been hired to do a shoot for an energy company's annual report.

Now Megan finished her sandwich, propped her elbow on her knee, and turned her head to gaze at the mound of rocks. A sadness rose unbidden in her throat. "I don't know why it took me so long to figure out that the tree where John found the arrowheads was right there at Alma's. I still don't understand why they killed her, and then buried her out here with what looked like all the trappings of a regular funeral."

"I guess it's because Miguel's people searched your place again and again without finding the emeralds," Ben said. "So when John told them he put the arrowheads back where he found them under that old oak, they figured Alma had them."

"But why would they kill her? They didn't do anything to John or Lizzie or me. Surely they didn't need to kill an old woman."

"Maybe they threatened her, maybe tried to kidnap her, and she died of a heart attack."

"I hope you're right. I hope they didn't hurt her." Megan hugged her knees, still eyeing the rocks. "The burial was probably Corazón's doing. I think Alma came into it about the time Corazón and Miguel were discovering their differences."

The sun disappeared behind a billowing cloud, and they watched the sky until it reappeared.

"I can't say I'm sorry the arrowheads are gone. Although for a while there, I thought I was rich. I guess I am rich—sort of—anyhow. Alma's paintings are selling. I almost don't want them to. I'm glad I set aside my favorites." She made a half-smile. "Some luck, huh? Alma leaves me her paintings, gets herself killed, and becomes a famous artist."

"Speaking of luck," Ben said, "when we were looking for that damn electric tower, how did you know that was the right road?"

"That night we waited for Miguel to call, Bernie said we would find him near a burned-down house. A road named Burnt Cabin had to have a burned-down house on it somewhere. Maybe people like Bernie can sometimes sense stuff like that. She says Lizzie can, too. I can't quite get used to that, but I'm not set against it anymore."

"Hey, I'm no disbeliever," Ben said. "My grandmother's best friend was a woman who had a little adobe house. She cured people with powders and herbs and little wax dolls. She even cured me once of a bad chest cold. Every time I saw that house, a hawk was sitting on the roof. Sometimes the woman would go out and talk to it."

Watching him, tracing his face in her memory, a profound sense of loss swept over Megan. She was grateful Ben had not pressed her for an answer, and she knew there would be long, intense moments of regret ahead.

With a small sigh, she broached the topic she had been avoiding since their abrupt and hasty drive to the Four Corners. "I appreciate that you've waited, that you haven't brought it up again."

"Brought what up?"

"Me . . . us . . . going with you."

"There's something I've been wanting to say," Ben interrupted. "I—"

She cut him off. "I wish I could go with you, I really do. But another major upheaval wouldn't be good for Lizzie. Aside from everything else, I couldn't ask her to part with Theodora, and I suspect it might be difficult to get a tortoise into a foreign country as a pet."

"I'm sure you're right."

Megan's eyes skidded to his, then darted away. "It's not just because of Lizzie. I've got an important client. I've already picked up two assignments. It's not exactly Ansel Adams or Dorothea Lange caliber, but it's a start. And I can hardly wait to try out the possibilities of prints on canvas. The only ones I've seen are color, but I think the new tricolor black-and-white would be stunning. It's expensive, and I couldn't print at home. I don't think many photographers are doing it yet." Not understanding the look on his face, her nervous chatter began to run down. "And maybe I can find a publisher for the work I did with Corazón. I'd kind of like to do that for her. That was good stuff."

"Yes, it was."

Gazing at the electric blue of the sky, she forced herself to say, "So when do you leave?"

He examined the toe of his boot as if it were the most important thing on earth, before looking up and pronouncing carefully, "I don't."

She stared at him, mouth open. "But this is the job you've always wanted." Little lines deepened across her forehead. "Don't give that up for me. You'd come to hate me for it."

He stood up, reached for the backpack, and withdrew a small brown grocery bag.

"When somebody decides to take your state—your land—away, it makes you think. And maybe you realize it means more than you thought. Here, I know every road, every mountain. I wouldn't be happy living anywhere else." With an awkward smile, he handed her the bag.

She looked inside, gave him a bewildered look, and removed a rectangular box. "Cracker Jacks?" The wrapper was taped. She peeled it back.

He tore the bag down the side, flattened it, and placed it in front of her. "Pour them out."

She did as directed, then shot him another puzzled look. When she looked back down, she saw it lying among the kernels of caramel corn and drew in a sharp breath.

"It's an emerald. I had to have it special made, but it seemed appropriate."

She picked up a slightly sticky silver ring set with a brilliant green stone.

"There's a condition," he said.

"Oh?"

"I want to travel. Like to visit Egypt and the Lost City in Colombia and . . ."

Fighting back the welling of tears, she held out her hands. "I think Lizzie will like that."

He helped her to her feet and pulled her to him.